continued . . .

Death-Fires Dance

"Engaging ... fascinating ... terrifying ... a fast-paced mystery you won't be able to put down."
—Carolyn Wheat, author of *Mean Streak*

The Dead Man and the Sea

"Janice Steinberg's characters sparkle. In *The Dead Man and the Sea* she masterfully creates a wide variety of people who are fun to hear, fascinating to watch, intriguing in the secrets they don't quite succeed in hiding—all of it in a La Jolla so appealing you want to hop on a plane."
—Susan Dunlap, author of *Cop Out* and *High Fall*

"An intellectually stimulating who-done-it ... *The Dead Man and the Sea* will appeal to a wide range of mystery fans."
—*The Midwest Book Review*

"Cleverly crafted and deftly written ... will please her many fans and undoubtedly create more."
—*San Diego Union-Tribune*

Death in a City of Mystics

Janice Steinberg

BERKLEY PRIME CRIME, NEW YORK

DEATH IN A CITY OF MYSTICS

A Berkley Prime Crime Book / published by arrangement with the author

PRINTING HISTORY
Berkley Prime Crime edition / November 1998

The Penguin Putnam Inc. World Wide Web site address is http://www.penguinputnam.com

ISBN: 0-425-16615-5

Berkley Prime Crime Books are published by The Berkley Publishing Group, a member of Penguin Putnam Inc., 375 Hudson Street, New York, NY 10014.
The name BERKLEY PRIME CRIME and the BERKLEY PRIME CRIME design are trademarks belonging to Berkley Publishing Corporation.

PRINTED IN THE UNITED STATES OF AMERICA

10 9 8 7 6 5 4 3 2 1

For my nieces
In Israel: Shira, Ronit, and Tamar
In the U.S.: Rachel and Maggie

Acknowledgments

The only way I could have written a book set in a city where I spent far less time than I would have liked was with the help of several wonderful Israeli correspondents: David Steinberg, Helen Bar-Lev, Phyllis Shalem, and Aviva Minoff. Special thanks to Phyllis for her delightful E-mail anecdotes.

On questions of theology, I received assistance from Rabbis Laurie Coskey, Alexis Roberts, Rami Shapiro, Moishe Leider, and Karyn Kedar. Also from Frances Thronsen and Renee Horowitz.

Thanks for their medical/herbal expertise to Sheryl Cramer, M.D., Steven Turchen, and Susan Albert.

Among the many books that made my way easier: *Safed: Six Self-Guided Tours in and Around the Mystical City* by Yisrael Shalem, *Major Trends in Jewish Mysticism* by Gershom Scholem, *What Do Jews Believe?* by David S. Ariel, *Jewish Literacy* by Rabbi Joseph Telushkin, *How to Run a Traditional Jewish Household* by Blu Greenberg, *Safed: The Mystical City* by Dovid Rossoff, and everything by Rabbi Lawrence Kushner. Also "The Mystical Kabbalah," audiotapes by Rabbi David A. Cooper. The article about the film *Men in Black* and the *lamed vav tzaddikim* mentioned in Chapter 22 is "Men in Black" by Arthur Taussig, originally published in *The Hi-Q Film Review*.

For literary advice, I'm grateful to Teresa Chris, Leagrey Dimond, and my writers group: Ann Elwood, Lonnie Hewitt, Janet Kunert, Martha Lawrence, Mary Lou Locke, and Lillian Roberts.

Thanks to Jack for taking the journey with me.

Character and Place Names

Safed (Ts FAHT)—an Israeli city slightly northwest of the Sea of Galilee; a center for the study of Jewish mysticism, Kabbalah (Kah bah LAH in Israeli Hebrew; in the U.S., often heard as Ka BAH la).

Mount Meron (Meh ROHN)—just west of Safed, site of the tomb of the sage Shimon bar Yochai (Shi MOHN bar Yo CHAI).

Margo Simon—reporter for a San Diego public radio station.

Alice Simon—Margo's mother, who is traveling and studying in Israel.

Audrey Simon Siegel—Margo's sister; director of marketing for a pharmaceutical company.

Barry Dawes—Margo's husband.

Batsheva Halevi (Baht SHEH vah Ha LEH vee)—Israeli poet; Alice Simon's spiritual teacher.

Nili Blum (NEE lee Bloom)—Batsheva's sixteen-year-old daughter from her second marriage.

Reuven Preusser (Roo VEN PROYS ser)—young man from an Orthodox family who studies with Batsheva on the sly.

Hillel (Hil LEL) Gebman—Israeli doctor treating Alice.

Dalia (DAH lee ah) Weiss—Safed artist who rents a room to Alice.

Gadi Halevi (GAH dee Ha LEH vee)—Batsheva's son from her first marriage.

Danny Rubicoff—American rabbinical student who studies with Batsheva.

Bernice Rubicoff—Danny's cousin, a retired nurse.

Rafi (RAH fee) Garfein—Israeli police officer.

Yitzhak Saporta (Yits HAK Sa POR ta)—Batsheva's cousin and opponent.

Ronit Laor (Ro NEET La OR)—young Israeli woman who studies with Batsheva; a spiritual seeker since she had a vision while serving in the Israeli Army.

Bruce Harris and Nancy Isley—Canadian students of Batsheva, known as "the flower children." Bruce and Nancy have an export business.

Yosef Gilboa (Yo SEF Gil BO a)—Israeli artist who studies with Batsheva.

Ma'ayan Gilboa (Mah ah YAHN Gil BO a)—Yosef's wife, also a student of Batsheva.

Lev Blum (Bloom)—Batsheva's husband; a physician.

Saul Halevi—Batsheva's brother.

Leah Halevi—Saul's wife.

Pincus and Efrati (Eh FRAH tee)—Israeli police officers.

The God who brings to birth and destroys, gives forth and takes away, judges my limitations and calls me to struggle, is terrifying not for God's distance, but precisely for God's nearness. That which is awesome, painful, or evil appalls or bewilders me not because it is far away, but because it is all around and as near as my own heart.

Judith Plaskow, *Standing Again at Sinai*

Religion is a more or less organized way of remembering that every mystery points to a higher reality.

Rabbi Lawrence Kushner, *Honey from the Rock*

Death in a City of Mystics

Part One /
The Counting of the Omer

Religious Jews ''count'' the fifty days from the second day of Passover to the holiday of Shavuot, which celebrates the giving of the Torah on Mount Sinai. Because this period coincides with the barley harvest, it is known as the Omer; the word means ''sheaves of a harvested crop.'' Possibly because of a plague that killed 24,000 students of Rabbi Akiva in the second century, the Omer is considered a period of semi-mourning in which religious Jews do not get married and do not cut their hair.

Prologue /

The snakes! Didn't anybody warn them about the snakes?

Standing at the edge of the Old City, the American woman called to the three young tourists walking—bare-legged, shod only in sandals—in the ancient cemetery below her.

"Hey!" She waved at them. "Hey!"

One of the three, a girl, glanced up. She looked scarcely older than the woman's teenage granddaughter.

"Snakes! There are snakes!" the woman yelled in English and then Hebrew, jabbing her finger toward the ground.

The girl shrugged incomprehension, and her friends, another girl and a boy, increased their danger by straying from the path. The American was about to run down the steep hill to warn them, when a black-coated Hasid went over and spoke to them. He must have mentioned the snakes—as well, no doubt, as chiding them for their immodest dress in this holy place. The young people returned to the path, and now they scanned the ground as they walked.

The girl waved at her and smiled.

The woman waved back. Then she murmured a prayer that restored the contemplative mood that this place, at this time of day, evoked in her.

With dusk descending, the fierce light of the Middle East—light that had turned her first, midday photographs into harsh zones of shadow and glare—had softened. Backlit by the sun sinking beyond Mount Meron, a dozen pilgrims, half of them black-clad Hasidim and the rest in colorful tourist garb, trooped over the hillside cemetery, approaching or departing from the tomb of the Ari.

The woman lingered until the sun set. Then, in the gentle, magical twilight of this most magical of cities, she followed Keren Hayessod Street to the long, broad stone stairway, the Ma'alot Olei HaGardom. The one perfectly straight route in a place where everything else conformed to the curve of the hill, the Ma'alot Olei HaGardom had been built by the British to divide the old Jewish and Arab quarters. It climbed all the way from Keren Hayessod to the Jerusalem Street pedestrian mall.

The mall was her destination, but the American chose the aesthetic route over the direct. Taking the stairs only partway, she progressed sideways and up through the former Arab, now the Artists' Quarter. Narrow, cobbled alleys led her past grilled gateways, many of them painted the same brilliant blue. A few days ago she had written to her older daughter, *I have tried to decide what to call this shade of blue. Azure? Peacock? If the soul has a color, I think it is this color blue.*

Occasionally she stopped to greet someone. After four weeks in a place where tourists seldom stayed more than a day or two, she'd become a familiar figure. She called out *erev tov,* good evening, to the Tunisian immigrants who had the café near the artists' exhibition hall. She was delighted that after a few weeks of daily study, she could chat with them in Hebrew.

From the café, she resumed her stroll and her musings, which were about the six hundred thirteenth *mitzvah.*

The last of the six hundred thirteen *mitzvot*—commandments—in the Torah concerned the Torah itself. Every Jew was supposed to write a Torah scroll during his lifetime. It was a commandment most people honored by proxy, by donating money toward the writing or repair of a Torah by a trained scribe. But wouldn't it be glorious to fulfill the six hundred thirteenth *mitzvah* as it was intended? She imagined the feel of the fine parchment under her fingers, and the letters. . . .

"The entire Torah is composed of the names of God," the thirteenth century Kabbalist Nahmanides had said. The act of writing each letter would be an act of prayer.

Reaching Jerusalem Street, she was assailed by tempting smells that came from everywhere along the pedestrian mall. She almost groaned with desire for a falafel. But even the bland fare she'd eaten lately didn't always prevent her from waking in the middle of the night, feeling like someone was stabbing her in the gut. She might as well consume battery acid as eat a falafel—deep-fried chickpea balls tucked into a pita, with delicious, garlicky tehina ladled in. Resigned to her fate, she bought two plain white rolls, one to have with dinner and another for breakfast tomorrow. She walked back into the Artists' Quarter, to the comfortable room with a private entry that she was renting in one of the lovely old stone houses.

She found a plastic bag of green leaves in the doorway. It must be the herbal tea Ma'ayan had promised for her digestion. The woman used the single burner to cook some fresh string beans while she put out the rest of her dinner—one of the rolls and a cold chicken breast she'd sautéed the day before. When the beans were ready, she spooned them onto her plate, then put a clean pot on the burner to brew the tea.

She performed a ritual hand washing and blessed the meal—practices her family had abandoned when they'd left the old country, determined to be modern Americans. Practices she cherished now.

Ma'ayan had said to let the herbs boil for at least ten minutes; the woman stewed them until she finished her dinner. Ma'ayan had also said the tea would taste awful. She hadn't been joking. It smelled disgusting, too. The woman nibbled a sugar cookie—a meager defense against the nasty tea—and got out a blank aerogram. Which of her children would she write to tonight? She didn't believe in following some kind of schedule, son one day, older daughter the next, and younger daughter the third. Rather, she felt sure she'd write each one an equal number of letters if she were guided by her mood, sharing funny stories with her firstborn, who had inherited his father's humor; and writing to her argumentative younger daughter when she wanted to argue with herself. In truth, the greatest number of letters went to her middle child, the older of her two daughters. It was to this child she felt closest in spirit and to whom she wrote when she was moved spiritually, as she had been this afternoon.

Dear Margo, she wrote as she sipped the vile tea. The night had become so warm. She wondered if one of the infamous *hamsin* winds were on its way from the desert. Slipping off her shoes, she cooled her feet on the terrazzo floor.

She'd only gotten down a cup of the tea by the time she finished the letter to her daughter. She forced herself to pour a second cup and lit one of the two cigarettes she allowed herself each day. She managed another half cup of tea as she smoked and tried to read a novel. Her vision was strangely blurred, however. Reaching for her glasses, she discovered she had them on; maybe they were causing the blurriness? She removed the glasses and noticed she had company.

"Lou!" She jumped up to greet her husband, vaguely aware that something was amiss but not remembering he'd been dead for four years.

She started to talk to him, but he wanted to go out. Of course! The evening here was lovely. And if she went out, she could mail the letter she found in her hand. Careful not to wrinkle it, she put the letter in the pocket of her slacks. Now, what was she doing? Going outdoors with Lou. Outdoors, it would be cooler, wouldn't it? What a relief, since she was so hot. Burning up. Raging with thirst, too. She turned on the tap, filled a glass with water, and gulped it.

"Come on, Lou dear!" she called.

She half fell into the courtyard and from there ambled into the dark street, chattering to her husband as they walked. Then he was no longer at her side, and a deep apprehension seized her. She started to run, faltering when her bare feet landed on pebbles and uneven cobbles.

At the Ma'alot Olei HaGardom, the long British stairs, she tripped and crashed down.

One /

Margo grasped the essentials. *Mother. Intensive care. Alive.* Sitting on an airplane somewhere above the Atlantic Ocean, dazed with fatigue and worry, she struggled to absorb the rest of what her sister had told her yesterday afternoon.

"What's wrong? Is it Mom?" she'd said, instantly alarmed to hear Audrey's voice on the phone. The two sisters, she in California and Audrey in New Jersey, had talked more than usual during their mother's trip. But Audrey never called her at work.

"Don't jump on me!" For a moment Audrey sounded like a tormented six-year-old kid sister. Then her more recent self, the aggressive marketing director, stated firmly, "Mom had an accident. She's in intensive care. I'm going there tomorrow."

"There? Where?"

Audrey said something that sounded like a sneeze, which Margo recognized as the name of the place their mother was staying. *Ts-faht,* though the English spelling was nothing like that. Alice Simon's letters were all about *Safed.*

"In Israel." Dully, Margo stated the obvious. The faster her pulse thudded in her ears, the more slowly her mind seemed to process anything. She even had the bizarre sensation of hearing her voice coming from outside her body, talking about a multinational police task force covering the San Diego–Tijuana border. *Good grief.* "Audi, hang on a sec," she said, and switched off her office radio, which was broadcasting a report she'd done for *All Things Considered* on National Public Radio.

"I'm catching a flight to Tel Aviv tomorrow morning," Audrey said. "Hank can't possibly make it, they expect Ellen to go into labor any minute. But do you want to meet me there? If you think you can handle it . . ."

"How sick is she?" Why were they being summoned, if not to Alice Simon's deathbed?

"I don't know. I was told she isn't in any danger, she just needs familiar faces around her and someone to take care of her for a while when she gets out of the hospital. But I couldn't get through to anyone official at the hospital. It's the middle of the night in Israel. The only person I talked to was the woman who called me. The guru."

"Batsheva." Margo felt comforted, just as her sister sounded disapproving, at the thought of Alice's—well, *guru* was as good a word as any. Still, Margo had a lot of admiration for Batsheva Halevi and, even more, a deep confidence in her mother's judgment. It was a confidence Audrey didn't share. They'd had this conversation already and would no doubt have it again.

"We can talk more when we see each other," Audrey said, as if reading her mind. "I've been calling airlines. We can get flights that will put us in Tel Aviv just a few hours apart. I booked yours. You just need to call and give them your credit-card number. My flight arrives first, and I'll pick up the rental car—"

"What kind of accident? When did it happen? When did you hear?" *Why the hell didn't you call me right away, instead of calling airlines and car-rental agencies?* Margo didn't say it, but knew that her sister heard her loud and clear.

"Did you really want to have to make half a dozen frantic phone calls back and forth while we tried to coordinate everything?" Audrey snapped. "I thought this would make the whole trip easier."

Margo could picture the injured look on her little sister's face. Growing up, she'd seen it more often than her own face in the mirror.

"Audi, I'm sorry. Please, tell me how she got hurt. Was it a car accident?"

"She fell down some stairs and got a concussion. Plus, she had a reaction to some kind of medication. They think that's why she fell. So, do you want to meet me there?''

"Yes, of course. Thanks for setting it up.''

"Now, this is going to be stressful. Are you sure you can handle it?''

"Yes!'' Margo regretted, not for the first time, that she'd told Audrey she was being treated for post-traumatic stress disorder, the result of a fire in which she had nearly died seven months earlier.

"Don't jump on me! You leave at ten tomorrow. You know you need to get there two hours in advance since it's an international flight? Give me your fax number and I'll send you the details.''

"My fax number. It's . . . it's . . . Hang on.'' Margo had to go ask someone for the number she gave out at least twice every day. She felt breathless.

Mom. Intensive care. Alive.

She was still trying to catch her breath on the plane thirty hours later. After Audrey's call, she'd gone into crisis mode, calling to confirm her flight, letting Barry know what was happening and asking him to arrange for the kids to have dinner with them so she could say good-bye. She had wrapped up things at work as best she could. There was a story on a photography exhibit for which she'd completed all the interviews and someone else could do a final edit; a feature she'd just started on local American Indian casinos that Claire, the news director, wanted to put on hold until she returned; and a sheaf of phone messages that Claire plucked from her hand when she burst into tears. She changed her voice mail to say she was out of town, got a hug from Claire, and rushed home. She resisted the temptation to stop and buy things—what things? what did she need for Israel in May?—only by repeating to herself like a mantra, *They have stores in Israel. They have stores in Israel.*

"Excuse me,'' came a shy voice.

"Sorry, I was daydreaming.'' Margo got out of her aisle seat to let the teenage girl through. The girl reminded her of Jenny.

Jenny and David had been lifesavers when she got home last night. Barry had persuaded her to have a glass of wine while he fixed spaghetti and salad. Still, she would have gulped the wine at the same time she stuffed things into her suitcase, if she hadn't had to sit down with the kids and re-assure them. They had asked about "Grandma Alice" in a way that touched her heart. Jenny and David were Margo's stepchildren, but they'd come to know and love Alice Simon on her annual visits to San Diego. Two months ago the whole family had gone to Connecticut for Alice's Bat Mitzvah, that passage into Jewish adulthood that few women of Alice's generation had made at the traditional age of thirteen. Alice invited all of her grandchildren, Jenny and David as well as Audrey's two sons and Hank's daughter, to join her on the *bimah* at the front of the synagogue when she read from the Torah for the first time. Tears pricked Margo's eyes as she remembered her mother standing proudly on the *bimah,* an embroidered tallit draped over her shoulders. The trip to Israel—Passover in Jerusalem—was Alice's Bat Mitzvah gift to herself.

Margo stood to let the teenager back into her seat. She covered herself with a blanket, put a sleep mask over her eyes, and tried to get, if not comfortable, at least only moderately uncomfortable. "I've got these great pills that'll knock me out for the whole flight," Audrey had told her. "They're not even on the market yet." Audrey was the head of marketing for a pharmaceutical company. Lacking Audrey's connections, all Margo had was melatonin. The hormone hadn't been enough to give her much sleep the night before. But that might have had something to do with what had happened after she'd finished packing at midnight.

"Hey, sailor," she'd said to Barry. It was their ritual when he was about to leave on an oceanographic research cruise.

"Got something for me?" he'd replied with a satisfying leer.

"Come here." She was wearing a satin camisole from Victoria's Secret. She slipped the strap off her shoulder.

Making love had been terrific. Hadn't it? Maybe it was only her anxiety about her mother that made her feel as if they still hadn't recovered from the uneasiness that had entered their marriage a few months ago.

The melatonin was having little effect now, either. She tried not to squirm in the position into which she'd wedged herself in the airplane seat. She tried the slow, steady breathing she'd learned in yoga class.

Half an hour later she accepted defeat. She turned on her reading light and scrabbled through her carry-on bag, past a Walkman, tapes, camera, contact-lens paraphernalia, a mystery novel, and odds and ends she hadn't managed to fit into her suitcase. She knew what she wanted, it was just a matter of finding it. There!

Her hand brushed against the turquoise silk bag, bought on a trip to Chinatown in San Francisco. The bag held her mother's correspondence from Safed. Earlier in the flight, she had put the letters and postcards in chronological order. Now she took out the first, dated a month ago. In the two weeks prior to that, there had been scribbled cards from Tel Aviv, Masada, and Jerusalem, where Alice had gone with a tour sponsored by the Hadassah women's group. "Mom, isn't the tour enough?" Audrey had asked. "Do you really want two additional weeks all by yourself?" Alice replied that she had cousins living just outside of Jerusalem. In fact, she had "promised," according to Audrey—"No, she didn't," Margo said—to spend all of the final two weeks of her trip with them.

The first Safed letter was written on lined paper torn from a spiral-bound notebook, the neat handwriting a testimony to sticklers for penmanship in both Alice's native Hungary and the New World to which her parents had brought her when she was eight. The letter stated that she had changed her plans.

Dear Margo,

I haven't had some of the strong feelings people told me to expect in this country. I didn't weep when the plane landed at Ben-Gurion Airport or when my feet first touched the ground of Eretz Yisrael. Even with women sobbing all around me, I wasn't deeply moved when we prayed at the Western Wall.

But this place, Safed! We spent only a day, not even overnight, here on the tour. But the moment I set foot in this city, no, the moment I laid eyes on it, it was as if the ancient stones called my name. (Margo, you would hear it, too.) Being here, I had no trouble understanding why Safed became the center of Kabbalah, Jewish mysticism, in the sixteenth century. The tour guide told us it was more or less accidental, that Kabbalah was flourishing in Spain and then came the Inquisition and the expulsion of the Jews. The Ottoman Turks, who controlled this piece of the world at that time, wouldn't allow the Spanish Jews to settle in Jerusalem but permitted them to come to Safed. Something about trade routes, all very mundane. But walking down the cobbled streets of the Old City, feeling the atmosphere of this place, I have to believe it was more than just an accident of history and economics that made Kabbalah reach its peak in Safed.

I keep thinking of something I read when I was studying for my Bat Mitzvah: the idea that Jewish spirituality is "life in the presence of God." I do feel that in this place, I am in the presence of God, whatever He/She/It may be.

When we came here on the tour, we visited several artists' studios—there's an Artists' Quarter here that you'd love. I met an interesting woman about your age, Dalia Weiss, who has a room she rents to visitors. I realized that what I most wanted to do, when the tour ended, was spend a few more days here. Dalia's room was available. So, here I am.

Must go now, Dalia is taking me to a lecture by "the religious leader who's shaking up the whole town."

Wish you were here (I really do),
Mom

"Sixty-six years old! And a grandmother!" Audrey had fumed; she'd received a postcard with the same news. "What's a sixty-six-year-old grandmother doing going off on her own in a foreign country?"

"Sixty-six isn't that old."

"Come on, Margo. You and I have traveled alone. But when has Mom ever gone someplace by herself, anything more than getting on a plane to come visit you?"

"She only plans to stay for a few days." Margo took her mother's side automatically, but Audrey had a point: Alice wasn't in the habit of traveling solo. Well, all the more reason to start now! "It took the letters a week and a half to get from Israel to the U.S. She's already in Jerusalem by now."

"No, she isn't. I called there. They said she's not going to visit them until next week. And she doesn't have a phone at the place she's staying!" Audrey made it sound as if Alice had ripped a phone out of the wall on purpose to avoid her calls.

The next letter arrived two days later. Margo grinned, remembering Audrey's reaction. In her phone call, the words *guru* and *cult* had figured prominently.

But the moment of amusement faded. *Mother. Intensive care.* She folded the letter and returned it to the silk bag. She wanted to savor each letter, to hang on to them for tense hours in the hospital, talismans that a woman who could write letters so full of life couldn't possibly die.

Two /

Thursday—the 29th day of the counting of the Omer

She hadn't given it any thought—hadn't in her rush and worry focused on anything except her mother—but the layover at de Gaulle reminded her that she was traveling to a politically volatile destination. Instead of getting to wander around the airport and snack on Parisian goodies, she and the other Tel Aviv–bound passengers were restricted to a sort of holding area, a large, utilitarian room with worn plastic seats, harsh lighting, and only one women's toilet that worked. Security personnel at the entrance scrutinized and admitted new passengers, but let no one leave. The room was stuffy, and after an hour she had a blasting headache—and another hour to go.

She popped a soothing Miles Davis tape, *Kinds of Blue,* into her Walkman and swallowed three aspirin. Even with a throbbing head, however, she couldn't resist people watching. Just among the passengers for this one flight to Israel, she saw more variety than in a year in San Diego. Young people sporting multiple piercings and jeans rubbed shoulders with Hasidic Jewish men in their long black coats and broad hats. Two olive-skinned children accepted a piece of candy from a Scandinavian-blond woman, then shyly ran back and pressed against their mother, who was dressed in flowing North African robes. Margo heard Hebrew spoken, as well as English, French, German, and other tongues she couldn't identify. She had never seen such a wide range of humanity gathered in one place. A small boy with the side curls of the Orthodox came barreling along and tripped in front of her. She helped him to his feet and handed him to his black-coated father, who flinched when she inadvertently touched his arm. She remembered that very Orthodox Jews taught that a man wasn't allowed to touch any woman except his wife.

Margo wondered if this man had heard of Batsheva Halevi, and what he thought of her. She reached into her bag and unfolded Alice's second letter, written on a thin blue aerogram in a tight, disciplined hand that had allowed her to squeeze in as much as possible.

Dear Margo,

The religious leader is a woman!

But that already sounds wrong, because it makes someone like you or me think she's some kind of feminist revolutionary. And that's such an idiosyncratically American way to look at her. It's something Batsheva herself would discourage. In fact, she did discourage it, vehemently, when I suggested it. A much more accurate way to describe her, the way some people here refer to her, is as a modern-day Deborah. But I'm getting ahead of myself.

In my last letter, I said I was about to go to a lecture by the religious leader who's shaking up the town. From the way Dalia, my landlady, said this, I thought we were going to see some kind of zealot. What a surprise, then, what a REVELATION!, to meet Batsheva Halevi.

Let me set the scene. Dalia and I walk up the hill from her house in the Artists' Quarter and then down the Jerusalem Street pedestrian mall. (Not the most direct route, Dalia has to do an errand.) Every inch of stone we pass sings with history, centuries-old tales and also major events that happened in my own lifetime. The old British police station, for instance, is pockmarked with bullet holes from the War of Independence in '48. Just past the police station are the stairs to Citadel Park, the highest point in the city, where you can see the ruins of a Crusader castle. That sounds old, doesn't it, but the history of the hill goes back much further. Centuries before the Crusades, Jewish spotters stood there and watched for signal fires that announced the new moon—

which was the beginning of the new month. Then they'd light their fires to alert the watchers on the next hill. The hilltop was part of a network that went from Jerusalem to Babylonia.

Farther along Jerusalem Street, we turn downhill into the winding streets of the Jewish Quarter, where the Jewish population lived beginning in the sixteenth century.

As we walk Dalia tells me a little about Batsheva Halevi. She is a noted poet and her first husband, Yehoshua Halevi, was a military hero who died in the Yom Kippur War in 1973. She's now married to Lev Blum, a doctor who escaped from Czechoslovakia. She kept the name Halevi because she had already published poetry under that name. She has two children, a son from her first marriage and a daughter, Nili, from her second. The daughter is about Jenny's age. Batsheva isn't a young woman, however. She had her second child when she was forty.

We arrive at a magnificent stone house. Batsheva, Dalia tells me, comes from an old Safed family, the Saportas, Sephardic Jews who came from Spain in the 1500s. Batsheva lives in one of several family homes that are all on this street. Dalia mentions a cousin living next door with whom she isn't on speaking terms. We enter a spacious, bright living room where there are plastic folding chairs set up in rows. About ten people are already here. During the next few minutes another ten arrive. Dalia makes remarks about "the Batshevites," people who apparently think Batsheva Halevi walks on water. By this time I'm beginning to realize that Dalia is a terrible cynic, as well as being one of the most high-strung people I've ever met. Still, her skepticism makes me feel skeptical, too.

But then Batsheva comes out and speaks! First in Hebrew—which I follow a little—and then in English.

Alice's writing became minuscule as she filled the last flap of the aerogram.

I'm out of space and also out of time, have to get to class now. "What class?" you're asking. I've decided to study with Batsheva for the next week. It means staying in Safed longer than I'd planned, but Dalia's room is available . . . and her skepticism ought to keep me honest.

Much love to you, Barry, Jenny, and David,
Mom

That her mother had developed a great enthusiasm for Batsheva Halevi hadn't surprised her. As Margo heard more about Batsheva and her ideas, she felt enthusiastic, too. But even Margo had been alarmed when the extra week in Safed stretched into ten days, and then Alice extended her stay in Israel to continue her studies. Alice Simon made some decisions with her heart, but she was ever-practical. Changing her travel plans seemed disturbingly capricious as well as expensive. "Don't you think she's been hyperemotional," Audrey asked, "ever since Dad died?" "You make it sound like a disease. She feels things deeply, it's a gift," Margo responded, in spite of her own misgivings. (Hank, too, was inclined to trust their mother's judgment. But Hank never got embroiled in arguments the way his sisters did.) Eventually, Alice's letters, as well as a phone call, reassured Margo that her mother hadn't stopped being a woman of tremendous good sense.

Her headache persisted during the flight to Tel Aviv. She felt thoroughly miserable when she dragged herself through Customs at three P.M., after traveling for nineteen hours.

Then she was swept up in Audrey's hug.

"Look at you! I'm so glad to see you!" Audrey exclaimed, almost jumping up and down in excitement.

"Your hair! You dyed it red! I love it!" Margo held her at arm's length, grinning.

For a moment they were two sisters who adored each other and were deliriously happy to see one another after their long journeys.

Then: "How can you look so fresh?" Margo asked, her admiration mingled with pique. No one should be able to fly halfway around the world and look as perky as her sister did. It wasn't just that Audrey's magic pills had allowed her to sleep on the plane. Her newly red hair fell in perfect waves to the line of her slightly pointed chin, her makeup was understated but just right, and her unrumpled calf-length print skirt and cotton sweater looked as if they'd just come from the cleaners.

"Is that all you brought?" Audrey looked askance at Margo's one suitcase and small carry-on bag. "Well, I've got some things you can borrow. Everything except pants, of course." Audrey was four inches taller than Margo, five-ten, and still as willowy as when she'd been a seventeen-year-old ballerina. "Do you need to stop in the bathroom, anything like that?"

I need a new body! Margo wanted to cry. But settled for a trip to the ladies' room, where she splashed water in her face and decided it would be torture to try to put her contact lenses in her eyes.

"What about food?" Audrey asked. "I'd rather wait to eat until we see Mom, if that's okay with you."

"Fine. They kept stuffing us with vile things on the plane. I just need to get a snack to have when I take three more aspirin."

She bought a peach yogurt in the airport, Audrey handling the language and money. Thank heaven Audrey had spent a year of college in Tel Aviv, Margo thought, and followed her sister into the parking lot.

"I talked to the guy at the rental place and he told me the best way to get there." Audrey unfolded a map on the hood of their rental car, a white Renault. "If you'll navigate, I'll drive."

"Bless you."

Margo spooned in yogurt while Audrey traced the route: from the airport they'd go north parallel to Tel Aviv and the Mediterranean. That would take them to a highway directly east into the interior of the country. Safed was in the mountains, slightly northwest of the Sea of Galilee.

"Here, I picked up a tour book," Audrey said when they got in the car. How had she managed to do it, along with getting ready to leave on less than twenty-four hours' notice?

"You can look up things we're passing if you want to."

"Thanks." Margo doubted she'd point out any sites of interest. She only hoped to stay alert enough to fulfill her role as navigator, an ability she began to doubt as they got on the highway. "Most of the signs are in Hebrew," she moaned. "I thought they'd be in Hebrew and transliteration."

"That's right, you didn't take Hebrew, did you?"

No, you were the overachiever, Margo thought with more sympathy than resentment. Audrey was the one who'd had a Bat Mitzvah ... and been valedictorian of her class ... and gotten a Harvard MBA. It was Audrey who'd followed her two-years-older sister into a ballet class and then, through talent and very hard work, become good enough to dance major roles when she was in high school. She still took a rigorous ballet class, compared with Margo's relaxed improv dance sessions. Margo looked on Audrey's achievements with pride, and on her drive—not just to achieve but, it often seemed, to achieve more than her big sister—with dismay. "Why can't she ever feel she's won?" Margo had asked a counselor after Audrey let it drop at a family gathering that, between salary and stock options, she made six times what Margo did. "Because you're the firstborn daughter, and you'll always have the power of place," the counselor said.

"I called Mom from the airport," Audrey said.

"Did you reach her? How is she?"

"She sounded weak, but she's glad we're coming. I only talked to her for a minute. Then that woman took the phone." Margo gave a mental groan; she was too exhausted to have the Batsheva argument now. Audrey must have felt the same. All she said was, "She wants us to call her when we get to Safed. She said the hospital's difficult to find and she'll take us there."

"How's your job going?" Margo asked, eager to move the subject away from Batsheva Halevi.

"Busy, and I'm loving it. We're about to launch a new medication for heartburn and I've been hip-deep in focus groups, working with the ad agency, and all that. I brought a sample for Mom to try."

"I didn't know Mom was having stomach trouble."

"Yeah, she called me to ask what I knew." Did Audrey

actually sound smug at having been confided in when Margo wasn't? "The food in Israel is delicious, but it's different from what she's used to eating. Spicier."

"You said she had a reaction to some kind of medication. Was it something she was taking for the stomach problem?"

"I don't know."

Somewhere around a place on the map called Yagur Junction, they stopped at a gas station to fill up the car and use a bathroom. When they went inside to pay, the proprietor, a dark man with a heavy mustache and an angelic smile, poured coffee into two delicate china cups. He proffered a cup to Audrey. She tried to refuse, but he insisted. Finally she accepted the cup, but only took a sip. Margo took her coffee from the man with a big smile and drank all of it.

"That man was an Arab," Audrey said as they drove away.

"I thought he might be. Arabs are noted for their hospitality."

"Margo, don't be an idiot. This is Israel. Neither of us may like the policies of the Israeli government toward the Arab population, but an individual Arab isn't going to ask about your politics and then decide you're all right. There are Arabs who hate us on sight. You have no way of knowing whether that man was one of them."

Margo almost admitted that she, too, had felt wary; that just as Audrey had responded to her fear by not drinking the coffee, Margo had fought hers by drinking it.

But she said, "The coffee was delicious. The syrupy Turkish kind but not too thick, and sweetened just enough."

It did occur to her to wonder briefly whether all the competitiveness was on her sister's side.

Three /

Nili Blum had long-lashed hazel eyes, green flecked with gold, that even she considered pretty. Not that anyone could see them behind her thick, disgusting glasses! Her best friend, Shira, had gotten contact lenses a year ago. Nili had tried putting Shira's contacts in her eyes, and she hadn't minded the feel of the plastic there. She hadn't even balked at touching her eyeballs to insert the lenses and pluck them out. But was Nili allowed to get contacts? "When you're eighteen," her mother said, every time she asked. "It's not that far away," her mother usually added, stroking her cheek as if she were a child instead of a sixteen-year-old woman. She was old enough that her family would be looking for a husband for her if they were strictly Orthodox, and only two years away from the army since they weren't. Nili couldn't wait to go into the army, to get out of here!

She knew better than to rage at her mother. Batsheva always triumphed in a rage match, as she triumphed in any direct confrontation. Limited by being merely her father's daughter when it came to rage, Nili's anger was a slow fire, never dying but never burning hot enough to give her the courage to say how she felt. Batsheva thrived on argument. Not that Batsheva would admit she was enjoying herself or that her arguments reflected anything but concern for Nili's welfare. Hypocrite! Batsheva wanted what Batsheva wanted. It had nothing to do with Nili. Batsheva's daughter had learned her weapons had to be deception and stealth. Refusing to wear her glasses, for instance, when she escaped from the scrutiny of her parents or teachers, who would badger her until she put them on.

Myopia was interesting. Walking down the pedestrian mall in the half-light of dusk, Nili's nonvisual senses leaped into alertness like those of a blind person. A doctor at the hospital, where she volunteered in the lab, had told her people who went blind had to work hard to train their other senses; it didn't happen automatically. But then why, without her glasses, was she so keenly aware of the smells wafting from restaurants and bakeries? Why, through her sandals, did she feel every irregularity in the cobblestones underfoot, keeping her from falling even when she walked fast? Okay, it didn't always work and she fell sometimes. Once she was almost run down by a kid on a bicycle when she didn't get out of the way fast enough.

The danger was part of what she liked.

Moving shapes were people, the tall ones adults and the smaller, more active shapes children. Occasionally a small shape was a shrunken old person, but the old moved haltingly whereas the children were in constant motion, playing with other kids or skittering impatiently beside their slow-moving lumps of parents. It was a choreography she would have missed if she'd had to see every shape as an individual—this man, that little girl, that two-headed blob a couple walking close to each other.

Nili liked to think of herself as a shape, too, a tall, thin stream of protoplasm as shadowy to everyone else as they were to her (so tall, so thin, that she was almost indistinguishable from the surrounding air). Invisible Girl, she called herself. She liked to go out walking before dawn, when everything was already indistinct, even more from not wearing her glasses. She liked to imagine the earth's atmosphere changing to a constant fog, so it would look all day the way it did when she walked at three or four A.M. In the fog, everyone would live a quieter, more interior life, a life in which you didn't have to constantly, politely say *erev tov* to everyone who said *erev tov* to you—a constant torment in this town where too many people knew her by sight (though they knew *nothing* of who she really was). Just coming down the mall, she had to greet Shira's dad and one of her teachers and awful Mrs. Gebman with two of her four small children. Mrs. Gebman was only thirty and already she was fat and always looked unhappy. Her husband, Dr. Gebman, who worked with Nili's father, seemed even more miserable.

"Hey, Nili!" She recognized the voice that pierced her invisibility as she passed the tourist office and turned down the street into the Jewish Quarter.

Nili felt as if every too-tall cell in her body were growing taller as she turned around and towered over the cutest boy in her class. Why did she have to be born in a country where the only tall women were Swedish tourists?

"Hi, Shlomo," she said.

"Wasn't that history test a bitch?" said Shlomo Drapkin.

"Yeah." Was that the best she could come up with? "Want some gum?"

"Yeah. No, I can't. Braces."

Nili, who'd already taken the pack of gum out of her backpack, figured it would look dumb if she didn't take a piece herself. She stuck one in her mouth, knowing she must look like a donkey as she chewed.

She and Shlomo stood wordlessly on the steps for what felt like three hours.

"Well, gotta get home," Shlomo said.

"Me, too."

The rest of the way home, Nili thought of the sparkling things she could have said and despised herself for not saying them. Approaching the courtyard of her house, she jammed her glasses back on so hard, her nose hurt. A shape to her left resolved itself into Reuven Preusser, sneaking away from one of Batsheva's classes. He nodded to her, but skittered away. They had played together as children, but after he'd entered adolescence, Reuven had started avoiding girls. Did Reuven really think his black-hat Orthodox family wouldn't find out he was studying with Batsheva on the sly? Batsheva let him listen from a side room so the other students wouldn't see him. But how did Reuven explain his absences to his family? Visiting rabbis' graves? There were a lot of famous rabbis buried in and around Safed, but how many times could Reuven use that story?

And how could Reuven, who was only a year or two older than Nili, be taken in by her mother? she thought as she entered the house and avoided the living room, where Batsheva was still teaching. It was one thing for people in their fifties, or even their thirties, to lap up her mother's words—especially the Americans, since everyone knew that Americans came to Israel with all kinds of romantic notions. But Reuven? It made Nili sick, the way people acted as if Batsheva were some kind of biblical prophet. She'd like to take them with her right now, upstairs to her room, to see the evidence of just what kind of person her mother was.

Her diary was on her night table, exactly where she'd left it that morning. That was no surprise. The trap she'd laid was more subtle. Proceeding as meticulously as when she helped with a test at the hospital, she reached into her backpack for the Polaroid photo she'd taken before she left for school. She placed the photo on the table. Only then did she open the diary, holding her breath in her determination not to disturb the ribbon that marked her place. The difference—the evidence—was so obvious, she needn't have been so careful. The ribbon had been moved a full inch since this morning. And, just as when Nili had first gotten suspicious, the diary carried a scent she had known all her life, her mother's l'Air du Temps perfume.

For an instant she wanted to run downstairs into the living room and shout to all the people who adored Batsheva, "Look what this woman—this monster—does! She reads her daughter's diary!"

But Nili wouldn't try to expose her mother in front of her students. Not that she cared what the students thought of Batsheva, just that it would never work. Batsheva . . . would she even deny what she'd done? Or would she just tell them that Nili had been so sad and withdrawn lately—"you see how she is"—that Batsheva felt obligated to read her diary, something she'd never do under other circumstances, but she had to make an exception because she was worried about her daughter? Somehow, she'd make it sound as if this were an act of love and not a sick need to control, an inability to give Nili even one tiny millimeter of space that was her own.

One of her mother's favorite videos, which she'd forced Nili to watch twice, was an American movie where a sophisticated woman from New York and her teenage daughter go to visit

their backwoods relatives who live in a swampy area of the
United States. Partway through the movie, when they haven't
been with the relatives very long, the mother asks about the
daughter's drug use and the daughter tries to hand over her
plastic bag of drugs. "Take it!" the daughter says, almost
begging. The mother refuses. "It's up to you to decide what
to do with this," she says. But by the end of the movie, the
mother has become morally stronger from being around the
relatives—which doesn't make any sense, because the relatives are uneducated, violent savages, but that didn't seem to
bother Batsheva. The mother and daughter are on a plane going back to New York, and the daughter announces she's going to move in with her boyfriend, who's about forty.
(Disgusting, but that's what she wants.) The mother takes her
into the airplane toilet and hits her. She yells at the daughter
that she will do no such thing. "You can't stop me," the
daughter says. "Yes, I can," says the mother. "I'm the parent
and you're the child." Batsheva said the movie showed the
mother accepting her responsibility for her daughter. She liked
to say that line when she told Nili what to do: *I'm the parent,
you're the child.* Like this proved what a great mother she
was.

Imagining how Batsheva would twist everything, Nili got
so angry she wanted to throw the diary across the room, right
through the window. Let everyone on the street read her private thoughts, all the neighbors! Why not publish it in the
newspaper?

Then she thought of a plan. Not to hide the diary or take it
to school with her every day. The whole point was that her
private papers ought to be respected as private. She shouldn't
have to lock her diary in a vault to shield it from her mother's
spying. No, if Batsheva wanted to read the diary, Nili would
really give her something worth reading. *Dear Jessica,* she
wrote—she called her diary Jessica after her favorite pop song.
Then *Shlomo,* she started, but she crossed that out and wrote
Reuven instead. Why not get one of her mother's prized students in trouble? Especially when he acted like Nili had some
kind of plague.

*Reuven has the softest lips. I know I shouldn't have let him
kiss me—well, on the mouth was okay, but not all the places*

he was kissing me—but the night was cold and it felt so natural to hold each other. Then the kisses started, like moths alighting on my lips. She paused a moment, then smiled and continued, *Moths that turned into fire! They say young people like us are in the grip of our hormones. When we're alone together, all I want to say is, Thank you, God, for hormones.* Was that enough? *I hope I'm not pregnant,* she wrote, but then crossed it out as darkly as she could. She only wanted Batsheva to worry, not to pack her off to relatives on a remote kibbutz in the Negev.

Four /

Sometime between dusk and night, they turned from the major east-west highway onto the road into the mountains around Safed.

"It must be beautiful here during the day," said Margo, scanning the hills; there was still enough light to see the silhouettes of trees. "We'll have to come back. With Mom," she added, half whispering, not wanting to jinx anything.

"What?" Audrey was concentrating on driving, a demanding task now that they were on a twisting two-lane road. They were crawling behind an elephantine farm vehicle, with half a dozen cars lined up behind them. Audrey nosed out, hoping to pass, but pulled back quickly—cursing eloquently about the rental car's lack of pickup—when another car rounded a curve toward them.

"Language!" Margo admonished, laughing. Not that she hadn't heard Audrey swear before, but it was still strange to hear such words coming from her baby sister.

Audrey giggled. "Did Miss Burton ever wash your mouth out with soap?"

"The third-grade teacher?" Just thinking about grade school brought back the smell of chalk. "Not mine, but some of the kids in my class. Usually boys. Did she ever do it to you?"

"Promise not to tell Mom?"

Margo delivered her part of the childhood ritual. "Cross my heart and hope to die. Audi, what did you say? *Darn? Phooey?*" None of the Simon kids had gotten in a lot of trouble in school, but Audrey was the best-behaved of all, the irritating sibling who was good as gold.

"*Bloody.*"

"Excuse me?"

"You know, *bloody,* like the British say. I must have heard it on public television."

The farm vehicle turned off the road. Audrey stepped on the gas. The little car did its best to leap uphill, but Audrey was right; it didn't have much power. They continued a desultory conversation.

"Are you still taking ballet?" Margo asked.

"Twice a week. You still doing the improv dance class?"

"Yes, and some yoga."

"You'll be interested in a place along this road that I read about in the guidebook," Audrey said. "A vegetarian community where they have several restaurants."

"I said yoga, not yogurt. I'm not a vegetarian."

"Yeah, but they usually go together."

"Right," responded the sister who had left the civilized east for La La Land. "And all Californians believe in reincarnation, engage in goddess rituals, and howl at the full moon." Okay, she had howled at the moon on occasion. It was cathartic.

"Kabbalists believe in reincarnation. Did you know that?"

"Kabbalists, as in Jews?"

"As in Jewish mystics. As in some of the stuff Mom's been studying."

"But she doesn't believe that."

"She doesn't know, she has a lot of questions about it," Audrey said.

Margo leaned back, watching the sky—dark and starry, dusk having given way to full night. Reincarnation . . . She remembered learning you go around once and create your heaven or hell on earth. Not that she'd had much in the way of religious education. Until she was confirmed at age sixteen, she'd attended a weekly religious-school class, about half of which focused on making her aware of accomplished Jews in various fields (the inventor of Esperanto! Itzhak Perlman!), while the other half dealt with social issues. At home, her family lit the Hanukkah menorah and had a Passover seder.

But they hadn't even lit candles on Friday nights, a practice her mother had recently resurrected from her girlhood. "After World War Two, we wanted to be so American, so much like everyone else," she told Margo. She regretted not having passed along to her children what she called the *simcha*—the joy—of the rituals. Audrey had always been more drawn to Judaism, having a Bat Mitzvah and going to Israel as a college student; and with a Jewish husband, she observed some traditions at home. As for Margo, it wasn't that being Jewish meant nothing to her. She was sometimes moved to tears when she heard klezmer bands play the wailing folk music of Eastern European Jews, and she felt a sense of pride when she heard of Jews taking the lead in movements for world peace or social justice. But she'd never felt her life was poorer for not including practices her grandparents had followed decades earlier.

"Look!" Audrey said.

Margo followed her gaze across a sweep of blackness to a hillside full of lights—too many lights to come from just another small village or agricultural settlement.

"Safed?" She tried to pronounce it as Audrey did—*Ts-faht*, like a sneeze.

The highway took a sharp right at a place called Meron. Fifteen minutes later they entered the city that had cast its spell on their mother.

"She said there'd be a gas station right away," Audrey said, pulling into the station that had appeared as promised. She hadn't yet, Margo noticed, referred to Batsheva by name.

In the gas station, Audrey conversed in Hebrew with the teenage attendant. Audrey spoke slowly—it was fifteen years since she'd studied in Tel Aviv—but the kid seemed to follow her. They talked back and forth in gutturals Margo didn't think she'd ever learn to understand, and the boy got out a piece of paper and drew a circuitous map.

"Aren't we going to call Batsheva?" Margo asked. "So she can show us how to get to the hospital?"

"So she can be on top of us from the minute we get here? No, thanks. The hospital's not that hard to find. There's a doctor I want to talk to. He took care of Mom when she was first brought in. Gebman, I think his name is."

True to Audrey's word, they found the hospital easily. Audrey was equally adept at getting them past the security guard at the hospital entrance and into the intensive care unit.

Alice was asleep when they approached her bed in the ICU. But even though they tiptoed (as only two women with forty years of ballet training between them can tiptoe), she opened her eyes, aware of her daughters' presence with some sense more primal than hearing.

"My girls! I'm so glad you're here." Alice smiled, but her voice was weak and her face . . .

"Omigod," Margo said under her breath.

She'd known Alice had fallen, but she hadn't anticipated the wicked scabs that covered most of her mother's right cheek and half of the left; the wounds glistened with some kind of ointment that must be aiding healing but made them look even more raw. Was the rest of her body as battered? Stifling a sob, Margo ducked past a tangle of tubes and electrical leads that connected Alice to some frightening-looking machinery. She kissed her mother's forehead softly, trying to find a patch of skin that wasn't damaged. Trying to smile.

"I feel better than I look," Alice said, then turned to Audrey, who had squeezed through on the other side of the bed. "Red? You went red?"

"Yeah." Audrey's tone was defensive.

It's a good sign if she feels normal enough to hate our hair, Margo wanted to reassure her sister.

"Mom, what happened?" Margo said.

Alice glanced past them, a nearsighted, helpless look that tore Margo's heart out.

"Did Batsheva bring you?" Alice asked.

"No, we got a map."

"Why didn't you call her? I was hoping she'd explain. I'm much better, really, but I get tired."

"Hang on." Audrey went to the nurses' station, which faced the row of beds.

Margo found her mother's glasses on the bedside table and put them on her—less, she realized, for Alice's benefit than because she couldn't bear the vulnerability of her mother's naked eyes.

"You don't have to talk, Mom," she said. "I'll just babble."

Holding Alice's hand, she chatted about Barry and the kids. She spoke softly to avoid disturbing other patients—the ICU consisted of a row of beds with only curtains between them to provide a shred of privacy. Audrey and the nurse, on the other hand, had gotten too annoyed with each other to keep their voices down.

"I told you, I want to talk to Dr. Gebman," Audrey said.

"It's seven-thirty at night. He's at home with his family." The nurse spoke Brooklyn English, but apparently she felt no special warmth for someone from her native land. Not that Audrey was doing anything to inspire warm, fuzzy feelings.

"Then call him!"

Alice rolled her eyes at the commotion. "My take-charge baby daughter."

"She is, isn't she?" Margo said.

"The doctor on call can answer your questions," the nurse was telling Audrey.

"I don't want to talk to the doctor on call. I want to see Gebman. Don't walk away from me, dammit!"

One reason Audrey got things done, reflected her sister, was that she had no fear of conflict. Maybe Audrey should have become the reporter. Not that Audrey would ever be satisfied with the salary at a public radio station or the rewards of doing in-depth stories on the arts and society. She'd be a television anchor in a major metropolitan area by now.

"It is all right, Dr. Gebman comes," said a third person, a woman whose English combined Israeli and British notes. Margo glanced toward the nurses' station as the woman continued, "I called him as soon as Lottie at the front desk let me know you are here. You must be . . ."

"Mrs. Simon's daughter, Audrey Siegel." Audrey sounded prickly.

"I am Batsheva Halevi."

Margo did a double take. She thought her mother had written about Batsheva's appearance, but she must have completely fantasized the mental picture she'd had—a big woman comfortable with her bigness, a powerful zaftig guru. The actual Batsheva was short and just a bit plump, with brown-going-to-gray hair pulled into a simple chignon. Not that she was so devoted to matters of the spirit that she didn't care how she looked. She wore a stylish peach-colored tunic over a calf-length matching skirt. Though she didn't wear much makeup, there was a hint of coral lipstick. And when she walked over to say hello, Margo sniffed a delicate floral perfume.

"How good to have your daughters here at last," Batsheva said, after giving Alice a kiss.

"Very good," Alice said.

"Why don't I go talk to them and we'll let you get some rest?" As soon as Batsheva mentioned it, Margo realized guiltily that Alice looked even more haggard than when they'd arrived.

Strong-arming Audrey, who would have resisted Batsheva on principle, she followed the "guru" into a lounge just outside the intensive care unit. She and Audrey sat on a newish, uninviting sofa. Batsheva pulled up a straight-backed chair.

"Audrey? Margo?" She paused to make eye contact with each of them. She had incredible hazel eyes; deep-set, with bruised-looking lids; intensely alive. "Dr. Hillel Gebman is on his way. He is an excellent doctor, trained in Boston, and he can give you the complicated explanation. Let me just go over a few things that you already know and some things we found out only after I called you. As I said on the phone, your mother became ill two nights ago. She was disoriented and fell down a stairway."

"I thought she was renting a single room," Margo said. "Where were the stairs?" And how hard had Alice fallen, to produce all those bruises?

"She fell outside, on steps called the Ma'alot Olei Ha-Gardom. Even though she was injured, in a way it was fortunate because people saw her fall and she was brought to the hospital immediately. The fall resulted in a concussion, but it is not a problem."

"What *is* the problem, then?" Audrey wasn't overtly hostile, but Margo recognized that distant, unemotional tone.

"She had certain symptoms that looked like an overdose of a prescription drug," Batsheva said, "so she was treated for that immediately."

"They treated her without even knowing what she was taking. . . ."

Batsheva held up her hand and Audrey was silent. "You can discuss this with Dr. Gebman. You want to know what the problem is. Your mother told the doctor what medicines she was taking. Nothing sounded like a drug that would cause the type of reaction she had. Dr. Gebman thought she might be confused about one of the medicines or maybe she was taking something new from the United States. Yesterday, the woman whose house your mother stays in and I went into her room to look for pill bottles to bring the doctor. We found a pot of herbs sitting in water, like she had made a tea. We brought it here to be tested. It was golden henbane."

"Isn't henbane . . ." Margo frowned. The word stirred up vague associations; the associations made her uneasy.

"Golden henbane is a poison," Batsheva said.

Five /

"Someone poisoned my mother?" Margo barely knew if she or Audrey asked the question. Both of them had jumped to their feet. The rapid movement and the shock, on top of her jet lag, made her feel giddy.

"Sit, sit." Batsheva didn't seem flustered, even though Audrey had grabbed her shoulders.

Margo sat down, pulling Audrey with her.

"As I said," Batsheva continued, "the henbane was in a pot of water, as if your mother had brewed a tea."

"Are you saying she poisoned herself?" Margo said.

"Not intentionally, of course not. But she might have picked the henbane by accident. It grows wild all over Israel. Ah, Hillel." Batsheva turned toward a man who had entered the room.

Dr. Hillel Gebman was tall and rangy, with springy reddish hair that made his long, lugubrious face even longer. He didn't look much older than thirty, but there was a nervous intelligence about him that made Margo feel her mother was in competent hands.

"Batsheva said my mom might have picked the henbane," Margo said, after Batsheva had made introductions. "What does *she* say? She must know if she picked it or not."

"Actually, she doesn't know." Gebman shuffled from one foot to the other, rather than taking a chair. "Because of the concussion, she doesn't remember anything that happened on the day she drank the tea. It's common," he added, cutting off Audrey's expression of disbelief. "The biochemistry of memory doesn't operate instantaneously. A trauma like a concussion can prevent us from forming memories of the most recent events that occurred before the trauma.''

"Why would she pick herbs growing wild and make a tea?" Margo asked.

Audrey spoke at the same time. "How could you decide how to treat her? If you didn't know about the henbane until the next day?"

"She exhibited classic symptoms of anticholinergic poisoning," he responded to Audrey. "Flushed, with huge pupils. Skin hot and dry. There's a mnemonic I learned in med school: 'Blind as a bat, red as a beet, dry as a bone, mad as a hatter, hot as a pistol.' Your mother had them all. And she was disoriented, talking to people who weren't there—someone named Lou."

"Her husband," murmured Margo. Alice's dead husband.

"Our first assumption was she'd gotten too much of a prescription drug—antihistamines and also some heart drugs are anticholinergics," Gebman said. "But whatever caused the symptoms, the treatment is the same."

"And that is . . . ?" Audrey said.

"There's really not much you can do to counteract the poison, it has to work its way through the system. You treat the effects. We knew she'd fallen, so we did a CAT scan and an EEG for the head trauma. Fortunately we didn't see anything but concussion. And of course, we administered physostigmine for the cardiac arrest."

"The what?" Audrey demanded as Margo fought a rush of dizziness. She had said she could handle the stress of this trip, and dammit, she was going to. She took deep breaths and focused her attention on the doctor's flustered response.

"I—I thought you knew." Beads of sweat appeared on his forehead and he looked helplessly toward Batsheva.

Audrey turned on the guru. "You didn't tell me she had a heart attack!"

"I didn't know when I called you the first time," Batsheva said. "When I found out, already you were coming—"

"It wasn't a heart attack!" Gebman broke in with surprising vehemence. "The henbane didn't give her a heart attack. Cardiac arrest is less serious than a heart attack, it doesn't involve damage to the heart muscle."

"Did the henbane cause the cardiac arrest, then?" Audrey demanded. "Is that why you've got her in intensive care? What's her status now?"

"Sh-she's coming along fine." Dr. Gebman, having rallied to correct the medical misinformation, showed no real zest for battle. As he spoke he edged away. "Cardiac arrest occurred because the henbane accelerated her heart rate. She's had some runs—some minor runs—of arrhythmia since then. It's nothing serious, but that's why we're keeping her here for a few days. Really, she's doing well. I'm sure we'll be able to move her out of the ICU on Saturday."

"And then what? When can she leave the hospital?" Audrey asked.

"Probably early next week. We'll know better in a day or two. I'll be here tomorrow, if you have any other questions." He'd made it to the doorway.

"Dr. Gebman," Margo said, and repeated the question she'd brought up earlier. "Why would she pick wild herbs and make a tea?" It was the kind of thing Margo might do, but her mother was more a Lipton's kind of person, maybe drinking a cup of Earl Grey if she felt adventurous.

Batsheva answered. "For her stomach. You knew she was having trouble with her digestion? One of my students knows a great deal about herbs and offered to prepare her a tea. We think your mother decided to make the tea herself, and she picked the wrong herb."

"Or else the henbane came from the herbalist?"

"Ma'ayan? There is no way she would mistake henbane for some other herb."

"Could the herbalist have done it on purpose, then?" Asking questions—reverting to her professional role—made Margo feel less shaky.

"Harmed your mother? Poisoned her?" Batsheva chuckled. "Not in Israel. The only violence in Israel comes from Arab terrorists or the Russian Mafia."

"Is Hillel Gebman the only doctor treating my mother?" Audrey asked.

Margo glanced over and saw that the physician had made good his escape.

"The doctors work as a team," Batsheva said. "But Hillel was here when your mother was brought to the hospital. He stayed with her that whole night, until he was sure she was going to be all right. He takes a special interest since then."

"I want a second opinion," Audrey said.

"Of course. But there is no one better than Hillel Gebman."

"I'm sure he's very good, but should she really be in the hospital here? What about moving her to Hadassah in Jerusalem? Couldn't that be done by helicopter?"

"Audrey . . ." Margo said. She was too exhausted to fight.

Batsheva met Audrey's gaze, and smiled. "You are exactly the way your mother described you to me! Both of you," she added, including Margo in a look that communicated both warmth and *Don't mess with me.* "You will not be able to move your mother anywhere tonight. Why not see how you feel after you have had some sleep?"

Sleep, Margo thought with a desire as strong as lust—and almost groaned out loud, realizing she hadn't given any thought to where she and Audrey were going to stay. Did Safed have hotels? But she had no need to worry.

"Dalia got your mother's room ready for you." Batsheva spoke as if it had all been arranged. Audrey seemed to have thought of everything. "You can follow me in your car."

"Just show us on the map," Audrey said. "I drive in New York City. I can get anywhere with a map."

"Believe me, you will need me to take you."

Mother. Intensive care. And now, *Poisoned.*

"The nerve of that woman," said Audrey at the wheel of the rental car as she tailed Batsheva out of the hospital parking lot and up a hill. "Withholding the information about Mom's cardiac arrest."

"Oh, Audi, I was worried enough on that flight. If we'd known, we couldn't have made the planes fly any faster." She didn't know if she agreed with Batsheva's decision not to tell them or she was just arguing because Audrey provoked argument. "Aren't youngest children supposed to be easygoing?'' she had once asked her counselor. ''Sure, in theory,'' the counselor replied. Sitting beside her combative little sister, Margo smiled ruefully. Audrey had emerged from the womb with something to prove.

''Bossy, arrogant, controlling,'' Audrey continued her complaint. ''Can you believe she had someone at the hospital call her to *report* when we arrived? Like having a spy system. She didn't want us to see Mom without her there.''

''Mom wanted her there. You should have seen the way she lit up when she heard Batsheva's voice.''

''Right, that's how cults work. They make you totally dependent.''

Bossy or not, Batsheva had been right about the difficulty of describing where they were going. The route, although short, doubled back on itself because of one-way streets. Margo was grateful to have a guide.

They followed Batsheva into a parking lot, stopped, and got out of the car.

''So that you can find your car tomorrow, we are on Ha-Palmach Street, close to the Saraya, the old Turkish government house,'' Batsheva said. ''We walk to Dalia's, she is in the Artists' Quarter. You should put on sweaters,'' she added.

Margo didn't need to be persuaded. Safed was in the mountains, and the night was chilly. She grabbed her jacket from the back of the car.

Even Audrey, after a moment's hesitation, put on a sweater. But made clear her opposition to the guru by her disgruntled tone, asking, ''Can't we drive in, unload our bags, and come back here to park?''

''Not in the Artists' Quarter. You cannot drive a car there. Where is your luggage?''

Audrey opened the trunk of the car. She'd brought two fat suitcases as well as two carry-on bags. *My sister the clotheshorse,* Margo thought, reaching for her single suitcase and carry-on. No wonder Audrey was always impeccably turned out and Margo looked more like Diane Keaton in *Annie Hall.* Audrey handed her carry-ons to Batsheva and hoisted the two big bags herself. Margo knew better than to suggest that she leave one of them in the car and get it tomorrow. Batsheva kept quiet as well, but she struck a swift pace and didn't look to see if Audrey was keeping up. Maybe Batsheva just walked fast. Or maybe, in spite of her surface composure, she was ready to smack Audrey in the face, a desire Margo could understand.

After a short walk down HaPalmach, they descended the hill by shallow steps placed a yard or so apart. Batsheva then led them down a narrow cobbled alley, the shadow splashed with light whenever they passed a doorway. Through decorative scrollwork, Margo peeked at the courtyards within.

"I feel like I've just stepped into my mother's letters," she said.

"Your mother reminds me of a saying I heard from a rabbi," Batsheva remarked, walking close beside her; Margo noticed the floral perfume again. "Some people come into a room and it is as if they say, 'Here I am. I am so important. Notice me.' Your mother comes into a room in a way that says, 'There *you* are.' She is interested in everyone."

"Yes," was all Margo could get out, her voice suddenly full of tears. Batsheva had touched both Alice's essence and, in knowing exactly what to say to her, Margo's deepest self. She had been ready to like Batsheva from her mother's letters; she was impressed by the obvious affection between Batsheva and Alice; and she'd admired Batsheva's strength in telling them difficult news and facing their reactions. Now she felt she was glimpsing firsthand the wise woman around whom students and seekers gathered—the woman who was herself a seeker, who wouldn't be satisfied with anything less than the truth.

Then how could Batsheva believe Alice had poisoned herself?

Six /

Thursday—the 29th day of the counting of the Omer

After a couple of turns down the alleys of the Artists' Quarter, Batsheva swung open an iron gate. They entered a courtyard with pots of flowers everywhere.

"Dalia!" Batsheva called out, followed by something in Hebrew.

"*Shalom!* Hello!" A small, wiry woman with cropped dark curls emerged from the stone house. She came forward with her hand outstretched in greeting, but quickly shifted focus when she saw the luggage they carried. "We go to your room and you can put those down. Come! Come!"

With an economy of movement that the dancer in Margo appreciated, Dalia led them to a door at the side of the house and inserted a key. She opened the door and switched on a light just inside, then held the door for them.

"How pretty!" Margo took in the wooden table with a lilac-print cloth, two framed pen-and-ink drawings of a synagogue (Dalia's work, she knew from her mother's letters), the vase of fresh white flowers . . . and a double bed. She held her breath, waiting for her sister to gripe. Audrey had balked at sharing a bed with her even when they'd visited their grandparents as children; however, the cozy little room had no space for a cot.

But Audrey said, "It looks great. Thank you, Dalia."

Dalia's accent was thicker than Batsheva's and her syntax occasionally tenuous, but Margo had no trouble understanding when she invited them to have something to eat. She'd thought she was more tired than hungry, but her mouth watered at the mention of hummus and pita.

They went around to the main door. Dalia Weiss's home was less conventionally pretty than her guest room, a true artist's abode. More of her drawings of synagogues—interiors and exteriors, peopled and empty—hung on the walls. It was work, Alice had written, that kept Dalia in shekels because the tourists snatched it up. Not that the drawings were inferior art. They were beautifully executed with a precise attention to detail. But some of the pieces in the artist's own home were edgier and more challenging—abstract drawings that had a passionate energy and jagged metal wall sculptures.

"You like that one?" Dalia asked. Margo had stopped in front of a sculpted hand, the palm raked with deep scratches that rent the metal. The piece could have been overdone, but the artist had stopped before the impression of suffering crossed the line into melodrama.

"I don't think it's the kind of thing you can like," Margo replied. "But it's strong. It refuses to be ignored. Your work?"

"Yes. Come, sit. You will take coffee? Or do you prefer mineral water?"

"Water, please. I plan to be asleep in about half an hour."

Dalia—"the most efficient woman in Safed," according to Batsheva—had already arranged food on a tray. She placed the tray on a round, glass-topped coffee table and poured coffee for herself and Batsheva, water for the jet-lagged travelers. Over the snack, the Israelis offered advice about places in the area to visit.

"How much memory loss does my mother have?" Margo asked. Fortified by tasty hummus and slices of melon, she'd finally stopped feeling as if her mind were suspended in some time zone between California and Israel, maybe over Iceland. "A few hours? More than that?"

"She remembers being in class on Monday afternoon. Nothing after that," Batsheva said.

"And she has no memory of picking the henbane, right?"

"It was in class on Monday that Ma'ayan offered to make the herbal tea for her. She wouldn't have had the idea of picking herbs until then."

"Did Ma'ayan say anything about what kind of herbs she would use? What they looked like?"

"Not in the class. Maybe afterward. Dalia, do you know?"

Dalia looked up from her coffee cup and shook her head.

"So, if she picked the henbane herself," Margo mused, "she could have done it Monday afternoon. But more likely Tuesday. Dalia, did you see her come back here either day carrying a bunch of herbs?"

"I'm sorry. More slowly?"

Margo repeated the question.

"No, but I go out a lot. Drawing in synagogues. I don't see her all the time anyway. I don't bother people staying in my guest room."

"It's okay." Margo hadn't meant to imply some kind of negligence. "What does *she* say about it? I know she can't remember, but does it make any sense to her that she'd pick the herbs herself rather than waiting to get the tea from Ma'ayan?" Was she the only one who doubted that Alice had picked her own toxic tea?

"She was surprised," Batsheva answered. "But she told me she used to gather herbs for her mother when she was a girl in Hungary."

"Sixty years ago!"

"Ma'ayan tells her an herbal tea will help her stomach," Batsheva said. "Maybe henbane looks like an herb she remembers that was good for stomach problems, and she decides to make the tea herself."

"Many of us here pick herbs for tea," Dalia said. "Sage, chamomile, mint, they all grow wild."

"Margo, what's the alternative?" Audrey said. "Do you think someone poisoned her deliberately?"

"No. I don't know. Whatever she did in Hungary sixty years ago or what people do here, for most of her life Mom's bought tea at the supermarket. Even if Ma'ayan told her what herbs to look for, she'd show them to Ma'ayan first to make sure she had the right ones. Everything I know about her says this is crazy."

She looked at Audrey; her sister merely shrugged. Batsheva, however, fixed her with those remarkable eyes.

"Are you sure?" Batsheva studied her face intently, as if

she expected to find the answer there. Margo had the weird feeling that if she were lying, even to herself, Batsheva would see it.

"I'm not saying anyone did this deliberately, but what if someone wanted to help her by giving her the herb tea, and *they* picked the wrong herb?"

"Batsheva!" Dalia said, and spoke urgently in Hebrew. Batsheva responded, evidently disagreeing. Margo expected Audrey to join in, but the Israelis must be speaking too fast for her. They argued back and forth for a minute or two. Then Batsheva returned to English.

"Dalia insists that I tell you what has happened to some of my students. A few of the students, especially the North Americans, have had acts of vandalism committed against them. Our young rabbinical student, Danny—someone threw ink on his clothes that were hanging on the line. Flowerpots were broken at a home being rented by a Canadian couple. We think this is done by boys who are threatened by the way I teach. But it is only vandalism, children's pranks—nothing like what happened to your mother."

"What about the dead bird by Kathy's room?" Dalia said.

"The bird could have died there on its own."

"With its neck broken, like a person twisted it in his hands?"

"Dalia, Dalia. It was just a bird."

"Do you know who these boys are?" asked Audrey.

"No, and not even if it is the same boy every time. All boys are naughty. I know, I raised a son. Who knows if the boys who did these things were even aware that these people were students of mine? Maybe they just resent Americans."

"She was lying," Audrey said, when she and Margo were alone in their room.

"About what?" Margo had unpacked enough just to find her nightshirt and toothbrush. Audrey seemed to be planning to stay awake until she'd put all of her things away.

"Not knowing who the boys are. When she and Dalia were speaking Hebrew, Batsheva said she'd talk to someone named Yitzhak. I'll ask Dalia about him tomorrow, when Batsheva can't interrupt. At least, Dalia seems to understand that these kids can be dangerous.''

"Does that mean you agree with me that Mom wouldn't have picked the henbane herself?''

Audrey paused, a stack of neatly folded shirts in her hands. "Margo, I don't know what to believe. I would never have thought she could fall under the sway of someone like Batsheva. Did you know about her picking herbs when she was a kid?''

"No,'' Margo admitted. "You even thought to bring photographs?'' she said as Audrey placed framed pictures of her husband and their two boys, nine-year-old Zach and six-year-old Bobby, on top of the bureau.

"I'd forget my underwear before I forgot the photos. It's really important to Zach. I don't know how I traumatized him when he was little, but he has a terrible time when I have to go away. I always prepare him in advance when I've got a business trip. We look at the map and we mark the calendar for the days I'm going to be gone. And I've never had to take a trip that lasted more than a few days. This time—I called home from the airport in Tel Aviv so I could talk to the kids before they left for school. Zach was such a good little soldier, he knows Grandma needs me. But he was freaked out. On the phone, he started to cry. And I brought my cell phone so he could call me, but it doesn't work here! Oh, hell. Bloody hell!''

Margo put her arm around Audrey's shoulder.

"It'll help once we know when Mom will be well enough to travel,'' Audrey said, leaning into her. "Then I can tell him exactly when I'm going to come home. He'll mark it on the calendar. It makes him feel like he has some control.''

She went back to unpacking while Margo got undressed.

"What else did Batsheva and Dalia say when they were speaking Hebrew?'' Margo asked.

"Batsheva asked how the boys would have known to give Mom herbs. Dalia thought maybe Ma'ayan mentioned something in front of her son, or else someone named Nili heard.''

"I think Nili's the name of Batsheva's daughter.''

"That must be why Batsheva got upset when Dalia suggested it.''

"We'll probably meet Nili when we go there on Saturday. By the way, what's Havdalah?" Margo asked. Batsheva had invited them to "Havdalah" and dinner on Saturday night, and she hadn't wanted to parade her ignorance in front of her mother's teacher.

"A service that marks the end of Shabbat and the return to ordinary life."

Ordinary life, Margo mused, lying in bed. She had thought ordinary life ended last fall, up in flames along with her house and most of her possessions. She hadn't understood how much more she could lose, not until what had happened with Barry three months ago. Was there a service that would return her to the ordinary? Any religion that offered one could sign her up as a believer.

Seven /

Dear Margo,

One of the things I love to do here is to go out walking very early, at five-thirty or six A.M. Did you know that the traditional morning prayer, said immediately upon waking, thanks God for giving back your soul? At dawn in Safed, I feel as if God has given back the soul of the world.

Love and XXXXX,
Mom

Funny—or was it more than funny? did it have some mystical significance?—that this postcard was next in the embroidered bag holding Alice's letters and that, without reading it, Margo put it in her jacket pocket at six when she quietly dressed and slipped out the door. She didn't look at the card until she was sitting outside a café on Jerusalem Street at seven . . . sitting and trying to quiet the inner trembling that had started when she'd seen the Ma'alot Olei HaGardom.

A stairway. Batsheva said Alice had fallen down a stairway. Technically that was true. But the Ma'alot Olei HaGardom was to ordinary stairways as the Beatles were to a garage rock band. Spanning the length of the hillside on which the Jewish and Artists' Quarters perched, it descended two hundred steps—she'd counted—interrupted only by an occasional landing where it intersected the street. And the stones! *Ma'alot* means "ascent," Audrey had told her. The whole name translated as "those that ascended the gallows," probably a tribute to people who'd died in the fight for the Jewish state, Audrey said. When she saw it, Margo thought of it as "the Gallows Stairs."

She took another bite of whatever was on the table in front of her—a poppy-seed roll, moist and still warm from the oven. She barely tasted it. She had also bought a cup of hot tea, which she gulped. She felt icy cold.

The Gallows Stairs were made of the same white-and-ocher limestone as the streets and buildings of the Old City. Decades of use had worn down the edges of the steps but had also left jagged spots where shards of rock had splintered away. Had Alice managed to slow her fall? Or had she blacked out immediately and kept falling, crashing against the rough stone?

Margo gave thanks to—God? Alice's own zest for life?—that her mother was still alive. And she set her heart on finding out what had really happened three nights ago.

Paper? Her napkin would do. She began to make notes. Finally she felt warm. She took a bite of the roll and discovered it was delicious.

A lovely floral scent made her look up.

"Batsheva, good morning."

"*Boker tov,* we say. *Boker* is 'morning.' *Tov* is 'good.'" Batsheva Halevi held a plastic sack from which the ends of two challahs protruded.

"*Boker tov,*" Margo said. She hadn't planned to ask questions so soon, but Batsheva was getting herself a cup of coffee, and why not?

"I've been thinking," she said, when Batsheva sat down with her coffee and a pastry.

"I, too." In fact, Batsheva looked like the one suffering from jet lag, her face pale except for purplish circles beneath her deep-set eyes.

"Did the police investigate my mother's poisoning?"

"We informed them. But no one thought a crime had been committed."

Margo watched, fascinated, as the older woman took an enormous bite of pastry, sending a shower of crumbs into her lap. Did Batsheva bite into life like that?

"Whoever picked the henbane," Margo said, "whether it

was my mother or someone else, they must have used a bag of some kind. Did the police find a bag? Did they test it for fingerprints?''

Batsheva sighed. ''Your mother tells me you have solved murders. If you had been with Dalia and me, you would have called the police the moment we noticed the pot of tea. But we . . .'' Pastry-flaked palms up. ''You are right, we found a plastic bag of herbs in your mother's room when we went there to see what medicines she was taking. We brought everything, the tea and the bag of herbs, to Hillel Gebman. He gave them to the police. You can talk to the police officer, Rafi Garfein.''

''Thanks, I will. I'd like to talk to Ma'ayan, too.''

''Ask Dalia to show you where she lives. That is the second most benign explanation, is it not?''

''What?'' Was Batsheva less proficient in English than she seemed? Or was she given to speaking in riddles?

''The most benign explanation for what happened,'' Batsheva said, ''is that your mother picked the henbane herself. That way no one has to feel guilty, only your mother feels a little foolish, but everything is all right because she recovers so well. Then the *second*-most benign explanation is that Ma'ayan gave her the henbane by mistake.''

''Why didn't Ma'ayan say something?''

''Out of fear? To protect her reputation? I do not say this is ethical behavior. But if all that happened is a terrible mistake, then there was no malice involved.''

''But,'' said Margo, responding to Batsheva's tone, ''you don't think that's how my mother got the henbane.''

''What I think?'' Batsheva demolished the last of her pastry. ''I think that Ma'ayan can identify golden henbane. Have you heard of the *yetzer ha-ra*? The evil impulse?''

Another riddle? She was intrigued by the way Batsheva's mind worked.

''Is it like original sin?'' she asked.

''Not at all. Catholics believe everyone is born sinful. Jews believe we have two possibilities that coexist, the *yetzer ha-tov* and the *yetzer ha-ra*—the impulse for good and the impulse for evil. You might think that means we try to manifest only the good and eliminate the evil, as the Catholics try to do. But we Jews make things more difficult. We say that both good and evil come from God. We see evil as part of divine creation. Without evil, free will means nothing.''

A book Margo had read as a child described God as the good that was in the world. Obviously a simplified version of the story.

''More than that,'' said Batsheva, ''the Talmudic rabbis saw the evil impulse as a source of strength and creativity. They said that without the *yetzer ha-ra,* a man would never marry and have a family. He would lack the drive to excel in his work.''

''Sounds a lot like testosterone.''

''American women always say that.'' Batsheva frowned, and Margo felt absurdly like a schoolgirl who had disappointed her favorite teacher. ''But the rabbis had a great deal to say about the evil committed by women. Women's evil, like that of men, is connected to the sexual drive. Take the figure of Lilith, Adam's first wife, who disobeyed him and was driven from Eden. Lilith is said to have become a terrible seductress, a demon who tries to tempt men from the path of righteousness. Some women now claim her as a heroine because she spoke her mind.''

''You don't?''

''As a matter of fact, I am very fond of Lilith. You must be wondering what any of this has to do with your mother.''

Margo nodded, although she was enjoying the theology lesson. She could see why her mother had been drawn to this lively mind.

''Shall we walk?'' Batsheva suggested, glancing around.

In the short time they'd been talking, Jerusalem Street had come to life, every table filled at the little outdoor café and shoppers striding purposefully along the mall. Many of them carried braided challahs—stocking up, as Margo and Audrey had been advised to do, before all the stores closed by early afternoon for the Sabbath.

Batsheva waited to speak until they'd left the crowded mall and turned onto a cobbled street that led downhill.

''At first,'' she said, ''when I learned the herb in your mother's room was henbane, I didn't think of the *yetzer ha-ra.* I thought—we all thought—she had picked the henbane by accident. Last night, after you insisted she would never do that, I asked myself what else might have happened. From the least evil possibility to the most." No wonder Batsheva's eyes were dull with fatigue.

"And you?" she asked Margo. "About what have you been thinking?"

"The boys you mentioned last night. When you say *boys,* what age are you talking about?"

"Fourteen, fifteen? Maybe a little older, maybe younger."

"In the U.S., kids younger than that are in gangs and carry guns. But the things you mentioned, throwing ink on someone's laundry, breaking flowerpots, even strangling a bird—that's awful, but it's still the act of a child. Poisoning someone and sending her into cardiac arrest, isn't that an entirely different magnitude of . . . evil?" she said, using Batsheva's word.

"Ah, but you confuse intention and result." Batsheva took a brisk left. The discussion seemed to give her energy. "Suppose a boy did give your mother the henbane. Would he have any idea she would make it into a tea?"

"She was expecting herbs from Ma'ayan."

"How would he know that?"

"If Ma'ayan mentioned it to her son."

Batsheva's laughter was surprisingly girlish. "Your sister hasn't lost her Hebrew, has she? But really, I'm sure Ma'ayan's son has nothing to do with this."

They must be in the heart of the Jewish Quarter, judging from the preponderance of women wearing long, shapeless dresses and the men in black hats and overcoats; and judging as well from the occasional man who glared at them or muttered as they passed. A woman sweeping outside her gate gave a hard push with her broom and sent dust into their faces.

Batsheva ignored them. Nor was the hostility universal. For every dirty look, several people said *shalom.*

"Tell me," Batsheva said, "what would you do if you found a bag of herbs outside your door?"

"I suppose I'd ask someone what they were."

"Someone like Ma'ayan, yes? And if you found out the herbs were poisonous, you might feel disturbed that someone gave them to you. It would be a cruel joke. But it wouldn't harm you, no more than Danny was harmed by the ink on his clothes.''

"How do you know someone left the henbane by her door? What if they handed it to her and said to make tea and drink it? How convenient for them that she had a concussion.''

"Ah, but no one could predict she would lose her memory, and would not be able to point her finger and identify him,'' Batsheva replied. She took a short jog to the left, then a right onto a street covered by a stone archway, and then—oh hell, Margo was losing track. She hoped Batsheva would walk her partway back to Dalia's. In the Old City's narrow alleys, she might be lost for hours. "Even if this person *did* think your mother might drink the henbane, she became more ill than anyone could have imagined.''

"Are you trying to excuse whoever did this?''

"Not at all. I want to understand his intention.''

"His intention?'' Margo stopped walking and faced her mother's teacher. "I have absolutely no interest in drawing moral distinctions between someone who never dreamed my mother would drink the henbane versus someone who *intended* to nearly kill her.''

"Margo, you misunderstand me. My point is, if we know why, it helps us know who.''

"And do you have any idea who?''

Batsheva bit her lip. "No.''

"One of those boys?'' Margo pressed.

"I don't know. I'm not being a good tour guide. Let me show you something.''

Bathsheva led her farther down the hill. The street dead-ended and she pointed to the right.

"Look. Up there!''

High across the narrow alley, attached to the facing walls, was a wooden frame in the shape of a Star of David; the frame was covered with pine boughs. They passed under it into a small square.

"The Lag B'Omer procession starts here on Sunday,'' Batsheva said. "I wish you had come for a different reason, but you'll love being in Safed for Lag B'Omer.''

Margo nodded in the right places as Batsheva described the procession that would start on the afternoon before the holiday, followed by a twenty-four-hour celebration on Mount Meron.

Batsheva had a point that if a boy had left the henbane, he probably didn't figure Alice would drink it. That eased Margo's reservations about seeing one of the local delinquents as the culprit. The kid must be quaking in his sandals over his prank gone so wildly wrong.

Still, Batsheva said she had considered all the possible explanations for Alice's poisoning, from the most benign to the most malicious. Surely she hadn't ignored the idea that the poisoner *had* known Alice was expecting an herbal tea. True, no one could have anticipated the fall and concussion or the cardiac arrest. But what if whoever left the henbane knew it would make Alice ill? Knew it—and desired it?

Where did that rank on Batsheva's hierarchy of evil?

Eight /

"So I tell those gonifs, those thieves, 'What do you think, I'm some kind of putz? Some teenage kid who can't find his own asshole?'

" 'Gadi, Gadi,' they say, big smiles on their faces now. No one smiles as big as Arabs when they're smiling. 'You know we had to test you,' they say. 'We need to find out what a man is made of, before we enter into a business relationship with him. You want some baklava?' they ask me. And then, real casual, 'Or how about some hash?'

" 'Baklava. And coffee,' I say. Ha, ha. I sure as hell wouldn't smoke hash in front of them, give them a lever to use against me. Wouldn't be much of a lever, anyway. I just do hash the way I take a drink sometimes. If it's there, I enjoy it. If it's not, I don't miss it."

Finishing his story, he lit the pipe and took a toke, then offered it to the girl lying next to him in bed.

"I don't really understand what kind of business you're in." The girl said it like she was about to pull out a pencil and start taking notes. "I mean, the cell-phone store I understand, but what else do you do? What kind of business are you doing with the Arabs?"

"I'm a broker. I bring people together who want to do business, especially people from different cultures," Gadi said carefully. When he'd met her at a café last night, she'd told him she was an undergraduate from—Yale? Princeton? one of those fancy American universities—doing a semester in Tel Aviv. Now he wondered if she could be some kind of cop.

He watched as she took her toke. She inhaled. Which didn't mean anything. A cop might inhale. But hell, would a cop have actually slept with him? Not that sleeping with him was an unpleasant experience.

"I could go for some baklava right now," she said.

"I could go for something sweet, too." Gadi stroked her muscled thigh. These American girls were made of iron.

"Gotta pee first." She got up, walked nude across the room to the bathroom. This one was a swimmer, the back of her body deeply tanned except for the white crisscross marks from her racing suit on her back, and her firm white butt.

He had another toke.

She took her time about getting back to bed, pretending to look around the room—strutting for him, arching her back a little to stick out well-developed breasts. Another benefit of the swimming? She had to be what she said she was.

"Who's this?" she said, coming to the photograph of him, Tamar, and the kids and picking it up.

"My sister's family," he lied. "Come here." She put the photo down and started toward him. "No, turn it," he said.

"What?"

"The photo. Turn it the other way. I don't want my niece and nephew watching."

"They might learn something," she teased.

"Sure. Okay. Let them watch. Now come here."

Gadi didn't disappoint her—he never disappointed any woman in bed—but his mind had already left his apartment in a dingy Tel Aviv suburb.

In his imagination, Gadi Halevi was on the road to Meron, on the way to the business opportunity that was going to set him up for life.

Part Two /
The Evil Impulse

To most Kabbalists . . . the existence of evil is . . . one of the most pressing problems, and one which keeps them continuously occupied with attempts to solve it. They have a strong sense of the reality of evil and the dark horror that is about everything living.

Gershom Scholem,
Major Trends in Jewish Mysticism

Nine /

"Just keep turning uphill wherever you can, and you'll get back to the Jerusalem Street mall," Batsheva had told her.

So why did Margo feel she'd wandered miles from the mall? Miles from her own century?

She'd continued walking beyond the square where the Lag B'Omer procession would start. As Batsheva had mentioned, the street led her past several of the synagogues for which Safed was renowned. Somehow she hit a dead end. She retraced her steps and found the next street that went up the hill.

Already, at eight-thirty A.M., the Mediterranean sun was baking the stones of the Old City. She took off her jacket and tied it around her waist, the sun hot on her shoulders whenever she had to leave the shade of the buildings. Had she remembered to pack sunscreen? *They have stores in Israel,* she reminded herself. But what kind of stores? Gazing at the Hasidim in their overcoats, it was hard to believe that the same city in which they lived would have ordinary markets. Hard to believe she had anything in common with them. Walking down a street in Africa or Papua New Guinea, would she feel any more foreign than she did here?

The street she'd hoped would take her uphill was only a short jog that stopped at a T. She turned again and paralleled the hillside.

She would have asked directions, but no one looked friendly. She had thought the hostile glances earlier were meant for Batsheva. Now that she was alone, however, she sensed even more disapproving looks. Even the men not in

Hasidic garb wore *kippahs* and had fringes showing at the bottom of their shirts that proclaimed them as Orthodox Jews. (What were the fringes called, and why were men supposed to wear them, anyway? Had that ever come up in her very non-Orthodox religious education?) Were the men really scowling at her, or was she so accustomed to smiling Americans that the Israelis' expressions seemed grim?

She walked faster. From the map she had glanced at last night, the entire city of Safed, both the Jewish and Artists' quarters, looked as if you could walk from one end to the other in less than half an hour. Even if she missed the mall, as long as she kept walking she ought to get somewhere.

A man addressed her in Hebrew. He sounded angry.

"English?" she said. "Español?"

He didn't answer.

She kept going. Faster.

Something small and hard hit her arm. She ran.

"Margo!" she heard someone call. "Margo Simon?"

The voice sounded American. She slowed to a fast walk.

The man ran up beside her. He was dressed in Western clothes, no *kippah* or fringes. "Are you Margo?" he said.

"Yes. How did you—" She stopped at last, panting.

"Your mom's proud of you. She carries photographs. I'm Danny Rubicoff."

The name was somewhat familiar and the face smiling. For the moment that was enough.

"You should put on your jacket," he said.

"What? It's hot."

"It offends them to see a woman in a sleeveless dress. They feel it's immodest."

"Oh." She slipped the jacket on, wishing she hadn't worked up a sweat running. Thank goodness her sundress was calf length; she hoped that would pass muster. "Am I just being paranoid," she said, "or did they throw something at me?"

"I'd be surprised. Usually that only happens in Mea Shearim, the ultra-Orthodox neighborhood in Jerusalem. Sometimes people flick pebbles at women who are improperly dressed. And that's nothing compared to what happens when someone tries to drive a car through there on Shabbat."

"I feel so dumb. I listen to my own radio station on occasion. I know about the tensions between Orthodox and secular Jews." She pulled the edges of her jacket closer

"The *haredim*—the very Orthodox—in Safed tend to be more easygoing than in Jerusalem. But there are a lot of tourists here this weekend because of Lag B'Omer. Can I help you get wherever you're going?"

"Sure. My mom asked us not to come see her until later this morning. I thought I'd buy some groceries. Just steer me toward the mall."

"I'm going there, too. How's your mom doing?" he asked as he fell in step with her. "I tried to visit her yesterday, but she was asleep."

"The doctor says she's making a good recovery." But as Margo said it she thought of her mother's abraded face—and the injuries that increased in severity the less visible they were on the surface of Alice's body. How easily did any woman in her sixties recover from a concussion and cardiac arrest?

"I've been praying for her," he said. "Hey, if you were going to Jerusalem Street from Dalia's, you really got lost."

"I ran into Batsheva and we took a walk. And then I felt like I entered a time machine and came out in nineteenth-century Poland."

"Wouldn't that be great! I can't wait to travel the way they do on *Star Trek*. You walk into a transporter station in Cleveland, say 'Beam me up, Scotty,' and five seconds later you rematerialize in Safed. And just think, your luggage stays with you. Gives a whole new meaning to 'carry-on bags.' "

"Wouldn't you worry about not coming out the same in Safed as you went in in Cleveland?"

"Like Jeff Goldblum in *The Fly*? Nah. I think if we ever get to that point in terms of technology, the questions will be more theological and psychological—not will you have the same DNA at the other end, but what happens to your image of yourself and especially your soul? Are you still *you* during the seconds when you're not connected to a body? Will we have a new category of mental illness, where people fear they've lost part of their essence in transit? On the other hand, will there be people for whom the state of dematerialization has a significant spiritual dimension? Will they feel that separating from their bodies brings them closer to God? Will they seek out the experience, not to travel from point A to point B, but as a mystical quest? Or, on a less spiritual level, as a way to get high?

"Well . . ." He laughed. "Believe it or not, I'm not the only Trekkie at Union Theological Seminary."

"Oh, Danny Rubicoff!" she said, finally placing him; finally emerging from the panic of running the gauntlet of antagonistic men. "The rabbinical student." The *cute* rabbinical student. Dark blond hair curled, Romantic-poet length, to the neck of Danny Rubicoff's shirt. His cheeks were slightly rounded and his skin so baby-soft Margo would have picked him for the kid who always got bullied on the playground—except for his chin, an assertive Kirk Douglas model. The rest of him looked sweet and accommodating, but that chin wasn't going to put up with any crap.

"What do you think of Batsheva?" he said as they took a serpentine stone stairway, much shorter than the Ma'alot Olei HaGardom.

"Fascinating. But I don't understand—or maybe I'm beginning to understand, after what happened a few minutes ago. Why is Batsheva so controversial?"

"Do you have fifteen minutes?"

"Sure." She and Audrey weren't planning to go to the hospital for another hour.

The stairway brought them to the far end of the Jerusalem Street mall. In a small area with wooden benches, they sat in the shade of a tree.

"How much do you know about Kabbalah?" he said.

"What my mom has said in her letters. That it's Jewish mysticism, and it was very big in Safed several centuries ago."

"That's a good place to start. In Safed at that time, you had one of the first big brouhahas over who should have access to Kabbalah. One of the greatest Kabbalists of all time lived here—Isaac Luria, who's usually called by the acronym of his Hebrew name, the Ari. His follower, Hayim Vital, wrote down things he said, sort of like Boswell and Johnson. Except instead of uttering bons mots, the Ari was, in some people's opinion, revealing the secrets of the universe. After the Ari's death in 1572, Vital became the leader of his students. Vital felt that only those students should know the Ari's teachings, and he swore them to secrecy. Later, when Vital lay ill, his brother accepted a bribe of fifty pieces of gold to let someone copy his writings.''

"Wow."

"Juicy stuff, isn't it? I always wonder what happened to the two brothers, if they reconciled. That's not part of the story that's come down. Anyway, it's probably thanks to that act of betrayal that the Ari's philosophy became as influential as it did. But that didn't settle the question of who should be allowed to learn Kabbalah. The purists believe it should only be taught to married men over the age of forty. That battle has pretty much been lost. But even the not-so-purists say you risk the wrath of God by having men and women study Kabbalah together, the way we do in Batsheva's class.''

"Why all the restrictions?"

"They say it's extremely powerful stuff and it's literally dangerous to study if you're not prepared. I think they have a point.''

"Do *you* think Kabbalah is dangerous?"

"Not dangerous, but I agree that you should be prepared. Kabbalah is based on interpretation of the Torah and the Talmud. How much can it mean to a person who isn't well versed in those texts? Can you develop a deep understanding of Jewish mysticism if you have no context?''

"Like going to a sweat lodge when you haven't grown up as a member of an American Indian tribe." All heat, no enlightenment, Margo had felt when she'd tried it.

"Exactly."

"You're the ink person, aren't you?" she said as they headed down Jerusalem Street to the shops.

"The poor schlemiel who had to replace half his wardrobe? That's me. At least they weren't thorough, they missed a few of the clothes on the line. The bad news is that every single thing I owned was out there, except for a pair of shorts and a T-shirt I had on at the time.''

"Where were you when it happened?"

"Hiking in the Golan. I did the wash early that morning, hung it out to dry, and left Safed around nine. Didn't get back until about five, and that's when I saw the damage.''

"You're staying . . . ?"

"Not far from you. In the Artists' Quarter, with my cousin Bernice."

"Did she see anything?"

"That morning, she did a first-aid training at a school. She retired kicking and screaming from nursing when she turned seventy, and she likes to keep her hand in. In the afternoon, she played bridge at her friend Chava's. Bernice is a hell of a bridge player. Chava says she cheats. By the way, did you know you're having dinner with us tonight? It's a Safed tradition to open our houses for Shabbat dinner. Batsheva wanted to invite you, too, but she's no match for Bernice."

"Thanks."

"We've got to stop here. They've got the best challah."

From the bakery, they went to the supermarket. Margo bought mouthwatering ripe tomatoes, dry soup mix, granola, yogurt—and chose from half a dozen different varieties of hummus. And she couldn't pass up what Danny told her was the best Israeli chocolate.

"Did you call the police?" she asked when they'd left the market and were walking toward Dalia's.

"About the ink? Yeah, but what could they do? There were no witnesses. No one conveniently dropped an ink bottle covered with fingerprints."

"What about the other incidents?"

"You've heard of Bruce and Nancy, the flower children? That's what everyone except Batsheva calls them, by the way."

"My mom wrote about them, but refresh my memory."

"Former hippies, Canadians, they have an export business. They're renting a house in the Jewish Quarter and they have a courtyard full of potted plants. One day as many as a dozen of the pots got broken."

"A little broken? Or smashed?" How much malice did someone feel toward Batsheva's students?

"Attacked with Scud missiles, to hear Bruce tell it. Then there was the bird. It was found with a broken neck outside where another student, Kathy, was staying. She's not here anymore, she went back to Boston. Not because of the bird, just that her vacation ended. Anyway, the bird might have been killed by a cat—cats are suspected of breaking the flowerpots, too—or maybe it flew into the side of the building. But it was weird that it happened at Kathy's place, since she's a real bird lover. That's why she came to Israel, because it's in the middle of bird migratory paths between Africa and Asia.''

"Does that mean someone found out enough about her to tailor the harassment to her?'' As someone might have known Alice was expecting an herbal tea? "Nasty kids in this town.''

Danny shook his head. "There's always the disgruntled-client theory. But personally, I think it's random acts by kids. Or else the cats.''

"What kind of client?''

They had reached Dalia's street. Dalia was standing by her gate. When she saw them, she came running, babbling in Hebrew. Tears drenched her face.

Danny spoke to her for a moment in Hebrew, then turned to Margo. "She doesn't know what the problem is. It might be nothing. But your sister is already at the hospital, and you should go there now.''

Ten /

Mother. Intensive care. Alive.

Mother. Intensive care. Alive. Alive. She had to be alive.

She barely heard Danny offering to drive her there or felt her legs moving as he, she, and Dalia rushed to where his cousin's car was parked. Margo would have preferred to leave the weeping landlady behind—her terror was infectious. At least she sat in the back.

"Talk to me," Margo implored Danny.

"About . . ." He was grinding the gears, trying to get into reverse; succeeded at last.

"Um. What disgruntled client? What does Batsheva have clients for?"

"Sure. Did you know about her being a mediator? She settles disputes—business disagreements, family problems. But actually, I'd be amazed if there's some unhappy client roaming around Safed, taking revenge on Batsheva through her students. The goal of mediation is compromise, so no one gets one hundred percent of what they want. But from what I hear, Batsheva's good at it. Bruce and Kathy had a falling-out after she borrowed his car. She picked up a Druze couple and dropped them off at their village, which meant driving on a crummy dirt road. When she got the car back, something was broken. Bruce said it was because of the dirt road and Kathy said it was about to break anyway. Batsheva got them to agree to split the cost of the repair, which made life easier for all of us. I don't know about any of her other cases. She's very discreet. Damn, there's usually not so much traffic."

"Lag B'Omer," Dalia said through sobs. "Everyone comes to Safed for Lag B'Omer. From all over the—"

"How does she get clients?" Margo cut off Dalia before she started sobbing, too. Whatever might be required of her at the hospital, she figured her mother needed her coolheaded rather than emotional. "Do they come to her?"

"Mostly," Danny said. "Every so often she approaches people when she feels they need to look at the ethics of what they're doing."

"That sounds like a way to make enemies."

"Not the way she does it. I . . . Never mind." They'd reached the hospital. "Why don't I drop you off right at the door and then go park?"

"Fine."

Margo jumped out of the car and ran to the intensive-care unit. *Mother. Alive.*

She braced herself for a welter of machinery around her mother's bed, Alice's body shuddering when they used those awful electric paddles to shock her heart into beating again. None of that was happening, and *not* seeing it was almost more frightening than what she'd imagined. Had they given up already?

"Margele!" Alice actually sounded stronger than she had last night.

"Are you . . . Oh God, are you all right?" She grabbed her mother's hand.

"All right? I'm ecstatic. Did you hear the news? Hank and Ellen had a little boy. Dalia, Dalia, what is it?"

Dalia must have been half a minute behind her. She fell to her knees beside Alice's bed, moaning in Hebrew. A nurse tried to pry her away, but Dalia clung to the bed. "It's all right," Alice murmured, stroking Dalia's head. "What's going on?" she asked Margo.

"We thought . . . Someone called. Oh, hell. Where's Audrey?"

"Audi, I'm going to kill you."

"Here? In the parking lot of the police station?"

"That's right. I don't care what they do to murderers in Israel."

"Dammit, Margo! How did I know Hillel would ask some teenage secretary to call Dalia's, and she'd make it sound like Mom was dying?"

"You're going to try to blame this on a pathetic teenager? You were the one who went to the hospital this morning without me and decided Mom had to be transferred to Hadassah Medical Center. When she said she didn't want to go, you—not some teenager—argued with her until she got so upset the nurse made you leave. How could you upset her when she's in intensive care?"

"Do you know why she wants to stay here for medical treatment? She's not planning to come home after she gets better! She wants to keep studying with that woman!"

"You bullied your way into using Dr. Gebman's phone to call Hadassah and make arrangements. You gave him the impression Mom wanted to go there. When he talked to her and found out the truth, you refused to leave his office . . . until in desperation, he asked the secretary to call and ask me to come here. And you're blaming this kid for making me think there was an emergency?"

"Margo, didn't you hear me? Mom nearly dies, and she's not planning to come home with us. Didn't you assume when you came here, that as soon as she got better, we'd take her home?"

"That's a discussion we don't need to have until she's stronger. She has the right to stay if she wants to."

"Are you really willing to get on a plane and leave her here? Especially—especially," repeated Audrey, "when you're the one with this idea that someone poisoned her? Could you possibly be that irresponsible?"

"Do you still think she poisoned herself?"

"Hey, I called the police, didn't I? I set up this appointment. Can we get out of the car and go in now?"

"Fine. Gee, Audi, could you slam the car door a little harder?"

Margo took several deep breaths before she sat down opposite police sergeant Rafi Garfein. She hoped—but doubted—that Audrey had done the same.

"Many peoples, they come to Israel, they act strange. You

ever hear of Jerusalem syndrome?'' Garfein said.

They both said no.

''Tourists, sometimes they get to Jerusalem and suddenly they think they are Messiah. They start walking around barefoot, wearing long white robes.''

''My mother doesn't own any white robes,'' Audrey snapped.

Garfein held up his hand. He was at least fifty-five, and the hand was dotted with liver spots. His expression suggested there was little that tourists—or probably anyone—did that would surprise him.

''The long white robes, the extreme cases, I do not say your mother is one of those. The point I make is this. People hear about Eretz Yisrael every day of their lives. Finally, they come. And they behave here not one hundred percent the way they behave at home in Los Angeles or Milwaukee, *nu?* The point I make is, if you say to me, your mother is not a person who would pick herbs like this and make a tea, I say to you, I believe you that at home she never pick herbs and make tea. If this happen at her home in . . .''

''Connecticut,'' Margo supplied helpfully. She recognized Rafi Garfein as a certain type of interviewee, who had to tell a story in his own time—and who would tell more and be more cooperative if he felt he was in control of the conversation.

''If she is back home in Connecticut, I ask right away, who tries to poison this lady? But in Safed, the place where is buried the Ari . . . In Safed today, you see people from all over world, people not brought up religious. Now they wear long coats like Polish aristocrats a hundred years ago, *nu?*''

Walking this morning, Margo had noticed a young man in Hasidic garb talking to an older man who wore a polo shirt and slacks. The older man, clearly the Hasid's father, was saying in American English, ''You're just doing this to hurt me.'' How much did this place change people? How much had it changed Alice? For a moment Margo doubted her suspicions: her mother had acted out of character by extending her stay in Israel, and she'd told Batsheva she used to pick herbs for tea when she was a girl, something Margo hadn't known. *Could* she have gathered her own tea leaves?

Even if Alice had picked the herbs, however, it was no excuse for half-baked police work.

"I heard the henbane was found in a plastic bag. Were you able to check the bag for fingerprints?" Margo said, careful not to sound confrontational.

"Did you even keep the bag, or did you just toss it in the trash?" demanded Audrey. So much for being conciliatory.

"Whose fingerprints, besides those of your mother, do you think we will find?" Garfein asked.

"Everyone says there are some boys. . . ." Margo began, but Audrey was better informed than she.

"We've heard about some problems with students of Yitzhak Saporta," Audrey said. "I want to know why you haven't questioned them."

"You want I should question every person in Safed? Hit them until they confess? You think this is police state?"

"What about talking to their parents?" Audrey responded. "Or to Yitzhak Saporta? Everyone knows these kids have been bothering people who are students of Batsheva Halevi."

"You know that for fact?" Garfein said. "You see them do these things? You want I should tell you, for fact, what I know?" He was clearly fed up with the Sisters Simon—the one who was trying to be diplomatic as well as the one who kept jumping down his throat. "I know that one or two students of Mrs. Halevi have things happen to them. I do not know—nobody brings evidence, nobody witnesses—if any of these things done by a particular person or students of a particular person. What else I know? I know Jerusalem has terrible problem between *haredim* and secular Jews. We are happy not to have such serious problems here. And we are careful not to increase tensions between the *haredim* and everyone else. If you excuse me, I need to do shopping for Shabbat. My wife wants I should bring home beautiful chicken."

" 'My wife wants I should bring home be-e-autiful chicken,' " Audrey mimicked savagely as they left the police station. "The unmitigated, arrogant, officious creep."

"You left out 'patronizing.' "

"God, I hate it that he has the same name as that singer my

kids love. Rafi! I bet he didn't even keep that plastic bag as evidence.''

"You got that across. Who's Yitzhak Saporta?''

"I bet it's in a landfill someplace. Yitzhak is Batsheva's cousin and her most outspoken opponent. He's also the head of a yeshiva. You know, a school for Orthodox boys. Do you think he'd talk to us?''

"Audi, if there's no evidence to make Yitzhak talk to the police, I doubt he'll have a heart-to-heart with us. Besides, didn't Batsheva say she was going to talk to him? When she and Dalia were speaking Hebrew last night?''

"Yeah, but will she? Dalia says they haven't spoken for over a year.'' Audrey paused, then said, "What about the herbalist who was going to make Mom a tea? What was her name?''

"Ma'ayan.''

"Why don't we go see her?

"Not this afternoon. *I* haven't had a chance to visit with Mom yet. I'd also like to take a few minutes to call our brother and congratulate him on his new child.''

"What about tomorrow?''

"You know, it might be less intimidating if only one of us talks to her, in case she feels at all responsible for Mom getting sick.''

"She ought to feel responsible,'' Audrey said. "And each of us might think of things the other one would miss.''

"Fine. We can play 'good cop, bad cop.' ''

"Which of us would play which?''

"Never mind.''

Eleven /

Friday—the 30th day of the counting of the Omer

Dear Margo,

Picture this. Hovering above every blade of grass, an angel, whispering, "Grow! Grow!" Do I believe this? I don't know. I don't know if I think there are really angels, nor, if there are, whether they would be concerned with the fate of every blade of grass. Would there be enough of them? I ask myself. How big are they? How many angels, as they say, can dance on the head of a pin?

Those are the questions that my intellect raises, the questions and the doubts. Then, beyond that, there is some part of me that is simply enchanted—and somehow deeply comforted—by the thought of those angels and their exhortations to grow, grow! When I go for a walk in the beautiful countryside around here, I look at the grass and trees, and Margo, I see them! Not the way painters show them, as individual angels with human faces and wings, but as a white presence like a light fog skimming the earth.

Margo looked at her mother, lying in the hospital bed on Friday night—moaning in her sleep. She tried to imagine angels whispering in Alice's ear, "Heal! Heal!"

I learned about the angels [the letter continued,] in a class whose title translates from Hebrew as "the Jewish

Soul," although Danny, our young American rabbinical student, calls it "Ecstatic Judaism." He says this in front of Batsheva, and she just laughs. It would be nearly impossible to get mad at Danny. He once called Bruce and Nancy "the flower children" to their faces, and Bruce got a little irritated, but not for long.

I was going to write next about the classes I'm taking, but I see I've already started talking about my fellow "Batshevites," as Dalia refers to us. There are always drop-ins, people like Dalia who come from time to time, but there is a core group of regulars and these are the people I'm really getting to know. I've mentioned Danny and the flower children, so I'll start with them.

Batsheva had said Alice was the kind of person who walked into a room and said, "There you are!" Alice had found her classmates fascinating, and her genuine interest had elicited their life stories.

My one regret about Danny is that I have no daughters or granddaughters the right age to introduce him to! The first thing you notice about him is that he's charming and funny. [No, thought Margo, the first thing you notice is that he's adorable. Then you notice the charm.] *Sometimes charming, funny people wear thin. But Danny has more depth than that. Not in terms of life experience. But he has a hunger not just for knowledge but for understanding. What makes a young man— not the son and grandson and great-grandson of a line of Orthodox rebbes but the son of a third-grade teacher (his mother) and a plumbing contractor (his father)— decide to become a rabbi? We've had several conversations about this, and every time I am ready to join Danny's congregation whenever he graduates from rabbinical school. He is better read in the Torah, Talmud, and other sources than the rest of us, sometimes including Batsheva, and he adds a great deal to our discussions. He doesn't just repeat what he's read, however. He comes up with his own insightful, sometimes irreverent interpretations.*

The flower children, Bruce and Nancy, are seekers of a different kind. Both of them were hippies in the 1960s, but not together—they met ten years ago. They both did all of the things hippies did, communes and meditation and, according to Bruce, every drug imaginable. He's the more classic example, a middle-class kid who dropped out of college. Nancy, I think, was destined to be a gypsy. She has a voice that makes me shiver, you should hear her on the blessings. When she was eighteen, she left the farm where she grew up and started singing in bands. They've both traveled to India and other places in the East. Like the hero of The Razor's Edge, *except that Bruce has a couple of teenage children living with their mother in Canada, and he takes seriously his responsibility to support them. Yes, I know this is his version of the story. But I think he would have figured out a way to make money without having kids to support. He strikes me as a natural entrepreneur. He started a business, which Nancy's gotten involved in, buying clothes, jewelry, etc. from the places they travel and selling them to boutiques in the West. They're helping Arab women in a village near here organize a crafts cooperative. Then they'll market the crafts. They promise to take me with them on one of their trips to the village. I'd love to meet some Israeli Arabs.*

Damn these aerograms! [She'd started to run out of space.]

Yosef and Ma'ayan Gilboa are also a couple [she continued in a chicken scratch.] *Yosef is one of Safed's best-known artists. He was brought up on a kibbutz, but it's hard to imagine such an individualist ever fitting into a communal setting. After he left for his army service, Yosef never went back there to live. He does wild, very witty sculptures, combinations of clay and things he picks up walking around—things from nature, children's toys, pieces of fabric. His personality goes with his art. He's expansive, talks not just with his hands but with his whole body, and he loves a good party. I went to one he and Ma'ayan gave two nights ago, and I danced until midnight!*

Margo's heart caught, feeling her mother's excitement. Alice was by nature an upbeat person, but she'd had to work at it since her husband's death. Until Safed. She was happier in this place than she'd been for several years.

She loved the people she had met here. None of them could have done her harm.

Then why was she lying in a hospital bed, needing to be monitored for the effects of golden henbane on her system? If this wasn't a horrid children's prank, had the henbane come from someone Alice believed was a friend? The herbalist, Ma'ayan Gilboa? The herbalist's husband? What about the flower children? Had their search for highs included experiments with naturally occurring drugs?

If one of them had poisoned Alice, was she still in danger? When Margo had returned tonight after having dinner with Danny and his cousin, a visitor was standing at her bedside— Ronit, a young woman with the long blue-black hair and glowing olive skin Margo had seen on Israeli travel posters. Any of Alice's friends might visit her here. Margo glanced at the nurses' station, staffed by a bright-looking woman about her age. At least in the ICU, patients were visible constantly. Other areas of the hospital would be less secure.

She went over to the nurse. "Dr. Gebman said he might move my mother out of intensive care tomorrow. Do you know if that's going to happen?"

The nurse, whose English was marginal, asked her to repeat the question twice. Eventually, she consulted a chart and answered that Alice was supposed to remain in the ICU.

"Why?" Margo didn't know how her mother's heart was doing, but hers was galloping in her chest. "I thought she was getting better."

The nurse said something about Dr. Blum—apparently Dr. Blum had given the order to keep Alice here? Who was Dr. Blum? Margo wanted to know. She peered over the chest-high barrier and tried to read the chart on the desk. The nurse snatched it away. Not that it made any difference, since the notes were written in Hebrew.

"Can I call Dr. Gebman?" she asked.

The nurse didn't have any trouble finding the English for no.

"Does the other nurse here speak English?" She'd been glad Audrey hadn't insisted on going with her that evening. Now she could have used her sister's knowledge of Hebrew—and her pushiness.

"Margo?" came Alice's weak voice.

"Mom, are you okay?" She rushed back to her mother. "Sorry I woke you."

"I was ready to wake up. I'm thirsty."

"Water okay? Or should I get you some juice?" She assumed if anything bad were showing on the machines attached to Alice's body, the nurse would leap into action.

"Water's fine."

Margo elevated the upper part of the bed, poured a glass of water, and unwrapped a straw.

"Who's Dr. Blum?" she asked as her mother sipped.

"Batsheva's husband, Lev."

"Is he one of the doctors treating you?"

"No, thank goodness. Lev's an oncologist."

After the first rush of adrenaline—they'd discovered cancer! they were keeping it a secret!—Margo thought of another reason Dr. Lev Blum might have requested that Alice remain in intensive care. What if he, too, was concerned about the less stringent security outside the ICU? In that case, she'd bet the request hadn't originated with Dr. Blum but with his wife—who had lain awake last night pondering the evil impulse. If Margo had questioned whether Batsheva was taking her mother's poisoning seriously, this was her answer.

"Would you read to me?" Alice said.

Was there any point in asking Alice if she had angered or threatened someone? If so, wouldn't she have already made the connection between that and being poisoned? Would suggesting it now help her protect herself or would it only upset her? How would that affect her recovery?

"What would you like me to read?"

"Something from the Torah? I don't know why, but I've been thinking about the Torah a lot lately."

"All right." It felt strange to pick up the Bible sitting on Alice's night table. Not that Margo saw herself an atheist, more an agnostic. In college, she would have registered for a course in the Bible as literature if not for a scheduling conflict with a pottery course. But for spiritual reading, she was far less likely to pick up a Bible than to read poetry by the Sufi mystic Rumi or maybe a novel by Ursula Le Guin. "Any special section?"

"You choose."

"How about the story of Deborah?" Margo suggested.

"I wrote to you, didn't I, about Batsheva being called a modern-day Deborah? It's not actually part of the Torah, it's in Judges, but that's fine."

Margo read aloud, saving her astonishment for when she finished.

"What does this have to do with Batsheva?"

"Do you know about Batsheva doing mediation?" Alice asked.

"Danny told me."

"Deborah was a mediator, too. She sat under a palm tree, not far from Safed, in fact, and people came to her for judgments."

"But the story wasn't about judging."

"Danny has a theory about that. You should talk to him." She yawned. "I can't believe I'm sleepy again. Why don't you go to Dalia's and get some sleep, Margele?"

"I will. Soon."

She had meant to read her mother's letters slowly, to comfort herself. Now, beside Alice's bed, she read them all in one sitting. She was no longer seeking comfort. She was looking for a poisoner.

At least it wasn't one of the fire nightmares she had had for months.

The place was dark and the throng of people dark-clothed and shadowy. In the obscurity, the press of people, she could see little; she was more aware of sounds. Conversations swirled around her in a bewildering, consonant-laden tongue. A nasal-voiced instrument wailed in a minor key.

Not a fire nightmare, but the fear and the feeling of suffocation were the same. Something terrible was happening—Deborah gripping a tent peg, about to drive it into her enemy's skull? Margo tried to escape, but the dense crowd crushed her. She fought to breathe.

"Are you all right?"

"Um. I . . ." She recognized the long face and goofy red hair of the man who stood over her—Hillel Gebman. "I fell asleep." In the chair by her mother's bed. She moved away, not wanting to wake Alice. "I'm fine," she said. "Just a nightmare."

"You should get some real sleep," he said. "Lying down."

"I will. I'm going now. What time is it?"

"Nine-thirty."

"You should get home, too," she told the strained-looking young physician.

No wonder Gebman seemed uncomfortable, she thought, recalling the scene that morning: Audrey planted in his office and he without a clue as to how to get rid of this opinionated woman who refused to leave. Did his wife crack the whip at home? Was that why he was at the hospital on a Friday night instead of home with his family?

"I just wanted to check on your mother," he said.

Or, she thought as he gently lifted Alice's wrist to take her pulse, was he simply a dedicated doctor who had come to care a great deal about a patient he had pulled through a crisis? Since the patient was Alice, she figured that wasn't hard to do.

Twelve /

Invisible Girl, Noiseless Girl barely disturbed a molecule of air as she crept downstairs, eased open the door, and escaped!!! at four A.M. *At one with the night*—that was what she'd write in her diary about moving through this chill, misty realm. She felt as if she were swimming rather than walking, her feet in tennis shoes so quiet she might be underwater; the diffuse halos of light around the street lamps were like the lights in a swimming pool at night, light softened and made liquid. Nili's vision without glasses was soft as well, just as it was when she swam.

Magic Girl!

Gliding past the sleeping houses, she clung to the opposite side of the alley when she saw a house with lights on. She felt a kinship with the other early risers but also an immense distance—*they* turned on lights to bring the day closer, while she wanted to blend into the night.

Through the Jewish Quarter, across the Ma'alot Olei HaGardom and then into the Artists' Quarter. The narrow alleys of the Old City always gave her the sense of something hidden, a mystery she never wanted to solve.

In HaMa'ayan HaRadum, the square where the Klezmer Festival took place in the summer, she saw them. Two lovers, pressed so close together that at first her myopic eyes saw only one large, misshapen figure standing against the wall across the square. Then she understood what the shape was, one figure taller than the other, the taller one bent over as if he wanted to fuse forever with his beloved. Their need for one another was so powerful that Nili felt it, too, and gasped.

The lovers pulled apart then. They looked toward her and ran from the square. "I can't see you," she wanted to call out, to assure them. "Even if I could, I would never betray you." But they were gone.

Dearest, darling Jessica [she wrote when she got home], *Isn't love the most wonderful and terrible thing in the world? And isn't a secret love affair the most romantic and tragic thing that can ever happen?* For surely the two people she had stumbled on—the poignant scene that she described in her diary—were secret lovers and not some boring husband kissing his wife before driving off to spend Shabbat in Tel Aviv. Why else would the couple be in HaMa'ayan HaRadum so early in the morning, and why run when she saw them? Why, above all, would married people have kissed with the passion and despair she had sensed? *How do I know that?* she wrote. *Because lovers, especially lovers outside at four-thirty in the morning, are night swimmers like me.*

Because, I, too, know what it's like to kiss someone and feel like I'd rather die than have the kiss stop, she added, grinning. That ought to drive her mother wild!

Something else she could write about this morning would drive Batsheva even wilder. But Nili closed her diary. She had told herself the point was that her mother should never read her private diary; not that she, Nili, was supposed to hide it more cleverly. She'd resolved to write whatever she pleased. But she couldn't take a chance on Batsheva finding out about this. Writing in her heart, she remembered what had happened when she returned home at five.

She hadn't needed her glasses to recognize the person she saw in the courtyard.

"Gadi!" She whispered and yelled it at the same time, and threw herself on her big brother.

"Little one!" He picked her up as if she were eight inches shorter, tiny and feminine like the woman she'd seen in the square. After a long hug, he put her down and led her outside the courtyard. She didn't speak again until they couldn't be seen from the house, and she continued to whisper.

"Are you here for a visit? When did you get here?" Her

half brother, from Batsheva's first marriage, Gadi was dearer to her than any full brother could have been.

"Sometime last night."

"Why didn't you come home? Where did you stay last night?" He looked tired and his clothes were rumpled and a little smelly, as if he hadn't yet gone to bed.

"I'm staying with friends," Gadi said, and she realized what a dope she was. Of course he wouldn't stay with them; she wouldn't either, if she had a choice. "Can you do me a favor?" he asked.

"Sure. What?"

"I forgot how cold it gets here. Can you go in my room and get a jacket? I think there's a jeans jacket in the closet."

No need to tell her to keep quiet. She snuck up to his room, which now doubled as a guest room, and was back in four minutes.

"Here's your jacket and a sweater, too, in case you're going to stay for Erev Lag B'Omer. It gets really cold on Meron, remember? You are going, aren't you? Gadi, can I go with you? Please?"

He had taken her the very first time she'd gone to Mount Meron for the holiday. Nili was only six, and she would have been terrified by all the noise and the people, but her big brother never let go of her hand. He even carried her when she got tired. He complained about how heavy she was, but he was teasing. She had been so happy, she still looked forward to going with him every year, even though it had only happened that once. That summer was when he got in trouble, and he hadn't spent much time at home since then.

Gadi laughed. "Little one, I don't know if I'm going to be here. I just have some business to take care of in Safed, and when it's done, I'll leave."

"Please? Can I see you while you're here?"

"I'll tell you what. Are you going to be at Meron?"

"Yeah, I was going to go with some friends. But they won't care if I go with you—"

"No, go with your friends. Like I said, I might be back in Tel Aviv by then. But if I'm at Meron, how about if I look for you around . . . ? Do you stay up as late as ten-thirty? Or is that past your bedtime?"

"Gadi, I'm sixteen!"

"Okay, I'll look for you at ten-thirty, by the women's entrance to the synagogue."

"I'll be there! And I won't tell anyone!"

"I know you won't. Gotta go now." He gave her a kiss and hurried off while the neighborhood was just beginning to wake up, before anyone might come out and see him.

Thirteen /

I'm not surprised I mentioned Yosef and Ma'ayan and then went on and on about Yosef [Alice's next aerogram had begun]. *Everybody overlooks Ma'ayan, because Yosef is so much more . . . well, he is so vital and opinionated. But there I go again, writing about him instead of her. The word* ma'ayan *means "spring," not the season of the year but a spring of water. It suits her. She makes me think of a spring running underground, only revealing a trickle of itself where it comes to the surface. People who are quiet and withdrawn often make you feel they have hidden depths, and sometimes they simply have nothing to say. I don't know her well enough to form an opinion about that. Before Yosef became successful with his art, she used to be a teacher. Now her main interest, besides their three children, is her garden. She's something of an herbalist. Nancy swears by a tea that Ma'ayan gave her for allergies. Everything is blooming here and Nancy was miserable until she started drinking Ma'ayan's tea.*

Quiet? Withdrawn? Margo asked herself as she listened to Ma'ayan Gilboa. A petite woman of about forty, Ma'ayan looked like the little mouse Alice had described, with lank, nondescript brown hair and a limp, long-sleeved white blouse over olive slacks. But there was nothing quiet about the way she hammered her points home.

"All I said was I would prepare a tea for her digestive

problem.'' Ma'ayan's English was flawless. Her family had emigrated to Israel from New York when she was six. "I told her the tea would taste bad but to drink as much as she could. She asked how to fix it. I said to put the herbs in a pot of water and let them boil for ten or fifteen minutes. That was all anyone said on the subject of tea. Then Batsheva reminded us we were there to study. Not like this tea; this tea is delicious.'' As abruptly as she'd shifted conversational gears, Ma'ayan snatched up the teapot and poured herbal tea; she handed cups to Margo and Audrey. "Have a cookie,'' she added. "Neither of you looks like you have to diet.''

Feeling as if she'd been dared to partake, to demonstrate her faith that her hostess wasn't a poisoner, Margo took a sip while the tea was still hot and murmured her appreciation. The tea was lemony and very good. The setting, at a wicker table beneath a pergola in Ma'ayan's garden, was idyllic.

And Ma'ayan seemed about to explode.

"We talked about it in class at Batsheva's on Monday afternoon,'' the herbalist continued. "We didn't discuss it anymore when the class ended, and your mother didn't come here. She's been here a few times, once for a party and once or twice to visit, but not after that class. Oy!'' Hearing a child's wail, she jumped up and ran inside the house.

"Methinks . . .'' Audrey mused. Remarkably mild, she had let Margo do the talking, mostly small talk while Ma'ayan prepared tea in her tidy kitchen and parried demands from her two younger children who were at home. Yosef and their older son were out hiking, she'd said. Once they sat in the garden, Ma'ayan had proceeded to defend herself without requiring accusations from Audrey or anyone else.

"Protesting too much? I agree,'' Margo replied.

From inside the house, they heard Ma'ayan speak sharply in Hebrew. A second child began to cry.

"She's so jumpy,'' Audrey said. "Maybe she has trouble concentrating and this isn't the first herbal tea she's screwed up.''

They fell silent as Ma'ayan returned, cradling her three-year-old son. "Tal and his big sister!'' she grumbled indulgently, and handed him a cookie. The boy's face was tear-streaked, but he'd stopped sobbing. He sat in his mother's lap, snuffling and chewing quietly.

"Does henbane have any medicinal uses?" Margo asked. Interested in Ma'ayan's volatility, she wanted to provoke it.

Holding her child, however, seemed to calm Ma'ayan down.

"As a folk medicine," she said, "it's used by the Arabs—topically, not internally—to treat a variety of conditions. Headache, backache, open sores. They mash up the stems and leaves and mix them with flour and water. Then they soak a dressing in it and apply the dressing. In Western medicine, henbane isn't used specifically. But it's from a family of drugs that's used in heart medications and antihistamines. You must know that. You work for a pharmaceutical company, right?"

"I don't, Audrey does. Do you ever keep henbane around?"

This time she hit a nerve.

"You mean do I grow it in my garden, in case I want to make a little extra income by robbing tourists? That's how henbane was used for years in parts of the Middle East, you know. The robber slipped some henbane into the tourist's drink, the tourist became incapacitated, and the robber took his money. Bim! Bam! Bom! If I wanted henbane, I wouldn't have to cultivate it. No one would. Come, see for yourselves."

Still holding her son, Ma'ayan stood and strode to the front of the house. The child whimpered. She rocked him but kept talking.

"Your mother wouldn't have had any trouble finding golden henbane." Ma'ayan cupped her hand beneath a yellow-flowered plant that grew from a crack in the wall. Similar flowers sprouted elsewhere on the housefront. "It grows wild like this on almost every wall in Safed, and in every empty lot, and all over the countryside."

The herb that had nearly killed Alice Simon was seductively lovely, its delicate golden flowers flaring outward from intensely purple hearts.

"Did you say what herb you were going to use? Did you give her any idea of what to look for?" Margo asked. She wondered why Audrey hadn't leaped in. Not that she minded carrying the conversation alone, but she wouldn't have expected Audrey to *let* her.

"I never use just one herb. I blend them. Do you want to

see the tea I prepared for your mother?'' She was already moving around the corner of the house; there was a side door like the entrance to Dalia's guest room. Putting down her son, she unlocked a combination padlock and pushed the door open.

"Ummm," Margo said, sniffing.

The room was an herbarium with fragrant bundles of herbs hanging to dry from the ceiling and herb-filled jars on shelves along the walls. The second most benign explanation, Batsheva had said, was that Ma'ayan had made a mistake. But Ma'ayan was no dabbler who grabbed a few leaves here and a flower there as she walked down the street. This was an herbal pharmacy.

"Your mother's tea." Ma'ayan held up a plastic bag, neatly labeled ALICE—DIGESTION. "I made it on Tuesday. I was going to give it to her in class the next day, but she was in the hospital then. Take it. She can use it when she's eating normally again."

She thrust the bag at Margo, then hustled them out of the herbarium and padlocked the door. Quiet? Withdrawn? The woman had so much nervous energy she jangled.

"Ai, Tal, didn't you want to play with your sister?" she said. The child whined. Sighing, Ma'ayan scooped him up again. "Will I see you at Havdalah tonight?" she asked Margo and Audrey. She moved toward the gate, clearly eager to end the conversation.

"If you could just tell us . . ." Margo went back to her chair and poured herself another half cup of tea. "Who was in class with you on Monday?"

"Who was . . ." Ma'ayan repeated impatiently. She joined them at the table, but didn't sit. "Danny came. I think that was the day he brought a friend from the States, I don't remember her name."

"What about the Israelis?"

"Yosef and me, of course. Why do you want to know about the Israelis? Oh! Because you think someone from our class gave your mother the henbane, and you think Israelis would know what it is?" Ma'ayan rolled her eyes. "Every child in Israel learns to identify protected plants because the Society for the Protection of Nature indoctrinates them not to pick those. But most Israelis only know henbane as 'that pretty yellow flower.' Bruce and Nancy would be more likely. . . . But the idea that anyone from the class would do that!''

''Were Bruce and Nancy there?''

''Nancy. Not Bruce, he had business in Tel Aviv. Ronit was there. She has something of a religious mania, but I don't think she'd poison anyone.'' Even as Ma'ayan scoffed, however, she seemed to relax. She sat down and the child in her arms stopped fussing. ''There are always a few drop-ins, don't ask me to remember who. Probably Reuven, too.''

''Who's Reuven?'' It was the one name, among the regular students, that Margo hadn't heard before.

''Reuven Preusser. He's a young man, about seventeen, from an Orthodox family. He studies with Batsheva in secret. He stands in another room to listen.''

''It's not much of a secret, if you know about it.''

''I'm the only one, besides Batsheva. I wasn't feeling well one day last week, a little sick to my stomach, and I ran out to the bathroom. I saw him then, and I promised not to . . . You won't give him away, will you?''

''What would happen, if his family found out?''

''They might watch him every time he went out. They might send him away. I think they have relatives on a religious *moshav*. . . . Ben!'' She turned toward an adolescent boy who'd come into the courtyard, and spoke to him in Hebrew.

The kid responded, but sullenly, head down. He wore a knitted *kippah* that identified him as an observant Jew.

Ma'ayan asked him a question. He shook his head and started into the house.

''Ben!''

He ignored her and went inside.

''How old is he? Fourteen?'' said Margo sympathetically. ''We have teenagers.''

''He's a good kid!'' Ma'ayan made it a declaration. ''Excuse me, I need to talk to him.''

''What were they saying?'' Margo asked as they headed for the car; they planned to spend the rest of the day with Alice.

''Ma'ayan wanted to know where his father was. I didn't catch what he said; it must be wherever they went hiking. She asked why wasn't he with his father? He didn't answer."

"Typical adolescent," remarked Margo.

"Did you notice she emphasized that he was a good kid? As opposed to the bad kids who've been harassing Batsheva's students?"

So Audrey hadn't been asleep during the conversation, just extremely quiet.

"Audi," her sister asked, "why weren't you saying anything?"

"You were doing fine."

"That doesn't usually stop you."

"Margo!"

Margo spent the next three minutes apologizing and kicking herself. That morning, they'd begun to talk about anything and everything as they pulled apart a challah and spread it with jam. The next thing they knew, both challah and morning had vanished, and each of them was feeling pleased to have a sister. Now they were acting like little Tal.

Finally mollified, Audrey said, "I was preoccupied. I called home before we went to Ma'ayan's. I was hoping, after I'd been gone a couple days and Zach realized the sky hadn't fallen, he'd adjust. But he wet the bed last night. He hasn't done that since he was five."

"If you need to go home now," Margo said, "I can handle this."

"Thanks. I want to be here for Mom. I just can't wait to get her out of here."

She might not come, Margo thought but refrained from saying. She was feeling some of the charm that had drawn her mother to Safed. After less than two days here, she had a sense of knowing the city—the inviting cobbled alleys, the hard clarity of the Mediterranean light at noon and its sweetness at dusk. Even the people already looked familiar, like the Orthodox teenage boy they passed whom she remembered seeing the day before.

Fourteen /

"I want to be philosophical about this," Alice said to her visitor. "Just think. It could be a springboard for considering the nature of experience and how we store experience as memory. Is an experience less if it isn't remembered?"

"So you still don't remember anything?"

"Nothing. As I said, I'd like to be philosophical. A bigger person would be. But I'm angry. Not remembering makes me feel old and helpless."

"Alice, it has nothing to do with age. A twenty-year-old could have a concussion and the same thing would happen."

"I tell myself that. And I tell myself I can't force it, that if I remember anything, it will come out of the blue—I'll be washing dishes or I'll turn a certain way on Jerusalem Street, see something out of the corner of my eye, and suddenly I'll get five minutes back. But I can't stop trying. I close my eyes and picture myself brushing my teeth, anything I know I must have done that day. I know what clothes I was wearing, so I try to remember putting them on. Losing such a big chunk of my life, it's as if I died for that day and a half. Did you see me at all that day?"

"You're worried about *your* memory. *I* don't remember. I guess I might have, on the street."

"Don't be upset. I'm sorry, I know I gave everyone such a scare. Let's talk about something pleasant. What's Simchat Torah like in Safed?"

"Celebrations at all the synagogues, I don't know."

"I really did upset you. I didn't mean to. Let me tell you

how we do Simchat Torah at my synagogue at home. First we carry the Torah around the sanctuary seven times, singing songs. It's like a parade. The kids love that part. I wish we'd done it when my kids were growing up, but that was a time when we let go of so many of the rituals. Then we unroll the entire scroll end to end. Everyone—there are eighty or even one hundred people—makes a big half circle around the room and we all hold the scroll very carefully by the top and bottom. It's incredible to see the entire Torah displayed like that!''

"I should go. I must be tiring you."

"I'm fine," Alice insisted. "The rabbi comes around and tells everyone what part of the Torah they have in their hands. Last time, I was holding Jacob's dream, where he sees the ladder to heaven with angels going up and down! You know, of course, that Simchat Torah is when you come to the end of reading the Torah for the year and start all over again. I never used to realize that you finish and start at the same time. You know, you read the last words and right after, you read B'reshit, "In the beginning," as a symbol that the study of Torah goes on forever."

"I'd better go now. Really."

"What icy hands! Are you sure I haven't terrified you? I promise I won't look so dreadful next time. I told my daughters to bring my lipstick."

Fifteen /

Saturday—the 31st day of the counting of the Omer

Nili Blum held aloft a candle that must have been a foot long. Each strand of the intricately braided candle ended in a wick; Lev Blum had lit the cluster of wicks before he handed the candle to his daughter.

Standing in the group of some twenty people, mumbling the prayers whenever she recognized a phrase, Margo suddenly found it all—the shy, willowy young woman, the beeswax candle, and the sense of ceremonies like this one being performed every Saturday evening for centuries—so beautiful that her eyes filled with tears.

"Nili's going to have to marry a basketball player," Audrey murmured.

"She's not *that* tall." The girl looked about Audrey's height.

"No, there's a tradition that you hold the Havdalah candle at the height you want your husband to be."

"Shh," said Batsheva, but she was smiling. It was hardly a hushed gathering, what with giggling and squirming from Ma'ayan and Yosef Gilboa's younger children and three of Hillel and Ofra Gebman's kids. Only the Gebmans' youngest was quiet; an infant, she slept in her mother's arms.

Lev, who was leading the ritual in his home, filled a wine-glass until it overflowed into a shallow bowl.

"You allow some of the wine to spill as a sign of prosperity," Audrey whispered.

Over wine Lev led the blessing that Margo had heard countless times growing up. She joined in, relieved not to feel a complete outsider. She lacked any frame of reference, however, for the object he picked up next. Of delicately worked silver, it was roughly the size and shape of two elongated sugar bowls joined head to head. He said a blessing, then passed the object around. When it came to her, Margo imitated everyone else; she gave the silver container a shake and brought it to her nose. Through pinprick holes, she inhaled . . .

"Wow. Cloves?" she mouthed to Audrey after she passed it on.

"Cloves and cinnamon." The reply came from Batsheva. "But any fragrant herbs can be used in a spice box. To remind us, as we reenter the week, of the fragrance of Shabbat."

Drawing Margo aside, she said that another reason for the use of spices was to comfort people for the loss of the special additional soul—*the what?* Margo managed not to blurt out—that we acquire on the Sabbath. She explained the next part of the service as well, blessing the candle while extending one's hands toward the light. "To show your fingernails are clean and therefore you have done no work on Shabbat."

Lev drank the wine he'd poured earlier and touched a drop of wine to each of his eyelids. This, Batsheva said, carried the Sabbath into the week.

"You know this song, about the prophet Elijah?" she asked, when the group started singing *Eliyahu Hanavi.*

Margo nodded and sang along. A rich alto drew her eyes to Nancy Isley. *A voice that makes me shiver,* Alice had written. It gave Margo the shivers, too; Nancy turned the Hebrew song into the blues. Next to her stood her partner, Bruce Harris—Margo had met them briefly before Danny had announced that Havdalah could begin because three stars were visible in the evening sky.

The service ended with a prayer for Alice's health; Margo noticed she wasn't the only person crying. Her mother was loved here—wasn't she?

What would you do, she had asked Batsheva yesterday, if you found out who gave her the henbane?

"What would *you* do?" Batsheva had countered.

"Tell the police, of course."

"No matter what the circumstances?"

"How could there be any circumstances where the person

who did this shouldn't have to answer for it?"

"Absolutely, the person must answer for what he did," Batsheva said. "But is putting someone in jail always the best way? You know what the rabbis say about repentance? The most important thing is if you have another opportunity to commit the same sin, not to do it. And you have to ask forgiveness from anyone you've wronged."

"Do you ever notice how some men immediately make you think of bed?"

Margo followed Nancy Isley's gaze toward the buffet table. "Danny?" Margo said. "He's adorable, but so are puppies."

"Not Danny. Hillel Gebman."

"Yeah?" Margo worshiped Dr. Gebman because he'd stayed with Alice all Tuesday night until her condition stabilized. His other charms were less apparent. "If you like the Lyle Lovett type," she remarked.

"God, that makes me feel old." Nancy laughed. "He reminds *me* of a red-haired Art Garfunkel. Anyway, I like just about every type. Which is often my downfall. Next time you talk to Hillel, check out his eyes."

Hillel Gebman finished filling several plates and took them to the three of his four offspring who had teeth.

"Are the Gebmans Orthodox?" Margo asked.

"Because they have four kids even though Ofra can't be older than thirty, and the poor thing's fat as a house? I think it's maybe because she's Moroccan—all the kids, not the fat— but I'm no expert on the branches of Judaism, a blond, blue-eyed shiksa like me. Do you eat meat?" she asked.

"Except when our twelve-year-old militant vegetarian is at home, and even then I sneak it sometimes."

"You're in luck. I'm a vegetarian, but I hear Batsheva's chicken is really tasty. Stay away from any green veggies, though. She overcooks them."

Margo helped herself to roast chicken, potatoes, salad, and bread—thank goodness the plate was huge.

People had spread through the living and dining rooms. She spotted a happily contentious group that included Batsheva, Hillel Gebman, Dalia, and Ma'ayan. Ofra Gebman sat with the young children, but she wasn't paying much attention to them. Her exquisite almond eyes were fixed on her husband, her fleshy face set in a scowl. Huddled cross-legged on the floor, Audrey and Nili chatted animatedly in Hebrew.

In the courtyard, Danny and Yosef Gilboa sat at a scarred wooden table lit by several bug candles. Danny beckoned her over and introduced her to Yosef.

"*Shalom, shalom.* I am sorry your mother is not well, but glad you and your sister are in Safed," Yosef said. He spoke a bit haltingly but with enthusiasm.

He took her hand; his was warm and callused, a sculptor's hand. His deep-set eyes and sensual lips, sculpted by the candlelight, reminded her of a Dürer woodcut. Had anyone mentioned Yosef's sexiness, she would have instantly agreed.

"Warm enough?" Danny said. "I can find a jacket for you."

"Actually, I am. It feels a lot warmer than last night."

"*Hamsin* is coming," Yosef said. "It's a wind from the desert, very hot. Do you feel it?" Now that he mentioned it, she noticed the breeze rattling the leaves.

"We have a wind like that in California, a Santa Ana," she said. "It can make people a little crazy. Does the *hamsin* do that?"

"Yes, yes." Yosef smiled—just happy to provide the information? She'd bet he liked wild weather.

She used to like wild weather, too; and she still exulted in thunderstorms. But not hot, dry winds. Hot desert winds made her think of death, an entire canyon roaring into flame.

"Tell me about Deborah," she said to Danny. "My mom says you have a theory about why people compare her to Batsheva."

"You know the story of Deborah from the Book of Judges?"

"I read it last night. For someone who's supposed to be a judge, Deborah sounds a lot more like a warrior."

"She goes to the battle," Yosef commented. "Like Golda Meir."

"Yes, and after this terrible battle, she sings a victory song. Rejoicing that her enemies have perished."

"Spoken with the disgust of a 1990s pacifist," Danny said. "She even sings about the Israelite woman who invites an enemy general into her tent, lulls him to sleep, and drives a tent peg through his head.''

"Hey, I have the same reaction. Still, it's only fair to look at Deborah as a woman of her time. Which was a warlike, bloody part of history. In the chapter of Judges preceding Deborah, the Israelites slaughter ten thousand Moabites like it's business as usual.''

"Danny, my friend." Bruce had wandered into the courtyard with Dalia. Yosef's older son had come outside, too; he stood stiffly behind his father's chair. "It's so limiting to think of the Bible as history. Adam and Eve, Abraham and Sarah. They're just our Judeo-Christian version of Chronos and the Titans or the American Indian Spider Woman. Every culture has its creation myth and its big stories to explain natural phenomena and teach moral lessons.'' Thin, ponytailed, and smug, Bruce reminded Margo of some of the New Agers she knew in California.

"I agree that Adam and Eve are mythological,'' Danny said. "But the later stories—I'm not saying they're literal truth, but I think they're based on real events that made their way into the oral tradition until eventually they were written down.''

"What was the oral tradition?" Bruce replied. "People sitting around the campfire, telling stories. Getting a better reaction from their audience if they spiced it up.''

Yosef's son spoke, his face dark with anger, his English nearly as good as his American-born mother's. "How can you speak about oral tradition and audiences, when the holy Torah was written by God and received on Mount Sinai?''

"Eh, Ben." Yosef turned and spoke to him softly in Hebrew.

"What does it matter where it all came from?" Bruce said. "Or what the stories say? More important than the words are the letters and even the white spaces between and around the letters. The early Kabbalists discovered that if they opened the Torah and brought all their concentration to just one Hebrew letter, they tripped out on God.''

"Bruce, how can you say in one breath that the stories are meaningless and in the next that meditating on any one letter is a holy experience?" Danny said.

"You talk like he is logical," Dalia said.

"Logic," said Bruce, "is the hobgoblin of little minds."

"I thought that was 'a foolish consistency,' " Margo murmured.

"What I like about Deborah . . ." The lilting voice was Ronit's. Half the party seemed to be joining their discussion. "Her song is one of the most ancient parts of the Bible, did you know?"

Across the table, the conversation in Hebrew between Yosef and his son got louder, and Dalia joined in.

"Whoa!" Margo cried, to no effect. Was it like this in Batsheva's classes, multiple impassioned arguments going on at once? No wonder Alice loved it. "Whoa! Danny!" Getting his attention, she leaned toward him and said, "I can see why people compare Golda Meir and Deborah. But why Batsheva?"

"Yes, tell us," said Ronit.

"Ah." A born teacher, Danny's eyes gleamed. "People say they make the comparison because of Deborah's role in settling disputes—which, by the way, is expanded on in Midrash, the teaching stories based on the Bible. Still, we come back to the original text, most of which, as you noticed, Margo, shows Deborah in a very different light. I think when people compare Batsheva with Deborah, they *are* thinking of the Deborah who leads the Israelites into battle."

"A woman who likes to triumph over her enemies?" It was a disturbing picture of Batsheva.

"A woman living in a time of conflict, who's very much a woman of her time."

"Are you talking about the Palestinians?" Margo asked.

"Actually I'm thinking of what's going on among Jews, with the ultra-Orthodox at one end of the spectrum, and at the other, the very secular who want nothing to do with God. You could say that, just as in Deborah's time, the future of the Jewish people is at stake. Batsheva is taking a stand."

"You talk like she is some kind of saint!" Dalia objected.

"Dalia, Dalia!" Ronit said. "What I think about this— Batsheva makes me think of the meaning of the word 'Israel,' you know this?"

" 'One who wrestles with God,' " Danny said. "I think so,

too. She's not afraid to wrestle with God, or other people, or her own demons. She enjoys the struggle.''

"What demons?" It was Audrey. Her flat tone of voice made Margo nervous.

"What demons does Batsheva struggle with? I don't know," Danny said. "But none of us is free of demons."

"Well, I wish someone would tell me," Audrey said, "why Batsheva's demons result in other people being harmed. If she's so willing to 'wrestle,' as you put it, how come she doesn't have to take the consequences?''

"You mean, why doesn't ink get thrown at *her* wash?"

"If her students are being harassed, why isn't she standing up to whoever is doing this?"

Batsheva appeared while Audrey was speaking. Audrey switched pronouns, but she didn't back down.

"Why haven't you made it clear to people in this city," she said, "that an attack against one of your students is an attack against you? Why are you protecting whoever is doing this?"

Batsheva stepped close to Audrey, chin jutting—whether from anger or because Audrey towered over her. "You think that is what I do? That I protect someone I know has done wrong?''

"I think it's an outrage that if people don't like what you're doing, they take it out on innocent people who come here to study with you."

"I agree with you," Batsheva said. "Only a coward does not come to me directly."

Mesmerized, as if she were watching her sister dance, Margo followed Audrey's expressive hands, fingers tensely splayed, the gesture inches from becoming a blow.

"I think," Audrey said, "that when someone comes here and takes your classes, you have an obligation to warn them that they are taking a risk."

"I agree," Batsheva said again.

"You agree, you agree!" Audrey's hands snapped into fists. "But I don't see you closing your classes and telling people that their safety is more important than anything you have to teach."

"If we stopped studying every time it got a little dangerous, would the Jewish people exist today?" Batsheva flared back.

"You know why we celebrate the holiday of Lag B'Omer? Because of people who went out in the country and pretended they were going hunting; really they studied Torah. They risked their lives to keep Judaism alive during the Roman occupation. As long as people want to study with me, I will teach. We will not be made afraid."

"*You're* not afraid." Audrey seized Batsheva's shoulders. The smaller woman flinched but didn't try to break away. "You're not afraid, and my mother is lying in the hospital. Why aren't you the one in intensive care?"

"I wish I knew," Batsheva said, and then, "Wait!" But Audrey had already run into the street.

"Why didn't anyone stop them?" Margo was asking herself as well as Danny and Yosef. They had remained in the courtyard with her after Lev adroitly moved everyone else indoors for coffee and cake.

"When they were having so much fun?" Danny said. "I don't mean it like that. But Audrey had things she needed to say. And Batsheva—"

"Batsheva doesn't need anyone to fight for her," Yosef said.

"I guess we're no longer invited for Erev Lag B'Omer," Margo mused. Batsheva had asked her and Audrey along for tomorrow's festivities in Safed and at Mount Meron.

"You heard Batsheva," Danny said. "She likes people who confront her. Margo, Yosef, do you want dessert and coffee? I've worked as a waiter. I can carry it all."

"Sure. Fine," Margo said.

Danny went inside, leaving her alone with Yosef—and aware of him in a way she had rarely been aware of another man since she'd met Barry.

"You are artist, no?" Yosef said.

"I do a little pottery."

"Let me see. You throw on a wheel?" He rubbed his thumb over the callused flesh on the edge of her hand. He'd taken her right hand, the one without the wedding ring.

"Yes. I was never any good at hand building." That was the specialty of the first man she'd loved.

"*Abba!*" Daddy. It was Yosef's youngest boy.

Quickly, guiltily, they pulled their hands apart.

Sixteen /

"At the Havdalah service last night . . ." Margo trailed off, head bent in thought.

Alice couldn't help herself. She knew it drove Margo nuts, but she reached up and brushed the unruly brown curls out of her daughter's pretty face.

Margo started over. "In one of your letters," she said, "you wrote that in Safed you felt you were in the presence of God."

Hearing a hint of a question mark at the end of the sentence, Alice answered, "Not just here. But I feel it more here than I ever have before."

"What does it mean to you, to be in the presence of God?"

"Ai, Margele, you only ask the easy questions." She sighed, but she was smiling. She felt more alert today, less drugged and far less damaged by the poison she had drunk five days ago. Bruises and scabs still covered her face, but life had returned to her eyes. She'd listened eagerly as Margo described the Lag B'Omer procession earlier this afternoon, and she had known, as shrewdly as she would have known it thirty years before, that Margo was lying about Audrey not coming to the hospital because she was taking a nap. She hadn't pushed it, however. She'd sensed that Margo had more important things on her mind.

"Let's take a walk," she said.

"Can you?"

"Since yesterday, they've been letting me get up and walk down the hall."

Margo helped her into her robe and slippers, and they headed out of the intensive care unit.

"To say how I feel God's presence," Alice said, "first I need to say how I think of God, because that's changed in the past month."

"Because of Batsheva?"

"Yes, and because of studying Kabbalah." Turning and looking into her daughter's troubled brown eyes, she saw her at six and eleven and twenty, all of those daughters coexisting in the tense thirty-nine-year-old woman who supported her under one elbow as she shambled along.

"I like the idea of God the Kabbalists came up with, at least as I understand it," Alice said. "They say that God is infinite nothingness, the *ein sof* they call it. The *ein sof* is so far beyond human consciousness, we can't begin to grasp it. As a way to explain God, intellectually, that feels right to me. But then you have the problem, how can we receive any comfort from a God who is so distant? The Kabbalists made it possible to get closer to God by creating an elaborate, beautiful way of looking at God's attributes such as loving-kindness or wisdom or justice. The idea is that even though our minds aren't great enough to comprehend the *ein sof,* we can experience God through those attributes, like knowing something is there because you see its shadow or you smell a scent it leaves behind."

"Do you want to rest?" Margo asked at the end of the corridor.

"Not yet." Walking felt unsteady, but wonderful! "Sometimes," she said as they turned back, "when I pray or read, or even more when I'm just taking a walk and I really notice things—the feel of the earth under my feet, the way a frond of purple bougainvillea drapes over a wall, a child crying and the voice of the mother comforting the child—at times like that, an enormous sense of compassion or understanding comes over me. I don't know, but I think that's God."

"Doesn't that come from inside you? That feeling of compassion?"

"It comes from inside, but it's more than that. It feels as if I'm connecting with something outside of me that's always there. I'm just not always prepared to connect with it."

"Oh."

Alice had been careful not to pressure Margo with questions, only to provide the answers she'd found for herself, imperfect as they might be. But now she asked, "Is that what you felt, at the Havdalah service?"

"I don't know. Probably what I felt was just a greater awareness of being Jewish, a cultural identity."

"There's a story Batsheva tells, about two yeshiva students who disagree on a point of law. Did I write to you about this one?"

"I don't think so."

"I must have put it in a letter to your brother. One of the yeshiva students goes to their rebbe and presents his side of the argument, and the rebbe says, 'You're right.' Then the other student goes to the rebbe and eloquently argues his side. The rebbe says, 'You're right.' A third student who has listened to all this says, 'One says one thing and the other says the opposite. How can they both be right? It makes no sense.' The rebbe says, 'You're right.' So," she said, slipping into a Yiddish accent, "you wonder why your mother is telling you this story?"

"It crossed my mind. I like the story. Back to bed?"

"Let's go down the hall one more time. Batsheva tells the story to illustrate the quality of paradox that's at the heart of Kabbalah," Alice said as they resumed walking. "The reason I'm telling you is, if you think the only thing you felt was a greater awareness of being Jewish, then you're right. If you think you felt God's presence, you're also right."

"How can I feel God's presence if I . . . I'm sorry, I'm tiring you out."

"I'm fine." Alice paused. If the woman beside her were anyone but her daughter, she might take the cue and talk about something else. But who except her daughter would have flown halfway around the world to hold her up when she walked down a hospital corridor? "How can you feel God's presence," she echoed Margo, "if you don't believe in God?"

"It's not a question of believing or not believing! I don't think God is dead or anything like that. He—or She—or whatever—is just irrelevant. Not a part of my life." Margo shook her head. "I have no idea why I'm getting upset."

"A brilliant rabbi in the United States, Abraham Joshua Heschel, said that God was in search of us, not the other way around."

"So God came looking for me last night?"

"God is always looking. We're just not always ready to be found. I want to say one more thing to you, and then we'll talk about something important, like when do I finally get to smoke a cigarette?"

"Mom, you're in intensive care."

"One more thing," she said. "Is everything all right between you and Barry?"

"Why do I feel like this is an impossible question? You wouldn't ask if you didn't think something was wrong, so no matter what I say, you're going to think you're right. The truth happens to be that everything's fine."

"If you say there are no problems, I believe you. I just thought . . ."

"Mo-om! . . . Okay, what did you think?"

"The last time I saw you, you and he seemed careful with each other. Have you had a chance to call him since you got here?"

"I tried last night. But it's ten time zones earlier and we don't have a phone at Dalia's. And I haven't seen that many public phones."

"The best public phones are at the Rimon Inn. And there must be a phone in the hospital. Why don't you call him before you leave here today? I don't mean to tell you what to do."

"Yes, you do. I thought you only smoked two cigarettes a day."

"I do. And I get a great deal of enjoyment from those two cigarettes. I wouldn't ask if I thought I still needed to be in intensive care. But since when do they let intensive-care patients get up and walk around? I thought they were planning to move me and give the bed to someone who was really sick."

"Maybe it was more trouble to move you than to let you stay a few more days," Margo said.

Margo had always lied so badly. *You asked them to keep me here, didn't you, so the person who gave me henbane couldn't slip in and finish the job?* Alice thought. She said nothing, however, because she shared Margo's concern. She was glad to have remained under the protection of the ICU. After she left the hospital—in two days, she'd been promised—she intended to make sure she was with someone at all times. That shouldn't be difficult, with Margo and Audrey here. To say any of that out loud, however, was to drop a boulder of accusation in the lovely, tranquil pool that was Safed. More than that, saying it gave it a reality that would make it impossible for her to justify to herself—much less to her daughters—remaining here after they left.

"Tell me about the procession again," she said. "You said the Torah was covered with flowers?"

"You know, there's the usual cloth cover over it, this one looked like white silk. Around that, there were garlands of yellow and red flowers. Audrey used up an entire roll of film in five minutes. They brought it out of the—I guess it's not a synagogue, but some historic building—where they'd been praying. One man would hold it for a minute; he didn't go anywhere, he just held it aloft. Then he'd pass it so another man had the chance to carry it. The women threw pieces of candy. 'Sweets for the sweetness of Torah,' Batsheva said. Mom, what is it?"

"I'm all right," she said, but she kept leaning against Margo. "This is so strange."

"Do you want to sit down? Should I get the nurse?"

"Let's sit down for a minute, there are chairs right here. I had . . . It felt like a memory, but it didn't make any sense. I remember being afraid of snakes."

"Is it a visual memory? Do you have a mental picture of yourself with a snake?"

Alice closed her eyes and tried—so hard!—to capture more than a fleeting impression. "No, dammit. All I get is 'snakes and fear.' I can't tell you if it was a real-life snake or a dream. Maybe I was reading Genesis! Maybe I went to the cemetery; that's the place in Safed where you have to be most careful. There's some kind of viper. Its venom can be fatal."

"What about outside of Safed? Could you have taken a walk in the country?"

Alice shrugged.

"About this cemetery, is it dangerous to go there?" Margo said. "Dalia and Batsheva told us we should go see the famous tombs."

"It's fine, as long as you cover your legs and wear closed shoes. It's nicest just before sunset. Now, let me tell you where I keep my cigarettes."

Careful with each other. What the hell did that mean? Margo stewed as she left the ICU and noticed the public telephones.

It wasn't as if she and Barry were having serious problems, she thought while she waited for the operator to connect her. They loved each other deeply; that hadn't changed. They still made each other laugh. They could still drive each other wild with pleasure—and thinking about that hadn't lost its power to send a tingle through her body. "Just calling to say I love you," she said when she got the answering machine.

Careful with each other. Barry hadn't committed an act of betrayal. But a certain trust had been shaken.

Approaching the glass doors to leave the hospital, Margo realized the sun had set. Erev Lag B'Omer—the eve of the holiday—had begun. She pushed open the door and gasped as she stepped from the air-conditioned building into the crushing heat of the *hamsin.*

Seventeen /

Sunday, Erev Lag B'Omer—the 32nd day of the counting of the Omer

Being separated from everyone hadn't worried her at first. How could she worry, when there was so much to take in— the black-hatted Hasidim dancing in circles, the bonfires, the crowd! Batsheva had told her (but she hadn't believed it, she couldn't have until she was in the midst of it!) that as many as two hundred thousand people from all over Israel visited Mount Meron on Erev Lag B'Omer. Secular Jews came for the excitement. For the Orthodox, this was a pilgrimage to the tomb of the second-century rabbi Shimon Bar Yochai.

"Bar Yochai wrote the Zohar, the most important Kabbalist text," Batsheva had said as they—she, her husband Lev, Margo, and Audrey—walked to catch the shuttle bus from Safed.

"Batsheva! You know it's been proven beyond a doubt that the real author was a thirteenth-century Spanish Jew named Moses de Leon," Lev had responded, leading to a lively discussion of the mystical versus the scholarly points of view.

Where were Batsheva and Lev? Where was Audrey? Hadn't they agreed that if they lost each other, they would check back each half hour at the stand that sold roasted corn on the cob? This was Margo's second trip to the stand, and she didn't see any of them. The road up the mountain to Bar Yochai's tomb was lined with booths selling all kinds of food, religious items, and trinkets, a scene reminiscent of the border crossing from Mexico into California. What if she'd gone to the wrong corn stand?

She glanced down the row of booths. One vendor special-
ized in red tarboosh hats and embroidered robes, the next offered sodas and ice cream, another featured stacks of cassette
tapes and a loudspeaker blaring what Lev had called "Jewish
soul music." There were loudspeakers all over; each one
blasted a different tune. But she saw no one else in the immediate vicinity selling corn.

Ten after eleven. There was nothing to do but try again at
eleven-thirty. Dropping her gnawed corncob in a trash can,
Margo plunged back into the crowd. She nearly stumbled into
a Hasid who held a metal collection box. She must have seen
a dozen of them already, asking for donations for yeshivas and
other religious institutions. There were also peddlers hawking
an incredible variety of merchandise—prayer books, amulets,
candles to light on Bar Yochai's grave, oil blessed by miracle
workers. Lev had even pointed out someone selling blessings.

The Hasid thrust the collection box toward her and said
something in Hebrew. Was he angry or was it just the harsh-
ness of the language? She shook her head, said, "*Lo midaberet
ivrit*"—*I don't speak Hebrew,* one of the half-dozen phrases
she'd mastered—and smiled. An aggressive solicitor, he kept
the metal box in her face. For a moment she was trapped there
by the crowd, so close to him she could smell his sour breath.
Fighting panic, she pulled away.

The crowd's momentum carried her back up the mountain.

The path veered to the right as it approached Bar Yochai's
tomb, now the site of a synagogue, and continued uphill. On
the roof of the synagogue, two concentric circles of men
danced with their arms around each other's shoulders, their
faces suffused with joy. Lag B'Omer was a happy holiday,
Batsheva had told her. No one was certain why, but on Lag
B'Omer the state of partial mourning between Passover and
Shavuot was lifted. Eager couples were permitted to marry.
Among secular Israeli Jews, it was mainly a children's holiday; on Erev Lag B'Omer, kids all over the country lit bonfires. There were fires on Mount Meron as well, blazing in a
couple of metal drums where the men danced. Looking down
to the women's side of the courtyard, Margo saw women praying and lighting candles. Some slipped pieces of paper into

cracks in the wall—prayers to have children, Batsheva had said.

Where the hell was Batsheva? And what about Audrey? Batsheva and Lev might have no sense of time, but Audrey was promptness personified! There must be a first-aid station, should she check there? But the thought of any medical setting, after the hours at Alice's bedside, made her cringe.

Suddenly it was all too much—the crowd pressing around her, the bright floodlights, the deafening music, the voices that were too loud and too foreign. Was this real or another nightmare? Spinning to escape, she came face-to-face with another Hasid holding a collection box—or was it the same foul-breathed man? She shoved through what felt like hundreds of people and ran, more by instinct than intention, higher up the mountain.

Here, beyond the synagogue, families had set up makeshift tents of blankets draped over clotheslines. Tomorrow morning, as part of the Lag B'Omer observance, three-year-old Orthodox boys would receive their first haircuts. (Batsheva had mentioned another Lag B'Omer tradition, the belief that if on the eve of the holiday a childless couple pitched their tent and made love near Bar Yochai's tomb, the woman would become pregnant. Several residents of Safed claimed to have been conceived that way.) It was no quieter here and the air reeked of smoke and cooking meat from dozens of barbecues, but at least she was free of the terrible crush of people.

She found a place to sit and focused on breathing slowly. After a few minutes she felt ready to return to the crowds and another try at the roasted corn stand. Finally she found Audrey and Lev. They were farther down the hill at a falafel vendor—didn't Margo remember, they had discussed the corn stand but then decided they'd prefer to eat falafel while they waited?

"Where were you?" said Audrey, munching a falafel.

"Up the mountain. It was Felliniesque." Making a story of it, distancing herself from the panic she'd felt and the sense of disaster that lingered like the smoke from barbecues clinging to her clothes and hair. Only Batsheva remained unaccounted for, however, and Lev was certain she'd simply met some friends and lost track of time.

Batsheva's husband was a good ten years younger than she,

a robust, thick-bodied man with an easy charm. He got them laughing, telling them how the Torah procession used to travel all the way on foot the five and a half miles from Safed to Mount Meron—"and those Torahs are heavy!"—but now the faithful carried the Torah only to the edge of the Old City, and a taxi conveyed them the rest of the way. Not just any taxi, however. "The same family drives the Torah taxi every year; it used to be the father and now it's the son."

As they joked and ate falafel, Margo kept glancing around for Batsheva. She couldn't shake the sense that the strangeness of the night on the Israeli mountain—the atmosphere composed of part carnival, part worship, and the eerie *hamsin* wind—wasn't merely entrancing but was somehow menacing.

By twelve-thirty, even Lev was concerned, though he didn't call it that. He talked about needing to find his wife so they could get home and get some sleep, since he was on call at the hospital tomorrow. Like many Israelis, he carried a cell phone. He used it to call home, in case Batsheva had caught the shuttle and gone back on her own. Nili answered; she'd been to Mount Meron with schoolmates and returned home already. Her mother wasn't there, she said, but she promised to have Batsheva call whenever she arrived. Still calm, Lev proposed looking around a little—if they left without Batsheva, she'd never let him hear the end of it. He went down the road and Audrey up, while Margo kept watch at the falafel stand. Occasionally she checked the corn stand, too, since Batsheva might have made the same mistake as she.

The hunt began in earnest an hour later. Lev asked the police and soldiers on duty—who were there in force, a necessary feature of any large Israeli gathering—to help. He enlisted several friends as well, people he'd run into when he made his initial search on Mount Meron and in the bazaarlike area at the foot of the mountain, where the highway was closed to traffic. Anyone who could actually recognize Batsheva was an invaluable searcher, since how could the police spot one small, gray-haired woman among the tens of thousands of people who streamed up and down the mountain, even at one-thirty A.M.?

One of Batsheva's friends checked the first-aid station—she

had no serious medical problems, Lev said, but she might have fallen or perhaps she'd eaten something that made her ill. Audrey took a turn waiting by the falafel stand while Margo accompanied a policewoman to all of the areas limited to women only. A male family friend and a policeman did the same in the areas restricted to men. A strapping young soldier volunteered to take the path all the way to the top of the mountain, in case Batsheva had decided to celebrate the holiday with a midnight hike.

A child found her at first light. The child, a twelve-year-old Orthodox boy, had awakened before his family and crept out of their tent to say morning prayers.

At first he thought the lady was sleeping, she was lying so still beside a bush. But it was a strange place to sleep, and equally strange that the woman had no blanket covering her against the cold.

The child, a bright, mature boy who was the head of the class at his yeshiva and the responsible eldest of seven siblings, ventured over to the woman and tried to wake her. He spoke to her, first standing and then kneeling closer—approaching gradually, not wanting to be disrespectful.

He knew he was forbidden to touch her, but what if she was very ill? He reached one finger to the woman's hand. It felt colder than anyone's hand should feel, even someone who had spent all night outside.

The boy's maturity fled and he let out a howl.

Part Three / Shiva

The traditional seven-day Jewish mourning period, *shiva* (the word simply means *seven*), begins when the family returns home from the funeral. ''Mourners must not shave, take a luxurious bath, wear leather shoes (which Jewish tradition regards as particularly comfortable) or have sex during the week of *shiva*.'' On the seventh day, the family's rabbi often comes to the house and ''escorts the mourners on a short walk around the block, symbolizing the mourner's return to the regular world.''

Rabbi Joseph Telushkin, *Jewish Literacy*

Eighteen /

Monday, Lag B'Omer—the 33rd day of the counting of the Omer

"It was a heart attack. That's all, a heart attack," Cousin Yitzhak said, for about the twentieth time that morning.

"Yitzhak," Lev said heavily, "there was never anything wrong with her heart." Poor Daddy. He was so quiet, wrapped deep inside himself, as if *his* heart was breaking.

"You never know with something like that," Yitzhak replied. "Eli Rabner, he was only thirty-six years old, and he drops dead one day when he's jogging."

"Eli Rabner's father died of a heart attack when he was forty, and for all we know, his grandfather and great-grandfather did the same," said Aunt Leah. Leah was bustling around serving coffee and pastry, and trying to force Nili to cry. *Don't be ashamed of tears,* she kept saying, bending close and looking at Nili through two layers of thick plastic, Nili's eyeglasses and her own. *Your tears are a sign of your love.* "But there's no heart disease in your family, is there, Saul?"

"Definitely not." Uncle Saul thumped his chest. Batsheva's only sibling, he and Aunt Leah had driven from their kibbutz as soon as Lev had called them this morning.

Uncle Saul was small and compact, just like Batsheva. Tall, skinny Cousin Yitzhak was the only one in the family that Nili resembled. The thought made her want to throw up.

"Well, I saw where it happened. Some of my students and I were camping near there," Yitzhak said. "She was stricken above Bar Yochai's tomb. So maybe Batsheva forgot she was a woman in her fifties and she ran up Meron like we used to do forty years ago. What else could she have died of, except heart failure?''

"That's what we need an autopsy to find out," Uncle Saul said.

"It's forbidden!" Yitzhak roared. "Even on your socialist kibbutz, you must know that an autopsy is a desecration of the soul. Until the body is properly buried, the soul can't ascend back to heaven. You do an autopsy only to immediately save a life, if you can find out about some disease threatening another person, or else to find a murderer. Right now the *Chevra Kadisha* women should be washing her body and preparing her for burial. Instead, she's in a refrigerator at the hospital. In a refrigerator, like a watermelon!''

"Stop it!" Nili cried.

Aunt Leah zoomed in on her, but she shrank away.

"Nili, come here." Her father looked as if he had to come back from thousands of kilometers away, when he opened his arms to her.

She covered the remaining distance herself and nestled against him, trying to absorb some of his grief; trying to feel her own. Any daughter, even a daughter who had hated her mother in life, should feel sad and awful that her mother was dead. But horrible, horrible Nili . . . She only felt scared and cold and also angry because of Uncle Yitzhak, who had barely visited their house for the last five years since her mother started teaching, and this morning he'd come over and started quoting religious law at them.

"Yitzhak," her father said; he still held Nili close. "I've listened to everything you have to say. Even though I'm not religious, if I felt completely convinced about Batsheva's death, I would respect your wishes."

"My wishes? *My* wishes? It has nothing to do with me. It's a matter of *Halakhah,* the laws that have sustained the Jewish people for centuries. Why do you think there was a land of Israel for you to come to when you left Czechoslovakia? Because generations of Jews followed *Halakhah.*''

"You don't say!" Uncle Saul's sunburned face turned violently red. "I suppose it had nothing whatever to do with the Zionist movement and the fact that the Western powers felt guilty after the Holocaust but not so guilty they were willing to take in all those refugees themselves? Where were the religious Jews when the Zionists were creating an agricultural base for this country's economy and taking up arms to defend it? Where are they today when they're asked to join the Israel Defense Forces? Claiming religious exemptions and leaving it up to the Zionists' sons and daughters to risk their lives."

"There are elite religious units within the Defense Forces."

"Serving by choice, when it isn't a choice for anyone else in the country."

As the relatives argued Nili felt as if her father simply left the room. His body stayed in his favorite old chair with the deep red brocade upholstery, but *he,* he was somewhere completely apart, maybe not even on the same planet. He didn't notice when the conversation came back to what to do with her mother's body.

"So, Lev," said Yitzhak, "can we call the *Chevra Kadisha* and tell them to begin?"

"What?"

Yitzhak repeated the question.

"Like it or not, Yitzhak, I haven't changed my mind," Lev said. "An autopsy will be performed this afternoon."

"Shouldn't you at least consult her own son?"

"I'll ask Gadi's opinion, if I can reach him. I left a message on his machine, and I'll talk to him as soon as he calls."

Nili bit her lip. She knew why Gadi hadn't been at his Tel Aviv apartment when they'd called this morning. But why mention it, since knowing why he was gone didn't mean she had any idea where to find him? He hadn't met her last night on Mount Meron, the way he'd said he would.

"Does he have a cell phone?" asked Yitzhak.

"He has a whole store full of them," Saul said. "That's his new business."

"Isn't it a little late to get in on the cell-phone business?"

"Yitzhak, since when are you an expert on cell phones?"

"I have friends in the business world. And I read the newspaper."

Lev sighed. "I tried Gadi's cell phone. I didn't get an answer. But ultimately, whether or not to do an autopsy is my decision. I'm making it based on my knowledge as a physician and also my knowledge of Batsheva and what I think she would want. Tonight, after the autopsy, the *Chevra Kadisha* can come. We'll be able to bury her tomorrow.''

"And then what?'' said Yitzhak. "You go to work the next day? You don't even sit *shiva*?''

Lev didn't answer; clearly he hadn't thought that far ahead.

"Of course we'll sit *shiva*,'' Aunt Leah said.

"I need to go lie down for a while,'' said Lev. "I think I'll take something so I can get a little sleep. Nili, how about you? You want a sleeping pill?''

"No, I'm okay.''

"I'll take care of her,'' said Aunt Leah.

It wasn't that Nili disliked Aunt Leah, but "Leah's Misfortune,'' as everyone in the family called it, was that her only child had died at the age of two and she hadn't been able to have any more. She made up for it by working in the children's house at her kibbutz. She also exercised her maternal instinct on all of her relatives under the age of thirty. There were times, especially when she was little, that Nili had adored this aunt who cuddled her and always had time to tell her a story or play a game. But Leah's idea of mothering involved being in your face constantly, and right now that was the last thing Nili wanted.

She sneaked out of the house when Leah was in the bathroom. She didn't know where she was going, just that she had to get away.

Nineteen /

"How old was she?" said Margo, curled up on Dalia's sofa and greedily inhaling secondhand smoke from Dalia's cigarette.

"Fifty-five, fifty-six," Dalia said.

"That's not very old." Would smoking just one cigarette destroy eight years of avoiding the evil weed?

"But if her heart was bad . . ."

"Did she have a history of heart disease?" Audrey said. "Or a seizure disorder?"

Dalia shrugged. "Israelis are not like Americans. We don't go on television and tell the whole world every illness we have."

"Jesus." Haggard with exhaustion and sorrow, Danny talked as if to himself. "I can't believe she's dead. Poor Lev. Poor Nili. She's just a kid." He gulped the strong coffee Dalia had made. He needed it even more than Margo did. She and Audrey had returned from helping with the search at four A.M. and had slept a little, in spite of the miserable heat. Danny had stayed on the mountain all night and was there a few hours earlier, when Batsheva was found. He had come to break the news after a stop at his cousin Bernice's. (Bernice, he'd reported, had insisted on going to the hospital to tell Alice. Having met Cousin Bernice, Margo felt the task was in hands far steadier than hers felt this morning.)

"Does Nili have someone she feels close to?" Audrey asked. "A relative or a teacher?"

"She and Lev are close," Danny said.

"The person she really adores," Dalia said, "is her half brother, Gadi."

Maybe another cup of coffee would quench the urge to smoke. Margo lifted the pot, but discovered it was empty.

"Sorry, I make more!" Dalia jumped up.

"Don't worry about it."

"No, it just takes me a minute."

"Can I help?"

"No!" Dalia said sharply. Although she'd skipped the celebration on Meron, she was as tired as the rest of them after spending half the night finishing a set of drawings for a gallery in Jerusalem. They'd had to stack half a dozen drawings, set out for fixative spray to dry, before they could use the coffee table this morning.

"Danny, could she have fallen from higher up the mountain?" Audrey asked.

"They had the area blocked off by the time I found out, but it didn't look like a place where someone would land after a fall. And if she'd fallen, she would have been banged up."

"Where was she?"

"Above Bar Yochai's tomb, where people were camping. But off to the side, in the bushes."

"What in the world was she doing there?"

A clatter followed by a loud curse came from the kitchen.

"Dalia, are you okay?" Margo came to the kitchen door.

Dalia sat on the floor, weeping, surrounded by spilled dry coffee. "It's so awful," she said.

"Do you want us to leave you alone?"

"No!"

"Here, why don't you let me make coffee?" She helped Dalia up, brushed the coffee off her shorts, and gave her a hug.

Dalia insisted on making the coffee herself, but let Margo sweep up the spill and get out some food; none of them had eaten today.

"What was she doing in the bushes?" Danny mused when they came in from the kitchen with fresh coffee and a tray of yogurt, fruit, and crackers. "Maybe she felt sick and wanted to get away from the crowd. Or . . . God spoke to Moses from a bush. Who knows? Maybe, if she was about to die, she heard the voice of God.''

What had Alice said about God yesterday? That she felt God's presence in a mother comforting a child, or a frond of bougainvillea? Margo hoped Batsheva had felt called by God on the holy mountain. Not a bad way for a deeply religious person to die.

''Has it occurred to anyone,'' said Audrey, ''that various hostile acts—including one that was nearly fatal—have taken place against Batsheva's students, and suddenly Batsheva drops dead?''

''Yes, but . . .'' Margo said. Danny had told them the story that had raced to every ear on Mount Meron: *She was lying peacefully. The boy thought she was asleep.*

He said it now. ''There was no sign of violence. The kid said she looked like she was asleep.''

''I bet he didn't look closely,'' Audrey said. ''The Orthodox cut the three-year-old boys' hair on Lag B'Omer, right? What do they use for that? Ordinary scissors or some kind of special knife?''

''Scissors,'' Dalia said. ''Only scissors.''

''Scissors can be sharp,'' Audrey replied.

''Murder is not an Israeli crime. No one but the Russian Mafia commits murder.''

''Yes, and no one but the Russian Mafia poisons people.'' Margo took Audrey's side by instinct. Logic followed, and it made her shiver in spite of the *hamsin.* They were basing their assurance of Batsheva's ''peaceful'' death on the word of a terrified child, a child who had seen her for no more than a moment. How did they even know that what they'd heard was what the boy really said? ''Dalia, can I bum a cigarette?'' she said.

''*Bum?* What is that?''

''Can I have one of yours?''

''Yes. Fine.''

''It doesn't compute,'' Danny said. ''Maybe some kid gave henbane to your mother. But murder someone? Absolutely not.''

''I agree,'' Margo said. ''I can't imagine a teenager killing Batsheva.'' Thank heaven, she didn't enjoy the taste of tobacco as much as she remembered. But oh, how she loved sucking in the smoke. "I think the point about the kids is that no one in Safed had any trouble believing Batsheva's students were being harassed, right? Because everyone accepts that Batsheva was threatening to a lot of people. What if she threatened someone who was capable of doing much worse things than a teenage kid would do?" *More evil things,* Batsheva would have said.

"If anyone stabbed Batsheva with scissors—or shot her or bashed in her head with a rock—there'd have to be blood," Danny said. "Someone would have noticed. And believe me, they wouldn't be able to keep it quiet with all of the people on Meron."

"You Americans!" Dalia hit the table so hard that Margo's half-full coffee cup tipped over. "You think, you think," she started, and then exploded into her own language.

Nili, crouching outside, had understood the English as long as they didn't talk too fast. And she followed perfectly when Dalia started yelling in Hebrew.

"You think this is some kind of game, turning people's tragedy into a murder mystery," she heard Dalia say. "It is a terrible, terrible thing to say that Batsheva is murdered and that some boys did it. You know how much pain you cause her family and the families of the boys if you start saying that? You know how much pain you're already causing, saying all over Safed that these boys poisoned your mother? You Americans, you come here and act like it is your country. You think we are just like you, but we're not!"

Nili agreed that Americans were really strange. Look at the way they virtually worshiped her mother. All except for Mrs. Simon's daughter Audrey. Audrey had told Batsheva off, in front of everybody! Audrey was as tall and thin as Nili, but she looked like a model. She used to be a ballerina! They had really talked the other night.

Nili hadn't thought, when she'd left her house, that she was going *to* anything or anyone; she only knew she had to get away. She was surprised when her feet took her to Dalia Weiss's house, and even a little surprised when she realized she was walking toward the side with the guest room where

Audrey was staying. Then she heard the voices, including Audrey's, coming from the main part of the house. She didn't want to have to talk to all those people. Neither did she want to be anywhere else.

There was a shady spot between a bush and the wall, right below a window. Just the place for Invisible Girl.

After Dalia stopped talking, a few seconds passed. Then Danny said in Hebrew, "Sorry, we've seen too many movies. Or in my case, too many episodes of *Star Trek*." Audrey apologized, too, and then said something in English to her sister. Nili didn't catch all the words, and she jumped when she heard the door open.

There was no time to run. When they passed her hiding place, she pressed against the wall; she didn't dare breathe. Thank God they didn't see her! She thought about going to their door then, as if she'd just arrived, but she felt too ashamed after eavesdropping on their conversation.

She felt even deeper shame as she realized that by scooting a few feet along the wall, she could hear the sisters talking in their room, and that she couldn't make herself leave.

"I probably would have apologized, too," Margo said, "if I'd had any idea what to apologize for." She rubbed an ice cube over her face and neck, and stood in front of the fan. How long would the *hamsin* last?

Audrey translated what Dalia had said and added, "Don't you think Danny was right? If Batsheva had been attacked, it would have been obvious when she was found." She lay down, and Margo ran the ice cube over her foot. "Mm, that's heavenly. Remember when we used to massage each other's feet after ballet class?"

"Lying with our heads at opposite ends of the bed so we could reach each other's feet?"

"Why don't you bring me an ice cube?"

"Bless you." Margo got an ice cube for Audrey and another for herself; her first was nearly melted. "I had a terrible dream the other night," she said after she'd lain down. "I was stuck in a huge crowd, I couldn't understand what anyone was saying, and I knew something terrible was happening. Last night felt like being in the dream."

"Sounds like culture shock," Audrey diagnosed. "That was only your fourth day in Israel. Plus, I would have been worried, too, if I couldn't find any of you and I'd been wandering around by myself."

"Weren't you?" Margo had somehow assumed they'd all gotten separated from one another and had stumbled around the mountainside while aggressive men shoved charity boxes in their faces.

"For a little bit. But Lev and I both knew where we were supposed to meet."

"That's right. The falafel stand. How soon do you want to go see Mom?" Margo said.

Audrey groaned. "Do we have to move, ever again?"

In spite of the hot day, Nili hugged herself, savoring the secret she shared with Audrey, the small lie Audrey had told her sister. But Nili knew.

There was no more sound from the sisters' room—maybe they were asleep? She heard nothing from Dalia's house, either. Invisible Girl crept from her hiding place and slipped into the street.

How weird that anyone thought her mother could have been murdered. Weird, and weirdly comforting . . . to realize that other people might have hated her mother even more than she did. Maybe her lack of sadness didn't mean she was the most terrible girl in the world.

Twenty /

"I smell cigarette smoke," Alice said. They were walking down the hospital corridor, Margo on one side of her and Audrey on the other.

"I'm sorry," Margo said. "I forgot to bring them."

"You forgot *what*?" demanded Audrey.

"Have you been smoking?" Alice said at the same time, sniffing Margo's hair.

"We were at Dalia's," Margo said to her mother.

"Dalia doesn't smoke."

"She did today." Dalia wasn't the only one, but Margo didn't mention her own fall off the wagon. Alice's two-cigarette-a-day habit hardly meant she tolerated smoking in her children.

"What the hell is going on?" Audrey said. "Margo, were you going to bring Mom cigarettes?"

"She begged me."

"She's in intensive care."

"Would you stop talking about me as if I weren't here?" Alice said, and burst into tears.

"Mom, I'm sorry," they said at the same time.

"Let's sit down," Audrey added, handing Alice a tissue.

For the next half hour the daughters maintained a truce, comforting Alice as she spoke about how devastated she was by Batsheva's death.

"I want to attend Batsheva's funeral tomorrow," Alice said

as they helped her back into bed. "It's going to take place right behind the hospital."

"We'll all go," said Audrey. "We'll come here beforehand with whatever clothes you want to wear."

"Pick anything. I'd like to go to the cemetery, too."

"Omigod. The cemetery," Margo said, suddenly reminded of her conversation with her mother—was it only yesterday? "Have you thought of anything else, Mom? Besides the snakes?"

"What snakes?" Audrey said.

"Not a thing," Alice answered Margo.

"What snakes?" Audry repeat.

Alice explained.

Audrey held her pique until they'd kissed Alice good-bye and were walking across the parking lot, the heat so intense through the soles of Margo's sandals it reminded her of covering a canyon fire.

"When did you and Mom plan to let me in on the secret?" Audrey said crossly.

"There wasn't any secret. It just came up yesterday. So much happened between now and then, I didn't even think about it."

"Mom finally remembers something after having amnesia for five days, and you neglect to mention it?"

"I wasn't keeping anything from you deliberately." Margo got into the car and swore as the vinyl seat seared her thighs through her dress. She started the engine and turned up the air-conditioning to full blast. It wouldn't do much good with the short distance they had to drive, but it gave her an illusion of control.

"You and Mom always have secrets. I can't believe you were going to bring her cigarettes."

"Audrey, I didn't just forget to tell you. With everything that's happened, I also completely forgot I wanted to go to the cemetery. Maybe someone saw her there on Tuesday."

"Were you planning to inform me about that?"

"Of course. Do you want to go with me? Later today?" The unshaded cemetery would be hellish now, in the early afternoon.

"Damn right."

They didn't speak again as Margo struggled to drive through the packed streets. Driving in Safed on Lag B'Omer was like driving in Tijuana, except the streets were narrower and the curses in a different tongue.

"It's not like you tell *me* everything," Margo said, once she'd managed to park. Walking through the Artists' Quarter to Dalia's, they hugged to the shade beside the buildings.

"What don't I tell you?"

"What you and Batsheva talked about yesterday afternoon. I asked about it at dinner and you changed the subject. Why did she ask you to come see her?"

"Gee, why would she have done that?" Audrey replied.

"To exchange recipes for gefilte fish?" They were too exhausted and hot and stressed to be having this discussion. And Margo was too cranky to let it drop.

"She wanted to make peace, after the argument we had the night before."

"I thought she liked it when people stood up to her."

"Sure, Margo, that's how she positioned herself. It was great PR. But who did she have around her? People who acted like she was the Shekinah."

"The what?"

"Shekinah." Audrey gave the *k* the clearing-your-throat Hebrew pronunciation. "It's the feminine aspect of God. The concept comes from the Kabbalah. Lately, Jewish women's groups have used Shekinah as a God they feel they can pray to. At my synagogue, we do Rosh Hodesh services, a traditional women's celebration of the new moon. All of the prayers are to Shekinah."

"That's beautiful. I didn't know you did things like that."

"You always feel somewhat excluded, even in a reform synagogue," Audrey said. "Then you find a God—a Jewish god, not some pagan goddess—whose image you're made in."

"Audrey?" Margo sensed her sister was holding something back about her talk with Batsheva. But she couldn't make herself bring up the touchy subject, when they had just achieved a rare closeness. And she felt hungry to know more about a Jewish God who was a woman. "Tell me about—what do you call it? Rosh Hodesh?" she said. "What do you do?"

• • •

The sun had set, but the parched earth of the cemetery still held the brutal heat of the day. Not that it seemed to matter to the Hasid standing amid a cluster of gravestones. He wore his long coat as well as his wide-brimmed black hat.

"Is it always this empty, or do you think it's the heat?" Margo asked Audrey.

Apart from the Hasid and a slender, dark-haired woman standing next to him, only a handful of people straggled down the hillside.

"There's a groundskeeper, it says here." Audrey skimmed a guidebook. "Listen. There's quite a story about him. He was on the Israeli fencing team that was supposed to compete in the Munich Olympics. But he had a recurring dream that God told him to leave the team and come here to take care of the cemetery. He did it, and he missed being at the Olympics where terrorists killed eleven Israeli athletes."

"Wow! Do you think that's him?"

They started across the hill toward the Hasid, both of them scanning the ground as they walked. How much protection did tennis shoes and thin cotton socks offer against vipers?

"*Shalom,*" Audrey called out as they neared the man and his companion.

He and the woman turned.

"Ronit!" Margo said, recognizing Batsheva's student. "I'm so sorry," she added. Ronit's cheeks were wet with tears.

"Oh." She looked at Margo and Audrey as if she barely knew who they were.

"We don't want to bother you," Margo said. "We were looking for the groundskeeper."

"The . . . Sorry, I do not know this word."

Audrey stated the request in Hebrew.

The man answered her.

"The groundskeeper isn't here right now," Audrey translated. "Lag B'Omer is a happy day, and on happy days people don't usually visit a cemetery."

"Except for special place like tomb of Bar Yochai on Meron," the man said in marginally intelligible English.

"Then why are you here?" Margo asked him.

"I . . ." He looked adoringly at Ronit.

"I wanted to lay a stone on the tomb of the Ari," Ronit

said. "Have you done this? No? Let me show you."

The tomb of Rabbi Isaac Luria, the Ari, lay in a group with those of four other Kabbalist rabbis. All of the tombstones were painted blue—a mark, Ronit told them, of the rabbis' holiness. Margo and Audrey each selected a stone from the hillside and placed it on the Ari's tomb; Ronit and Natan had already laid stones there.

How beautiful the city was, and how bleak this place, Margo thought as Ronit and Natan murmured prayers. If God was present in the rocky cemetery, then it was an austere, harsh presence—the punitive Old Testament deity who unleashed floods and destruction. She preferred the Shekinah.

After they finished praying, the two Israelis held a whispered conference.

"Natan would like to read your palms," Ronit said. "He knows to read palms from studying Kabbalah."

"I . . ." Margo felt intrigued but wary.

"He lives just up the hill," Ronit said.

"Margo!"

Audrey's disapproval sealed it.

"Sure," Margo said. "Why not?"

"He's not reading *my* palm," Audrey muttered, but she went with them into the Jewish Quarter.

"How is your mother?" Ronit asked.

"Much better," Margo said. "She's being released from the hospital tomorrow."

"*Mazel tov.* Will you stay at Dalia's then? All three of you?"

"No, there isn't room. We're doing a trade with Danny. He'll take the room at Dalia's and the three of us are going to stay with his cousin Bernice."

"Your mother, does she remember anything?"

"Not really."

"You come to Bruce and Nancy's tonight, yes?" Ronit said. "All of us, we want to be together. Please, your mother would be there if she could."

They arrived at a house in the Jewish Quarter where Natan rented a room. He motioned them to sit in the courtyard while he went inside; every surface Margo glimpsed through the open door was covered with books.

The Kabbalist palmist came back out wearing plastic bags on his hands.

"He has to protect himself against touching you because you're a woman," Audrey whispered, "and you're going to let him read your palm?"

Margo followed Natan's request to hold out her left hand. Intellectually, she shared Audrey's irritation. But she liked Natan. And she was fascinated by the obvious attraction between the young Hasid and Ronit. Did they ever touch? What had Natan thought of Ronit studying with Batsheva?

In a combination of fractured English and Hebrew translated by Audrey, Margo heard that she was married to a good man and she had children in her life but not her own. She was a woman of heart and spirituality, Natan said, and it took a great effort for her to succeed materially. That definitely sounded like something he'd heard through Alice, who never seemed to fully appreciate that Margo had come a long way from the twenty-year-old who had "thrown away her future" by dropping out of college and making a hand-to-mouth living as a potter in New Mexico.

"I see here fire," Natan said, his finger through the plastic tracing a line on her palm.

"I was in a fire."

"Your physical body . . ." He switched to Hebrew.

"I'm not sure I understand," Audrey said. "Your body . . . it emptied? It prepared for death."

"But your soul," Natan said, "she not ready to die."

Margo felt numb as she heard that she should eat only raw foods, and she would be very "popularic" in ten years. She'd told no one except Barry and her therapist for post-traumatic stress what had happened to her in the fire, not just the heat searing her eyes and throat but the humiliation of losing control over her body.

She wanted to leave, but now Ronit asked if Audrey wanted her palm read. Audrey said, "Why not?" in a tone Margo recognized—*If my sister can do it, I'm not going to be left out.*

Natan told her that she was a dancer. (Why had he only seen that on Audrey's palm? Margo wondered. Had Alice spoken of just one daughter who danced?) That she had children, although he erred and mentioned a girl as well as Audrey's two sons. He said she had a demanding job that she performed well, but she would be even happier in her work if she started every morning at five.

"Who's going to get my kids off to school?" Audrey said, laughing.

Then came a mildly contentious exchange entirely in Hebrew. Margo kept catching one word Audrey said—*lo. No*. After that, Audrey brought the palm reading to a rapid close.

She explained while they walked to Bruce and Nancy's; Ronit had said she'd join them later.

"He said I'll learn many things from being in Safed for Shavuot," Audrey said. "Do you know what that is?"

"Of course. It celebrates the giving of the Torah on Mount Sinai." Margo didn't mention that she'd heard this from Batsheva only a few days before. "But isn't Shavuot more than two weeks from now?"

"Right. And I told him I won't be here, I'll be home, since Mom is supposed to be well enough to travel in a week. But he kept insisting. Margo, if I don't get home when I promised, my son is going to need therapy for the next five years. The poor kid has wet his bed almost every night since I've been gone. Did you know that bed-wetting is associated with torturing animals and moving on to more sophisticated forms of torture as an adult?"

"Audi! Audi! Zach has never hurt an animal, has he?"

"No."

"You're getting upset because a man with Baggies on his hands said a few things he heard about you from Mom and made up the rest."

"And because I'm the most guilt-prone mother in New Jersey. I know. It's just that—this is stupid, but there was one thing he couldn't have found out from Mom. What he said about starting work at five? I've been thinking about getting up early to do some writing. It made me feel like he could see things about me, private things. Did you feel that way about anything he said to you?"

"No," Margo lied.

Twenty-one /

Monday, Lag B'Omer—the 33rd day of the counting of the Omer

"Lev, where are you going?" said Uncle Saul, unaware of Nili curled up behind the high back of a chair in a corner of the dark courtyard.

"The hospital," her father said.

"What for?"

"I want to run a few more tests."

Having eavesdropped once, Invisible Girl felt less guilty about doing it a second time. Besides, it wasn't as if anyone ever told her what was going on. Or anyone noticed her. Her mother would have known she was there without even having to see her, she thought, with a sudden, surprising sadness.

"What kind of tests?" Uncle Saul asked. "They did the autopsy and said she had a heart attack. What more do you have to test for?"

"You, too?"

"What? You mean you think I'd take Yitzhak's side?" Uncle Saul spat to show his contempt for his holier-than-thou cousin. "I was one hundred percent for the autopsy. But what's with more tests? You've got relatives arriving from all over the country. Misha is here, and David and Hana. Tamar and the grandchildren are on their way, aren't they?"

"I think so. Leah called them."

"So. Come inside and talk to people if you want to, or ignore them if you want to do that. But rest now."

"I can't."

"What? Do you suspect something? Did the police tell you something?"

"I . . ." Lev didn't speak for a moment, and Nili heard a comforting, familiar sucking sound as her father lit his pipe. "In Czechoslovakia," he said so softly she almost had to hold her breath to hear, "when I first graduated from medical school, I didn't just work at the hospital. They also assigned me to a prison. Sometimes—not often—they called me if a prisoner was sick. And I examined the dead. Do you have any idea how many times I had to sign a death certificate saying someone died of a heart attack when I didn't believe it?"

"Lev. That was Czechoslovakia."

"Czechoslovakia, Israel. Wherever, I'm still being asked to accept a cause of death that makes no rational sense to me. The difference is that this time I don't have to keep my mouth shut and do nothing."

"What about the funeral? Are you going to stop the funeral from taking place so you can do more tests and more tests? I don't believe all the crap that Yitzhak does, but I want my sister to be buried."

"Don't worry. The funeral can take place tomorrow. I had them save blood and tissue samples. I'll use those for testing."

Saul sighed. "How many tests will be enough? What do you think you're going to find?"

"Lev! Uncle Saul!" A third man entered the courtyard, and Nili's heart sang: Gadi!

It was all she could do not to leap up and run to her brother. But she was still Invisible Girl. She stayed hidden as Gadi explained that he'd been out all day and his cell phone was broken. The moment he came home and finally got the message about his mother, he jumped in his car and drove as fast as he could to Safed.

"Did you talk to Tamar?" Uncle Saul asked.

"Uh . . ." Gadi fumbled.

"Leah called her and she was going to come, but she was having some car trouble."

"Oh yeah, I tried to call and I guess she'd already left. I got the answering machine."

Even Nili could tell he was lying. He wouldn't have called Tamar. But Nili understood, as Lev and Saul didn't seem to, how mean Tamar always was to Gadi, how when they were married she complained and complained every time one of his business projects didn't make a million dollars overnight. He'd be working so hard and Tamar would make him feel worse instead of helping him. And now that they were divorced, he had to beg to get to be a father to his own children. That was why he saw them only once every two or three months. He wanted to spend more time with them, but Tamar wouldn't let him.

"What happened?" Gadi asked.

"Come on. Let's go inside and we'll talk," said Uncle Saul. "Lev, come on. You're not going back to the hospital tonight, are you?"

"No. Not tonight."

Nili heard the door open and close as they went in. Quietly she unfolded herself from the chair. If she waited a few minutes, she could say she had just come in from a walk. She counted the seconds, then made herself walk inside slowly, without excitement, pretending she had no idea that Gadi had arrived.

She didn't have to pretend the happiness she felt at seeing him. Running into her big brother's arms with a cry of joy, she didn't even feel mad anymore that he hadn't met her the way he'd promised, last night on Mount Meron.

Twenty-two /

Monday, Lag B'Omer—the 33rd day of the counting of the Omer

Bruce hugged them and asked them to remove their shoes. Margo slipped off her tennies and added them to the half-dozen pairs of footwear in the foyer of the flower children's house in the Jewish Quarter.

More hugs greeted them in the living room. (Was Yosef's hug longer and closer than the rest, or did she just imagine it? Did she *wish* it?)

"Wine?" Bruce picked up a glass from the coffee table, where four candles provided the only light in the room. "Red or white? Or we've got soda."

"White wine, please," Margo said, and helped herself to some food, the ubiquitous hummus and pita bread as well as some cheese. She had no appetite, but if she didn't balance the wine with something solid, she'd have to be rolled home; Safed's cobbled streets would make that a truly memorable experience.

The gathering was disjointed, everyone upset and tired. Over on one side of the room, Yosef was giving Nancy a neck massage; neither spoke except for Nancy's occasional groans when he kneaded a tight muscle. The rest of them—Ma'ayan, Bruce, Danny, Audrey, and Margo—sat in the irregular circle of sofa and chairs around the coffee table.

"I want to know what happens when one of the *lamed vav* dies," Bruce said. "Does a newborn baby instantly become the next *tzaddik*, the way the Buddha got reborn in some kid from Seattle?"

"What are you talking about?" Margo was glad to hear her sister ask; she was tired of constantly being the ignoramus about anything Jewish.

"*Lamed vav* just means thirty-six," Danny said. "The idea is that in every generation there are thirty-six special *tzaddikim*—extremely righteous people. The Talmud says that without them, the world will end."

"So when one dies," Bruce said, "does a new one have to show up immediately, or else boom?"

"Bruce, do you think Batsheva was one of the *lamed vav*?" Ma'ayan asked. "And now a baby has taken her place?"

Margo pictured a baby with Batsheva's pinched, intense face and managed not to giggle. She hadn't realized how exhausted she was until she'd taken a sip of wine. The sofa was too vertical; she slid off and half reclined on the carpet.

"I think Batsheva was a *tzaddik,* a wise, righteous person," Danny said. "But the *lamed vav* are supposed to be really low-profile. I've heard them called the hidden saints. You want to hear about a wild article that got passed around rabbinical school? It said the movie *Men in Black* was a modern version of the story of the *lamed vav*."

"What movie?" asked Ma'ayan.

Bruce responded. "*Men in Black*. Guys in black suits go after aliens."

As they talked Margo swallowed more wine and became closely acquainted with the carpet. Unlike the newish but plain furniture, the rug wasn't the standard you-can-spill-anything-on-it-and-it-won't-show issue she would have expected in a rental house; it was a plush Persian in a rich dark blue with accents of white and crimson.

"The number thirty-six is believed to come from Jewish astrology," Danny was saying. "And there are twenty-six men in black, like the twenty-six letters of our alphabet. So they both have numerological sources."

"Everything has a numerological source, if you read enough into it," Audrey argued.

"Sure, but isn't it a great parallel, these alien hunters who have to save the world and the *lamed vav* who save the world? The article also said the Hasidim probably figured the *lamed vav* dressed the way they did. In other words, they're men in black.''

"Speaking of the Hasidim . . .'' Bruce started. "Hi, babe,'' he said to Nancy, who'd come up beside him.

"Who wants to bliss out next?'' Nancy said. "Margo?''

"Um. Someone else must be ahead of me.'' She hadn't realized Yosef was treating everyone to neck rubs.

"Hey, I'm ready to bliss out.'' Danny went over to take his turn under Yosef's fingers.

"Speaking of the Hasidim,'' Bruce said again, "we should all be dancing.''

"Are you insane?'' The response came from Ronit; she must have arrived while Margo was studying the carpet. "You would dance at a time like this?''

"The Hasidim sang and danced when their hearts were full of sadness. They knew a great secret! They knew that God dwells in the cells of our bodies, in the intracellular spaces and the mitochondria. When we dance, when we open our cells, God dances.''

"Bruce, don't be such a stereotype!'' Ma'ayan said affectionately. Folding her compact body, she sat on the floor beside Margo. "I'm glad your mother feels better,'' she said. "I went to visit her on Erev Lag B'Omer when Yosef took the kids to Meron—I never go, I can't stand the crowds. She told me she could only remember one thing, being afraid of snakes. Has anything else come back since then?''

"No.''

"I don't get it,'' Ma'ayan said. "It's one thing to forget what happened after she took the henbane and it affected her thinking. But how could she lose the whole day before that?''

"The doctor said it has to do with how we create memories. They're not cemented in immediately,'' Margo said warily. Too many people were interested in her mother's memory. But wasn't it natural for people who cared about Alice to ask? Nevertheless. "The thing about snakes probably wasn't a real memory. It was probably a dream,'' she stressed, and added, "Did you see her that day?''

"I already told you no,'' Ma'ayan said, but she sounded less defensive than she had the other day. In fact, despite her sadness about Batsheva, she seemed far more relaxed in general. "There was no class with Batsheva. But I bet your mom had her Hebrew lesson. Ronit? Nancy? Gee, I don't know where Bruce is. Did your Hebrew class meet last Tuesday? Was Alice there?"

"Tuesday? Yes," Ronit said. "Nine to ten A.M."

"Do you remember anything special happening that day?" Margo asked.

"My problem," Nancy said, sighing, "is I never remember anything from class. No matter how hard I study, the letter *dalet* still looks like the letter *resh,* and the *zayin* looks just like the *vav.* Then, just when you think you might have a slim chance of figuring out the *aleph-bet,* you discover that most written Hebrew doesn't use any vowels."

"How can they leave out the vowels?"

"The vowels go *under* the letters. Except, as I said, in most writing."

"How many people are in the class?"

"Just your mother and Bruce and Nancy," Ronit answered. "I am not regular teacher of Hebrew. But I taught in army. When I come here, they ask me to teach them."

"We were in a big class before that," Nancy said. "The teacher told us we were going against God by studying with Batsheva."

"Did my mom say anything about her plans for the rest of the day?"

They both shook their heads.

"She and Bruce might have talked," Nancy said. "They like to discuss philosophy. Don't look so surprised! I know Bruce can sound like he dropped too much acid at a formative age, but there's something beautiful about the way his mind works."

Spoken like a woman blinded by love, Margo thought. Not that a cosmic bullshitter like Bruce would ever attract her. Artists, she thought uneasily, were her weakness.

As if on cue, Yosef came over and touched her shoulder, which leaped tensely toward her ear. "You could use a neck massage," he said.

It would have looked silly to refuse, Margo thought, sitting in a chair while Yosef stood behind her. And the massage was fantastic, Yosef's strong hands coaxing the tightness from her neck as if he were wedging air bubbles out of clay. That felt great; so did the little additional tingles in her body that had nothing to do with loosening muscles.

"Ma'ayan is different than I thought she'd be," she said. Always a good way to defuse sexual tension: talk about your spouse or his.

"Oh?"

"I had the idea she was shy. She's much more outgoing than I expected."

"She's happier now," Yosef said, but *he* didn't sound happy. Margo reconsidered her choice of tension-reducing subject.

"Where are people buried?" she asked.

"You mean modern people? Not rabbis who died four hundred years ago?"

"Yes. Ooh!" she yelped. He'd gotten the part of her neck that turned into a rock whenever she was stressed.

"Just breathe and relax." He caressed her trapezius muscle.

"I should give someone else a turn."

"Another minute, this muscle will let go. People today are still buried in cemetery, but lower down the hill from the Ari and other rabbis. You know what is at the top of the hill? The Ari *mikve.* For men only."

"I thought *mikves* were for women."

"Religious men use it to purify. In the Ari *mikve,* the water is so cold, people say anyone who bathes there is immediately forgiven for all their sins. There's a newer *mikve* down the hill, it's heated. You should go while you're in Safed."

"To a *mikve*?" It was one thing to attend a Havdalah service. She wasn't about to dip in a ritual bath, whose purpose for women, as she understood it, was to combat inherent female impurity. *Stories about women and the evil impulse,* she heard Batsheva saying, *have to do with sexual desire.*

"Thanks for the neck rub," she said. "It looks like Nancy's about to give my sister a tour of the house. I don't want to miss it." She squirmed from under Yosef's hands.

The house the flower children were renting was unremarkable. What made Margo ooh and ah were the personal touches

Bruce and Nancy had added—the indigo Persian carpet in the living room, a dozen framed antique textiles from Asia and the Middle East on various walls. Another carpet, this one a pale rose, covered the bedroom floor, and a century-old Japanese kimono hung on the wall.

"What we keep for ourselves are things we can pack easily, that can't possibly break," Nancy said.

Movable assets—and expensive ones. For old hippies supplying Pier 1 shops, Nancy and Bruce did remarkably well. Margo wondered if they limited their exports to clothing and ethnic jewelry; and if not, did that have anything to do with her mother being poisoned? Had Alice wandered into the room whose door Nancy hadn't opened, the room she said was just for storing merchandise? What kind of merchandise? Drugs? Or maybe she and Bruce dealt in exotic reptiles, and that explained Alice's fear of snakes. What if she'd entered a room full of them!

"We're checking into buying some texts in Israel," Nancy was saying.

"Like a Torah?" Audrey asked.

Why poison Alice, however, when they couldn't have known she'd suffer a concussion and amnesia? Maybe to put her out of commission while they got rid of evidence?

"No," Nancy answered Audrey. "A used Torah, even one with no historic value, costs as much as five thousand dollars. There are other kinds of texts—the writing of scribes, things like that. If they had vowels, I might even be able to read them."

"What does Ronit do?" Margo asked. At least Bruce and Nancy had a legitimate business, and they could have gotten incredible deals on the rugs, kimono, etc., from their regular suppliers. Did Ronit have any income, other than a three-student Hebrew class?

"Ah, Ronit's a real seeker," Nancy said. "She had a vision when she was in the army five or six years ago. Since then, she's taken odd jobs—grunt work on archaeological digs, waitressing, whatever—so she can leave her mind free for spiritual study. She lives cheaply, and whenever she saves enough money, she stops working and studies full-time. Oh, here's Bruce." She opened the door to a sort of study.

Bruce was sitting at a desk talking to Danny, their heads close together. They both jumped back—guiltily? Or did Margo just feel suspicious of everyone? And guilty herself?

"Audi?" she said when they were walking back to Dalia's. "Do you ever get passes made at you?"

"Now that I'm a thirty-seven-year-old married lady with stretch marks? Not often enough. Not that anyone's dumb enough to do that at work and risk a sexual-harassment suit, and where else do I ever see men? It'd be weird if one of the soccer dads came on to me. Although, come to think of it, there's this one dad I wouldn't mind. . . . Why? Did someone make a pass at you?"

"I don't know. Yes."

"Yosef?"

"How'd you know?"

"Seems like the type. More to the point, Margo, he's *your* type. Did he nuzzle your neck when he gave you a massage?"

"Did he do that to you?"

"No, he just used those magic fingers." Audrey giggled.

"It's not a joke. He's married."

"So are you. But don't you think flirtation has become a lost art? It's politically incorrect, but it's so wonderful for your ego. As long as you don't do anything. You're not going to do anything, are you?"

"Of course not."

That's all it was, Margo told herself. A small "flirtation." A flattering reminder that she was still attractive at thirty-nine. And her response—well, who wouldn't enjoy being flirted with by a handsome, vital man? Still, there were the hints she'd had of trouble in Yosef's marriage, not to mention the rocky time she was going through in her own. *Will you and Barry be there for each other when it gets rough?* The woman who'd said that was lashing out and trying to hurt her. But Margo hadn't been able to forget her words.

Instead of returning immediately to Dalia's, she went to the Rimon Inn and used one of the public phones. She caught Barry in his office. It was a joy even to chat with him about the mundane; and it did her soul good to discuss her mother's progress and Batsheva's death. Thank goodness Alice had told her about the phones at the inn. She'd tried calling once from Jerusalem Street and could barely hear herself, much less the overseas operator. At the charming hotel, the only background noise was a low rumble of Hebrew from a man at another phone.

Turning to leave, she glanced at the other caller. It was Hillel Gebman. He noticed her, too, and abruptly ended his conversation.

"I'm sorry, I didn't mean to interrupt," she said.

"You saved me. I thought that patient would go on forever." They walked outside together. Gebman continued shyly, a bit nervously, "You see before you the only doctor in Israel who doesn't own a cell phone."

"I don't think I've ever thanked you for what you did for my mother," Margo said.

"With four kids, sometimes I just have to have a little peace and quiet to make calls."

Nancy had him nailed, Margo thought. He was much less Lyle Lovett than Art Garfunkel.

Twenty-three /

Dear Margo,

Water is so precious in this desert country that even a scummy pond no bigger than a child's wading pool might inspire reverence. But here is the miracle. When water does appear, it is often in settings of extraordinary beauty. A spring emerging from a cleft in a mountain. A waterfall that you reach after hiking for half an hour under a sun more intense than I've ever felt when I've visited California. Suddenly the trail turns and you enter a cool, wooded glade, the air shimmering with drops thrown up by the force of the waterfall. It amazes me that when our ancestors came up with monotheism, they didn't decide the One God must be a god of water.

Today I went with Bernice (Danny's cousin, I'll tell you about her) and two of her friends to Sachne. Sachne is an Arabic word meaning "warm," and the name has stuck in spite of official Israeli efforts to get people to call it something in Hebrew. At Sachne, Ein Harod (the spring of Harod) comes to the surface and forms a natural swimming pool so large that it's divided into four different pools with walkways between them. There is even, between the first and second pool, a small waterfall. Each of the pools is larger than most man-made swimming pools. The water feels delicious to swim in—it maintains a nearly constant temperature year-round. And the setting! Because of Ein Harod, the precious wa-

*ter, the pools are surrounded by trees and bushes, and
there are grassy lawns for relaxing and picnicking.*

*We swam a little. Ate a lot—Bernice makes mouth-
watering tsimmes.*

Margo had tasted Bernice's *tsimmes* when they'd been invited for dinner the preceding Friday. The stew of sweet potatoes, carrots, and prunes was so delicious she'd be happy to
eat it, prepared by Bernice's hands, at every meal for the rest
of her life.

*We played some bridge. And I indulged in people watch-
ing. Sachne is special in that it attracts both Jews and
Arabs, just people of all kinds who want to relax with
their families in a peaceful setting. I watched a group
of schoolgirls who all had beautiful olive skin and long,
shining black hair. They might have been Arabs or they
might be Jewish girls whose families came from North
Africa. The wonderful thing was, it didn't matter. One
girl carried a drum, and she beat the drum as they
walked around. The other girls sang.*

*Sachne is in the Jordan Valley, not far from a re-
markable archaeological dig, Beit Shean, which we visited on the tour. Archaeologists have found the ruins of
twenty different civilizations there. We started talking
about Beit Shean, and one of Bernice's friends brought
up a story about Batsheva's son, Gadi (from her first
marriage, to the air-force pilot) and a problem related
to an archaeological dig. I won't go into the details—
they aren't important and besides, did you know that
one of the Torah's 613 commandments is a prohibition
against lashon ha-ra, saying something bad about another person even if it's true? But it gave me new insight
into Batsheva. What her strong sense of ethics might cost
her.*

Now let me tell you about my dear friend Bernice . . .

Sitting in the covered courtyard behind the hospital before
the funeral, Margo kept glancing at Batsheva's family, clus-

tered to one side of the simple bier. Which one was Gadi? What had he done?

"Doing okay, Mom?" she asked.

After Alice had dressed that morning, Hillel Gebman officially discharged her. Everything went so smoothly, they even had fifteen minutes to relax in the hospital cafeteria and drink iced tea. Still, it was more activity than Alice had done in the entire week since she was poisoned and fell. And the *hamsin* continued to bathe Safed in brutal heat.

"Physically, I'm fine." Alice dabbed at her eyes.

Bernice, who sat with Danny in the row behind them, put a comforting hand on Alice's shoulder.

Alice had been struck by the similarities between her life and Bernice's—and the vast differences. Both women were widows with grown children, Alice had written. Like Alice, Bernice was born in Eastern Europe and left as a child. *But my family came to Brooklyn and hers emigrated to Israel (Palestine, then), so she was here when the country was born. The same year I graduated from high school and started my first full-time job in Uncle Ira's dress store, Bernice was a member of the Haganah! Mostly she carried messages, but she also learned to use a gun, and she was sometimes in groups that came under fire. After Israeli independence, she studied and became a nurse. She took a job in public health here in Safed, and her husband taught chemistry in the high school. She probably knows everything that's gone on in Safed for over forty years.*

Bernice spoke excitedly in Hebrew. Danny, sitting beside her, translated. "That man with the white hair is the poet Elazar."

While they waited for the funeral to begin Bernice handed them keys and urged them to move in as soon as it was convenient; Danny was already packed and ready to trade them for their small guest room.

Bernice also filled them in on the differences between funerals in Safed and in the U.S. Although the prayers would be led by a rabbi, a major role was sometimes played by a friend of the family—in this case Moshe Elazar, a noted poet who had known Batsheva ever since she'd first published poetry as a young woman. Batsheva would return to the earth not in a casket but a burial shroud in which she had been wrapped by female members of the *Chevra Kadisha,* the burial society that was part of the government Ministry of Religion.

"Gadi! . . . There's Gadi," Margo heard several people murmur.

Heads turned toward a rumpled, slightly built man in big, dark sunglasses who had just arrived. People pushed him toward the front row, and someone put a *kippah* on his bare head. Nili left her father's side to cling to him. Gadi clung back. It wasn't clear to Margo which of Batsheva's children was holding the other up.

People fell silent when four men carried the shrouded body of Batsheva Halevi to the bier. The rabbi recited a blessing. With a razor blade, he made a small tear near the necks of the shirts worn by Gadi, Nili, Lev, and a scrappy-looking, sunburned man about Batsheva's age—her brother, Margo guessed, since only members of the immediate family had their garments "rent" to symbolize their broken hearts. Or could this be the dread Yitzhak, the cousin with whom Batsheva hadn't exchanged words for the last year of her life?

Following another prayer, Moshe Elazar spoke and read several of Batsheva's poems. Even without understanding the words, Margo appreciated the complex rhythms Batsheva had given to the throaty Hebrew syllables, sometimes sharp and choppy and sometimes like a rough caress.

Individual mourners were invited to speak next. A few read prepared remarks, but most of the tributes seemed spontaneous. The Israelis didn't try to hide their tears, and Margo's handkerchief was damp by the time the rabbi led a final Kaddish, the mourner's prayer.

She broke away the moment the service ended to get the car air-conditioning going, to make the ride to the cemetery more comfortable. Alice had refused to be dissuaded from attending the shadeless graveside service; she'd barely promised to rest before paying a condolence call on Batsheva's family.

Margo picked up her mother and Audrey at the entrance to the hospital and followed the procession to the lower end of the cemetery. Would you absolve any sins if you bathed in the Ari *mikve* today? she wondered, sweat soaking her back.

Or did you earn no points with God if the frigid mountain water felt too good?

It wasn't until she stood on the harsh hillside that she thought about the vipers.

"Mom, should we be here in sandals?" she asked. "Because of the snakes?"

"With so many people here, I think the snakes are smart enough to stay out of our way," Alice said. "Shh, they're starting."

Margo gazed across the hillside. Bernice had told them the cemetery was a microcosm of Safed history, with the sixteenth-century sages buried near the top, their painted graves splashes of blue; and at the bottom of the hill, children killed in two terrorist incidents in the modern State of Israel.

"Oh!" Alice suddenly whispered. "Oh!"

"Mom, what is it? Should we take you back to the car?"

"I'm fine." Sweat beaded Alice's face, however. Margo, who was holding her hand, slipped her fingers up her mother's wrist, uneasy until she found the strong pulse. Audrey uncapped a water bottle and held it to Alice's lips.

Following the graveside service, Alice insisted they stay for the ritual hand washing. Audrey got them to the head of the line, immediately after Batsheva's family.

"I'm all right, really," Alice said as Margo started the car. "I didn't mean to scare you. It's just that I remembered something else. I know why I was afraid of snakes."

Twenty-four /

Tuesday—the 34th day of the counting of the Omer

"I was standing above the cemetery, on Keren Hayessod Street," Alice said. "I saw three teenagers walking around with bare legs and sandals. I yelled and tried to warn them about the snakes."

"When did it happen?" Audrey asked. "Morning? Afternoon?"

"Sunset. I came to see the sunset. Margo, you need to drive. We're blocking other cars."

"What about the henbane?" Margo put the car in gear. "Do you remember anything about the henbane?"

Alice shook her head. "The doctors said I was most likely to remember things that had a strong emotional content. With the snakes, I was terrified one of the kids would get hurt—they reminded me so much of Jenny. Whatever happened when I got the henbane, it mustn't have had the same emotional charge."

"Were the kids all right?" Audrey asked.

"Damn," Alice said after a moment's thought. "All I have is that one minute, nothing else. But it should be easy to find out if a young person had a snakebite that day, we can ask. Margele, what's on your mind?" she added, touching Margo's cheek.

"You really know how to make a girl feel transparent."

Margo waited, however, until they'd settled Alice at Bernice's and she and Audrey had fetched their bags while Alice napped.

"Mom?" She sat cross-legged on Alice's bed, enjoying the

respite from the heat; Bernice had one window air conditioner and she'd moved it to Alice's room. "Don't ask if anyone was bitten by a snake that day."

Alice regarded her shrewdly.

"It's just a gut feeling," Margo said. "I'd rather not let people know you're remembering things. Okay?"

"Okay. I have a gut feeling, too, something to discuss with you and your sister. But right now I want to go to Batsheva's. Are you ready? With your hair like that?"

"Like what?"

"Just let me run a comb through it."

"Mo-om!"

"Have you ever been to a *shiva*?" Alice asked.

"No. Ouch!"

"Sorry, hit a snarl."

"I didn't think Batsheva's family was Orthodox."

"Not really. But a lot of people in Israel follow Orthodox customs of mourning, more or less. . . ."

White sheets cloaked the mirrors at Batsheva's house, and a candle was lit that, Alice said, would burn throughout the week of *shiva*. Although the family didn't sit on the traditional low stools, all of them were gathered in the living room to receive visitors.

Except for Gadi.

Margo scanned the room but didn't see him. She wondered if Nili was looking for him, too. Nili acted pleased when Audrey arrived, but after a moment her eyes began traveling to the doors.

Margo chatted with Lev for a few minutes, then made way for other visitors. She wandered into the dining room. No black sheep son there, either.

"Would you like some lemonade?" a man offered. A strong-looking fifty-something, he had thick salt-and-pepper hair and a matching beard. Like Batsheva, he spoke British-accented English; and he regarded her with Batsheva's burning hazel eyes.

"Thanks," she said. "You must be a relative."

"Batsheva's cousin, Yitzhak Saporta."

Margo introduced herself, murmured condolences, and wondered if alarms were going off in Yitzhak Saporta's head, the way hers had clanged the instant she heard his name. She sternly told herself this was neither the time nor place to question him about the actions of his students. But she wanted to ask him *something,* if only to get a feel for Batsheva's zealot cousin. She groped for some topic. . . .

"The thirty-six people," she mumbled; she'd forgotten the Hebrew and doubted he'd have any idea what she was talking about.

"The *lamed vav*?" he asked. "The *tzaddikim*?"

"That's it. I understand you're a teacher. Someone was talking about them and asked what happens when one dies. Does a newborn baby become the next *lamed vav*?"

"*Lamed vavnik*. Sit, please." He poured a lemonade for himself and sat as well. "I used to worry about just that question when I was a boy. Since the *lamed vavnikim* keep the world from ending, doesn't there have to be a new *lamed vavnik* immediately after one dies? I thought there might be one split second when there are thirty-seven, the *tzaddik* who's dying and a new one about to take his place. I've seen many ways of talking about this. An idea I like very much I heard from an American rabbi, Rami Shapiro. He says someone may be a *lamed vavnik* for some period of time—a month, a year, eighty years—and then it passes to someone else. It isn't tied to a human lifetime, but to when a person is ready to take on the burden of sustaining the world. Rabbi Shapiro, and here I think he goes too far, even says there may not be thirty-six men the way it says in Talmud; he thinks anyone may go in and out of—what does he call it?—a *lamed vav* state of mind." Yitzhak shook his head and smiled. "Shapiro's a brilliant man, but I think he spends too much time around Buddhists. Please excuse me, there's someone I need to speak to."

"Of course."

If Yitzhak had answered one question—delightfully, she loved the idea of a *lamed vav* state of mind—he had raised several more. Such as, why had no one mentioned that Batsheva's ultrareligious cousin was friendly, reasonable, even humorous? Maybe, she cautioned herself, because he wasn't. What if he'd known who Margo was all along and had sought her out because he knew she suspected his students of poisoning Alice? Was the reasonable, charming Yitzhak only a skillful act to deflect her suspicions?

She poured another lemonade and returned to the living room, hoping to be surprised by another of Batsheva's relatives.

But Gadi didn't show up.

"He promised Nili he'd only be half an hour," Audrey fumed as they walked back into the Artists' Quarter. "He went to put his kids down for a nap down the street, where his ex-wife is staying. That was two hours ago."

"I'm sure his children were upset about their grandmother dying," Alice said. "Maybe they needed him to stay with them."

"Nili needed him more."

"Audrey, you don't know that," Alice said. "She's not your daughter."

"Don't make this about my not having a daughter," Audrey said with such heat that Alice had clearly struck a nerve.

Had she, her mother, and her sister ever stayed under one roof with no other family members as buffers? Margo wondered. All she could remember was an occasional weekend when her dad went on a Boy Scout outing with her brother. Would the three of them make it through the next few days?

"Mom, what did Gadi do?" she asked.

"What do you mean?"

"In one of your letters, you talked about some kind of problem with an archaeological dig."

Alice sighed. "If I tell you, I want you to make me a promise."

"You're going to negotiate about gossip?"

"I want both of you to promise me something."

"Good. Then we know you're feeling better." Margo tried to catch her sister's eye, but Audrey was staring at the ground.

"I told you earlier I had a gut feeling," Alice said. "I want you to stop trying to find out who gave me henbane."

"But we—"

"Don't think I didn't know."

"Why didn't you tell us to stop before?"

"In case someone *was* trying to hurt Batsheva's students, I thought it was important to stop them before they did more harm. But no one will be studying with Batsheva anymore, so it doesn't matter."

"What about justice?" Margo asked.

"What about mercy?" Alice countered.

"I'm in favor of mercy, once the person has been brought to justice."

"I wasn't thinking about the legal system."

"What were you thinking about?"

"Actually, God." The Kabbalists, Alice explained, placed contrasting attributes of God opposite each other on the tree of life. Thus, the attribute of judgment contraposed that of mercy or loving-kindness; one needed to find the balance between them. "The point is, if someone gave me henbane and did the other things against Batsheva's students, think how they must feel. They've been punished.

"I want you both to promise me something," Alice repeated. "For the next week I want you to have a vacation. Take the car and explore. Have fun."

"Can I do laundry tomorrow, and then have fun?"

"Margo, is that your idea of a vacation?"

"It's my idea of necessity. I'll do yours and Audrey's, too. Now tell us about Gadi."

"You're going to be disappointed. It's not a very dramatic story."

"Just tell it!"

"Ten years ago, Gadi was an undergraduate at Hebrew University. Perpetually broke like most students. He had a summer job on an archaeological dig, and he tried to sell a few pieces of pottery—nothing of major historical value and he wouldn't have gotten much money for them. But to a starving student, it must have seemed like a fortune. . . . Why are you laughing?"

"Because of what you said about justice and mercy," Margo said. "Everything about the way you tell the story minimizes what he did."

"I guess it's because of the way Batsheva dealt with him."

Alice knew part of the story. Over dinner—to which they'd been invited along with Danny—Bernice filled in the rest.

Caught and charged with stealing cultural treasure, Gadi had pleaded with his mother. First he'd asked her to help him get out of the country. She refused. If she wouldn't help him flee, would she intercede on his behalf? She was a well-known poet, a member of an old family, the widow of a war hero; she knew people in the government. Couldn't she keep the matter from coming to trial? At the very least, could she get him a reduced sentence?

"You have to understand the way we feel, those of us who lived here when the State of Israel came into being," Bernice said; Danny translated, with Alice and Audrey throwing in bits. "Whether someone immigrated from another country or, like Batsheva, they were born here and had to live under the British colonial rule, we all knew what it was like to have the law operate differently for people with influence—people who weren't Jews. It isn't just an abstract principle, it's an essential part of our identity, that in the country we made, everyone is treated the same under the law.

"I know what you're going to say," she added, seeing Danny's raised eyebrows. "We don't practice what we preach when it comes to the Israeli Arabs. So, we're not perfect. All I'm saying is, that was why Batsheva told Gadi he had to pay for his crime, just as he would if he came from a poor family who didn't know anyone important in Jerusalem."

"He was so young," Alice said.

"Yes and no. Remember, by the time boys enter the university here, they've already served in the army for three years."

"Would you have done what Batsheva did, if it were one of your children?" asked Danny.

"Everyone talked about that at the time. 'What if it was your son?' What mattered more, your loyalty to your family or your loyalty to the laws of your country?"

"How did people know Gadi asked her to help him leave the country?" Margo said. "Wouldn't that have been hush-hush?"

"Forgive me for giving you a long answer, but it will help you understand. This is a nation, especially in its early days, of heroes. Gadi is the son of not just one hero but two of them, a poet whose words are taught in every school and a brave pilot who died when Gadi was only six—when he was growing up, his father wasn't even a real live person but a legend. My husband taught Gadi in his class one year. He was a sweet boy, very funny, and he always had friends. But he was a boy who thought life owed him something. Frustrating for his teachers. And it hurt Gadi more than anyone else. It made him less strong than he might have been.

"You asked how people knew he asked Batsheva for help and she refused," Bernice said. "Gadi complained about it to anyone who would listen. I think that was what Batsheva couldn't forgive. Of course, she was furious about what he'd done—of all crimes, to try to sell a part of the nation's heritage. But when Gadi, as she saw it, whined and cried that his mother wouldn't save him from taking the consequences for his own actions, it was as if Batsheva truly looked at her son for the first time. And the man she saw was someone for whom she felt no respect. I think Gadi truly saw her then, as well. I think that's why he was so bitter. He thought Batsheva was bigger than life, maybe bigger in her love for him than an ordinary mother would be. And she failed him."

"My aunt is a very wise woman," Danny said when he finished translating.

Margo had heard the rest of Gadi's story from her mother. He'd spent two years in prison. And although he saw Batsheva once or twice a year, the rift between them had never healed.

"How do you do it?" Audrey asked as they got ready for bed.

"Do what?"

"Get Mom eating out of your hand. And don't say you don't know what I'm talking about."

"You and Mom always clash. I'm always the peacemaker. We could be talking about anything, and the same dynamic would happen."

"What, she'd take a dig at me about seeing Nili as the daughter I couldn't have? And she'd have a lively philosophical discussion with you? Margo, it's just that she adores you and she disapproves of me. You're the one with the socially relevant job. I'm the yuppie drug pusher."

"You're the one she takes seriously enough to argue with.

I'm the nice one that she sees as never really accomplishing anything.''

''She argues with me because she *doesn't* think I'm serious.'' Audrey leaned close to the mirror to tweeze her eyebrows. ''She thinks I'm frivolous because I like to shop and I do funny things to my hair, and I'm not introspective like you and she are.''

''Have you ever heard her talk about *my* hair? She insisted on combing it today. Hey, Audi?''

''Yeah?''

''I didn't know you were trying to have a daughter.''

''I'm not, anymore. With Zach in third grade already and Bobby going into first next year, I don't want to start all over with an infant.''

''Remember what Natan said?''

''The palmist with the Baggies?''

''He said he saw three children, two boys and a girl. What if the girl *is* Nili? Sort of a spiritual daughter?''

''I like that.'' Audrey turned off the light and climbed to her bed; they were sleeping in the bunk beds once used by Bernice's children.

''Um, do you feel that cool breeze coming through the window? The *hamsin* must be breaking.''

Twenty-five /

Wednesday—the 35th day of the counting of the Omer

Nili didn't actually *want* to go to school. Who would want that? But it wasn't fair that her father got to go to the hospital, and she was expected to sit at home doing nothing for the rest of the week.

"We don't really observe *shiva*," Lev had said to her before he left that morning. "But it's not right for you to be in school so soon. Aunt Leah and Uncle Saul will be here. And Gadi."

Except Gadi had gotten up at five to say good-bye to his children before Tamar left with them; then he'd gone back to bed and was still sleeping at ten A.M. Nili waited for fifteen minutes, sitting cross-legged on the floor outside the guest room. Maybe he was awake and he just hadn't come out yet to join the family. (Who would blame him?) But she didn't hear a sound.

She hung around in the hallway for another quarter hour. Lying on her back, she watched a spider spinning a web above one of the windows. Then she wandered into her bedroom.

For the first time since she had found out her mother was dead, Nili opened her diary. She lay on her stomach across the bed with her pen poised, sniffing the l'Air du Temps perfume that lingered from the last time Batsheva had read the diary. Nili couldn't think of a thing she wanted to write. She was a complete idiot, she knew, but somehow knowing that her mother would no longer spy on her by reading her diary took some of the fun out of writing in it.

What was there to say, anyway? "Mother died today. Or maybe yesterday?" That was the beginning of a famous book she had read in school, about a man who was so terrible and numb to all feeling that even his mother's death had no effect on him. That was supposed to be a sign that the man was very sick.

Nili put down the pen. Instead of writing, she read the last thing she had written; she'd done it on Sunday morning, when she was a girl whose mother was alive. Batsheva hadn't reacted to what she'd put in the diary about her "boyfriend," even though Nili knew she had read it. So this time . . .

Dear Jessica,

At last, I'm a woman. Reuven and I knew we shouldn't have done it. Afterward we both cried. But who says it was really wrong? The adults who tell us that, either they've never really loved or else they know they have to say such things to young people but they don't believe them. They know that none of the moral principles they say we should practice make a difference when your body is melting to join with the body of your beloved.

Like Reuven and me. Like the secret lovers of HaMa'ayan HaRadum.

I saw them again early this morning. And this time I understood why they must keep their love a very deep secret. They are both married! To other people!

Even though they no longer feel any love for their spouses, and they feel like they are only half-alive every second they must spend apart, they can't possibly leave their marriages and be together. They both have young children, and their love for their children is even greater than the intense passion they have for each other.

They didn't see me, because they were devouring each other with their eyes, and they were weeping because they loved their children so very very much.

Writing about them being so devoted to their children was the best part of making up the story, the part that brought tears to her eyes. Nili remembered thinking, I'm going to be a writer one day. Not a poet like her mother but a real writer, someone who told stories where people loved and hated and did thrilling things. Already she was a natural observer, one who liked to sit in the shadows and watch other people . . . and look what a good imagination she had. She had only glimpsed the lovers a few days ago, and already she had created whole lives for them.

As she read it over she asked herself how the lovers could have devoured each other with their eyes and wept at the same time. That was a good thing in a writer, to always ask if what she'd written could really happen. She tried to look at her stuffed turtle, Koko, as if she were devouring him with her eyes and imagined crying at the same time.

She put the ribbon back in the diary, at first exercising her usual care, but then she remembered it didn't matter anymore—her mother wasn't going to open the diary.

And then she *was* crying, so hard it felt as if she would never stop.

She cried for almost an hour. Finally she washed her face and checked again to see if Gadi was awake—he wasn't. Downstairs, a few people were visiting with Aunt Leah and Uncle Saul, *shiva* calls. Nili said hello and escaped as quickly as she could. She was wandering from room to room when Audrey Siegel came to see her.

The tall, beautiful American woman had brought a bottle of Diet Pepsi with her, and suddenly Nili realized it was exactly what she wanted to drink.

When Audrey suggested watching a video, that was exactly right, too.

"Do you have a favorite video?" Audrey asked, when they went into the den.

"There's one I used to watch with my mom," Nili said. "It's an American movie about a mother and daughter."

Audrey didn't say, the way Aunt Leah would have, "Are you sure you want to watch that movie today?"

She just said, "Great," and kicked off her tennis shoes. She had polish the color of raspberries on her toenails! She saw Nili looking and said, "Next time I come, I'll bring some polish and we can do yours. If you want to."

"Oh, yes."

Twenty-six /

Wednesday—the 35th day of the counting of the Omer

If Margo had known that Yosef would be at the Laundromat that morning . . .

Would she really have put off doing the laundry? Wasn't it a lot pleasanter to have company as she waited for the clothes to wash and dry? And really, what could happen, when there were always two or three other people doing their wash and Yosef had his youngest child in tow?

What could happen was that, once again, Margo felt as if all the cells in her body were more alive. What had Bruce babbled about? Mitochondria? Whatever they were, they snapped to attention, too.

"What kind of clay do you use?" Yosef asked her. They sat on the edge of the sandbox outside the Laundromat, where his son played. He kept glancing at Margo's toes, bare in her open sandals—and wildly red since she and Audrey had applied toenail polish that morning.

"Black Mountain is my favorite," she said, reminded uncomfortably of the sensualness of working the earthy, chocolate-brown clay. "Tell me about your work."

"You have to see it! But I tell you a little. In newest pieces, I work things into the clay. Leaves, sticks, feathers."

"Do you go into the countryside to gather materials?" Thank goodness, her initial intense awareness of the sculptor faded—softening to a string quartet instead of a symphony—as they talked about his art.

"I find things everywhere. That's why Ma'ayan makes me do the laundry now, so I empty my pockets myself and I don't get mad at her for throwing valuable art materials away. See what I found already today.'' He lay the contents of his pockets on the sand: several small stones, a shred of bark, a knot of brown string.

"Is difficult to be stepmother?'' he asked as they transferred their wash into dryers. ''To feel love for children who aren't yours?''

"It isn't difficult to love Jenny and David. It can be hard dealing with their mother, especially if the kids play us against each other. For instance, when Jenny wanted to get her nose pierced, I agreed with her that it was her body. I also told her she had to get her mother's permission. Next thing I knew, she had a hole in her nose and she'd told her mother I said she could do it.''

Yosef sighed. ''I wish Ben would just get a ring in his nose. Easier to have a kid who's an artistic rebel than a kid who decides to be *haredi*—you know that word? Means a person is very Orthodox?''

"At home, do you try to be more Orthodox for his sake?''

"We light candles and bless wine every Shabbat now. Before, sometimes we do and sometimes we forget. We let him go to the school he wants, even though the leader of the school is . . . You know how some rebbes, you don't believe the same as they believe but still, they look at you and you feel like they love everyone? This rebbe isn't like that.''

"Yitzhak Saporta? I met him yesterday. He was a lot friendlier than I expected.''

Yosef shook his head. ''Friendly, maybe. And learned. But I think he is angry man.''

"Is there any chance Ben heard Ma'ayan say she was going to make an herb tea for my mother, and he told someone he knew from school?'' All right, she had promised Alice she'd stop looking. But better to discuss Yosef's son than other, riskier subjects.

"Ben never listens to *anything* we say. Do your kids listen to you?''

"Sometimes when we least expect it. Did you and Ma'ayan mention it at home that night? Maybe at dinner?''

"What night?''

"Last week Monday, the day it came up in Batsheva's class."

"I . . . I wasn't home that night. I mean, not home for dinner. I . . . I got home late."

Wondering where he'd been and why he seemed so nervous about it, she had a sudden vivid image of Yosef passionately tangled in someone's bedsheets. The decorous string quartet she'd heard in her head swelled to an orchestra playing something lush and romantic—Mahler.

"I bet my clothes are dry," she said, getting up.

"Mine, too." With a word to his son in the sandbox, Yosef followed her back into the Laundromat. "What do you do this afternoon?" he asked. "Will you be with your mother?"

"No, she went to play bridge with Bernice. I was thinking of going to some of the galleries in the Artists' Quarter."

"Good. I know the best galleries. Studios, too, not open to tourists. We meet at the General Exhibition Hall and I show you, yes? What's funny?"

"Just laughing at myself." And humming a little Mahler.

There was no graceful way to turn him down, she imagined defending herself to Audrey. Besides, Yosef hadn't made a pass since he'd taken her hand a few nights ago. For all she knew, the visceral awareness she felt around him was completely one-sided, and he was just a friendly native offering to show her the sights. *I would have brought you along,* she'd tell Audrey, *if you hadn't been taking Mom to the hairdresser.*

When she met Yosef at the artists' exhibition hall, he insisted they go first to "the most beautiful work of art in Safed."

"What's that?"

Not replying, he led her across the Ma'alot Olei HaGardom into the Jewish Quarter.

"Have you heard the story of Avritch Synagogue, the miracle?" he said. "Safed has many, many earthquakes. One day in 1837, the Avritch rabbi suddenly stops in the middle of praying and yells, 'Whoever wants to live, draw close to the Torah!' Everyone runs to ark. A second later there's a terrible earthquake. Half the synagogue is destroyed. But not the part by the Torah."

"Is that where we're going? The Avritch Synagogue?" Margo was glad she'd taken to wearing a T-shirt under her sundress to cover her shoulders. She would have liked to hide her painted toenails as well; they were garishly visible in her sandals.

"No, this is where we go." Passing through a gate, they entered a tree-lined courtyard. "Abuhav Synagogue. You know why there's an outer gate and then the courtyard? It's like the ancient temple in Jerusalem. The temple had two gates with a courtyard between, so after you go through the first gate, you have more time to prepare to meet God. Margo, are you prepared?" His sly grin made her wish she had Audrey at her side.

But hell, she didn't need a chaperon!

She got one, anyway. Dalia sat sketching on one of the benches that lined three sides of the synagogue.

Margo said hello but barely noticed either Dalia or Yosef as she drank in the color.

"It's so blue!"

The vivid cornflower blue she'd seen on the gates in the Jewish and Artists' quarters dominated the interior of the synagogue, coloring the central wooden *bimah* on which the rabbi led prayers. The last time she'd talked to Barry, he had read her Alice's latest postcard, mailed two weeks earlier. About the gates of Safed, Alice had written, *If the soul has a color, I think it is this color blue.* Feasting her eyes on the Abuhav Synagogue, Margo thought her mother had the right idea. In addition to the searing soul-blue of the *bimah,* the birds and Hebrew letters decorating the inside of the dome were a darker, rich shade that reminded her of Mexican ceramics. Yet another blue—a vibrant turquoise—showed on the elaborately carved wood of the arks against one wall.

"Religious people say there is so much blue because of a commandment in Torah to put a blue thread in the prayer shawl," Yosef said.

"We copied the blue from the Moslems," Dalia countered. "Like the Moorish arches on the *bimah.*"

Dalia hadn't looked happy to be interrupted. She continued to apply pastel crayons to a piece of creamy white paper she'd taped to a lap easel.

"I never thought about it," Margo said, "but the synagogues in the U.S., at least the Reform synagogues, look more like Christian churches. Stained glass windows, the *bimah* up in front."

"The Abuhav is Sephardic," Yosef answered. "The style of the Jews who came from Spain. That's why the *bimah* is in the center and you have Moorish influences like arches and the blue and the birds painted on the dome. Do you want to hear story of synagogue?"

"I'd love to." She sat on the bench, where it was easier to look at the synagogue dome.

"It's named for Rabbi Yitzhak Abuhav," Yosef said, sitting beside her. "A Spanish rabbi of fifteenth century."

Muttering something in Hebrew, Dalia crumpled the sketch she'd been doing and dropped it on the floor; Margo noticed half a dozen discarded sketches there.

"Dalia, are we bothering you?" she asked. She had glimpsed the drawing before Dalia trashed it—an image from the dome, a bush with delicate yellow flowers. She'd thought it lovely, but it clearly hadn't satisfied the artist.

"No bother," Dalia said. "I don't like color. In black-and-white, you see the real forms of things." Frowning, she taped a fresh piece of paper to her easel. "But tourists who come to Safed, they all want color, color, color. Color and fairy tales, like the flying synagogue."

"You think no miracles ever happen?" Yosef replied.

"I think people who want to believe in miracles invent them. But tell the story, it's a good story."

"Rabbi Abuhav never lived in Safed," Yosef said. "He designed the synagogue in Spain, with many Kabbalist symbols. Some people say Abuhav's followers built the synagogue here using his design. But a legend—what cynical people call a fairy tale—says the synagogue wasn't built in Safed, it was built in Spain. When Abuhav's followers came here, they carried a Torah scroll he wrote himself—a famous Torah, it's still here. The Turks, who ruled Israel then, didn't allow people to make synagogues, so there was no place to keep the Torah. One night the leader of the congregation had a terrible nightmare—"

"Several nights," Dalia interrupted. "I thought he had the same dream three nights."

"I thought you didn't believe any of this." Yosef grinned. "One night or three, he dreamed he had to wander all over the world because the Torah had no home. He told everyone they should pray and fast. For three days they washed in the *mikve,* they ripped their clothes, they did various holy things."

"They say names of the great rabbis, don't forget that." Dalia whittled at the tip of a brown crayon with a pocketknife, the blade gouging close to her fingers; had she been Jenny or David, Margo would have grabbed her arms and forced her to cut more carefully. As Yosef continued she couldn't tear her eyes from the knife.

"In Europe, a terrible storm came, the worst storm anyone ever saw. What do you think? The storm lifted Abuhav Synagogue in Spain into the air and put it down here."

Margo flinched. Rather than tapering the crayon, Dalia had hacked off the end of it.

"Is the Torah written by Rabbi Abuhav here in the synagogue?" she asked, forcing herself not to watch as Dalia started again with the knife.

"Over there," Yosef said, "in a special ark. The Abuhav Torah is read from on only three holy days—Rosh Hashanah, Yom Kippur, Shavuot. Anyone who takes it out or even looks at it at the wrong time is supposed to die a horrible death. They say that once after an earthquake, the Torah had to be moved to another synagogue while the Abuhav was repaired. Ten men volunteered to carry it. All ten died within a year."

"*They* say." Dalia sniffed. "You know what else *they* say? *They* say if a couple on their wedding day sits in special chair in the Ari Ashkenazi Synagogue, in a year they will have a boy and boy may be the Messiah. You know how many people sit in that chair, and where is the Messiah? *They* say anyone who opens the ark here just to take a photograph, the person gets sick and dies. How many people drop dead in the Abuhav Synagogue?"

"Nobody opens the ark to take a photograph," Yosef said. "The ark is always locked."

"No, it isn't."

"It is. I'll show you."

"Don't," Dalia said when Yosef got up. "Yosef, don't." Her voice rose, panicky, as he took several steps toward the ark.

"Nothing will happen. I told you, it's locked."

The elderly synagogue caretaker started toward him. But Yosef was younger and closer.

"No!" Dalia shrieked, and ran outside.

Twenty-seven /

Wednesday—the 35th day of the counting of the Omer

"I have to admit, I was relieved Yosef didn't actually try to open the ark. What if it turned out not to be locked? I almost ran outside after Dalia."

"Because of a superstition?" came Audrey's voice from the top bunk in the dark.

"You had to be there. Look at Dalia. A total skeptic until she thought she had to face the curse of the Abuhav Torah."

"So, enough about the Torah. Did Yosef come on to you?"

"There was no gracious way to turn him down when he offered to take me to the galleries," Margo said. "I would have asked you to come, if you hadn't been taking Mom to the hairdresser. Audi, you're brilliant. She looks ten times healthier without the gray roots. I'm an adult woman. I understand I can feel attracted to someone who isn't my husband, and it's just part of being human."

Margo realized she was babbling. Audrey didn't interrupt her, however, and she couldn't seem to stop.

"After the synagogue, he took me to a bunch of studios and introduced me to the artists. It was great to be with someone who knew them. He helped me pick out some great prints to buy. You want to see?"

"In the morning."

"Oh, and I saw his studio! His stuff is fantastic. Very whimsical, but it involves an incredible amount of artistic skill. You've got to go there."

Yosef had also talked about his life —growing up on a kibbutz, serving as a medic in the army. An individualist in a country that exalted communal values, he had rebelled against both kibbutz and army life. He thought he'd found salvation when he left Israel and studied art in Italy for a year. "I wasn't going to come back," he said. "But this country gets into your blood."

Nothing had happened between them physically, other than their hands occasionally brushing as they looked at prints and, at least on her part, that heightened awareness, the Mahler playing in the background.

Audrey said nothing for several minutes, and Margo figured she'd drifted off to sleep. Then Margo heard her climbing down from the top bunk. She sat on the floor by the head of Margo's bed.

"You're tempted, aren't you?" Audrey's tone was serious.

"To go to bed with him? Sure, I wonder what it would be like. Don't you ever wonder about someone?" She was starting to babble again. "But seriously tempted? No."

"What about, tempted that if you happened to be alone someplace and he started kissing you, you wouldn't immediately tell him to stop?"

"Audi, aren't you the one who said flirting can be fun?"

"But I didn't realize . . . Is everything all right between you and Barry?"

Margo almost gave the same automatic yes she'd given her mother. But she was feeling closer to Audrey than she had for years.

"Don't tell Mom, okay?" she said.

"I promise."

"We're basically okay. I found out about an affair he had—"

"He cheated on you!" Audrey sounded ready to eviscerate her sister's husband.

"No, it happened before we ever knew each other, although I appreciate your outrage on my behalf. And it was only a one-night stand. It's just that it was with someone he worked with, that we saw socially. It was weird to think I'd known this person for years without knowing that. It wasn't cheating."

"But it felt like it?"

"Yes." Margo *did* know how it felt to be cheated on,

thanks to the potter who'd been her first love. Learning about Barry's affair had provoked some of the same sense of betrayal.

Neither sister spoke for a minute. Then Audrey said, "When was the last time you talked to him?"

"Just two nights ago. Really, we're working things out. We're going to be fine."

Early the next morning, she took advantage of Bernice's offer to use her telephone for credit-card calls.

"Barry!"

"Hey, what time is it there?"

"Six-thirty tomorrow morning. I mean, it's tomorrow for you."

After he'd put each of the kids on for a few minutes, she caught him up on her mother's health. "She walked with Audrey and me at dusk. We were out for half an hour, and she did great."

"You bet I was great, and wait till you hear where we're going today." Alice came in with two cups of coffee; she handed a cup to Margo. "Is that your handsome husband? Let me talk to him."

As Alice and Barry chatted Margo sipped her coffee beside the window. An Orthodox teenage boy seemed to be looking through the grillwork of the gate. Was he the same boy she'd seen in the street two or three times already, or just another Orthodox teen with the identical dress and side curls?

"Mom?" she called. "Come look."

But the kid was gone.

"So, where are we going today?" she asked after they had told Barry good-bye and hung up the phone.

"The Lebanese border."

"To see if we can get shot at?"

"To eat the most delicious trout in the world."

Twenty-eight /

Thursday—the 36th day of the counting of the Omer

"Lev, why did you have to keep testing for this and testing for that?" Aunt Leah moaned.

"Leah, listen to yourself," said Uncle Saul. "Lev finds evidence that someone killed Batsheva—someone who had to plan in advance so they could bring that terrible stuff with them to Mount Meron. Some animal does this, and you'd want him to get away with it?"

"That terrible stuff" was pancuromium bromide. It was a drug, and Nili's father had found it this afternoon in the samples he had taken from her mother's body.

"Who says they *won't* get away with it?" Leah said.

"Even if the police don't catch this animal," Saul replied, "at least he'll know that we know."

"Oh, you think that's going to give him trouble sleeping at night? Someone who could do that to her?"

"Daddy." Nili went over to her father. He'd been slumped in his chair, lost in thought. "How does pancuromium bromide work?" she asked.

"Nili, it doesn't matter," Aunt Leah said.

"It's all right." Lev pulled up a footstool for Nili to sit close to him, and he held her hand. "Pancuromium bromide—it's usually called by the commercial name, Pavulon—is a very strong muscle relaxant. It paralyzes the muscles that control breathing and movement."

"Why would anyone make a drug that does that?"

"Pavulon can be an excellent drug. Doctors and paramedics use it when they need to insert a tube in a patient's throat to establish an airway, and the patient is fighting them. It immobilizes the person so the doctor can insert the tube and save his life. As long as the person gets air from a respirator, it's all right that he isn't breathing for himself."

"And if he doesn't get air from a respirator?"

"Then the person's heart stops beating from lack of oxygen."

For a moment he squeezed Nili's hand so hard it hurt. She wriggled her fingers and he relaxed his grip.

"Nili, can I ask you a question now?" Lev said gently.

"Okay."

"On Erev Lag B'Omer, when you were at Mount Meron, did you notice your mother there?"

"Um. Um, no." She wished she hadn't hesitated. She wished even more that she hadn't stolen a glance at Gadi, who sat, head bowed, and said nothing. She'd bet he didn't even realize he was clutching his cell phone as if he expected a call from God. "The Pavulon, how did someone give it to her?" she asked Lev.

"It's given by injection."

"Did someone just walk up with a needle? Like the Mossad when they sneak up on somebody and drug them?"

"I suppose so." Lev gave her a hug. "Honey, I need to go talk to the police some more. Will you be okay?"

"Nili and I will make cookies," Leah said.

"Thanks, Aunt Leah, but I think I'll just go to my room and read."

"Nili," her father said, his eyes searching her face. "Are you sure you didn't see your mother that night?"

"Yes, I'm sure." The second time, the lie was easier. "There were so many people. Except for my friends that I came with, I didn't see anyone I knew."

Aunt Leah mumbled something to Lev in Yiddish as she left the room. Nili understood enough of it: *Such things to tell a child!* Even though the things her father told her made her sick to her stomach, she was glad he didn't treat her like a child.

Audrey hadn't treated her like a child, either.

Nili didn't know why, when Audrey came to visit yesterday,

she had suggested seeing the same movie her mother used to make her watch, *Shy People*. The second she said it, she figured it was dumb. But it turned out to be a great idea.

"Wow! Is that Barbara Hershey?"

That was the first thing Audrey said when the New York mother and her daughter got out of the boat at the home of their relatives in the swamp and the mother of the weird swamp family came to meet them. Audrey didn't say anything before that about how terrible the teenage daughter was for being rebellious or why the mother was right to force the daughter to go with her to see their relatives. She just talked to Nili as if she were a person. She said the actress playing the mother of the swamp family, Barbara Hershey, usually looked really beautiful. Then she and Nili decided Barbara Hershey looked beautiful in *Shy People,* too, but in a way that wasn't glamorous.

It wasn't even a big deal when the daughter tried to hand her drugs to the New York mother (played by Jill Clayburgh), and the mother said she had to decide for herself whether to take drugs. Audrey said, "I can't believe Jill Clayburgh's doing that." But she didn't act like she assumed Nili was probably taking drugs, or like Nili needed to be told that the mother was being irresponsible.

Gadi had gotten up by then, and he came into the den and watched the movie with them. Gadi thought the movie was hilarious, especially the parts that were supposed to be really dramatic and meaningful, that Batsheva had insisted on discussing with Nili afterward. When Jill Clayburgh slapped the daughter and said, "I'm the parent and you're the child," at first Gadi said the line a few times, using funny voices in English and Hebrew. Then he started playing with the words— *I'm the zookeeper and you're the monkey. I'm the mouse and you're the cheese.* The things he said made less and less sense and made Nili and Audrey laugh more and more: *I'm the bicycle and you're the vacuum cleaner. I'm the ocean liner and you're the balloon. I'm the pumpernickel bread and you're . . .*

"The handkerchief!" Nili had supplied.

"I'm the bus to Haifa and you're . . ."

"The falafel," said Audrey.

They laughed so hard their sides hurt.

"Milk and cookies." It was Gadi's voice outside her door.

"Come in!"

He carried a tray with a plate of cookies and two glasses of milk. He set the tray on her bed, lit a cigarette, and sat down across from her. The telephone—one in the house, not the cell phone in his pocket—rang and he jumped up. Aunt Leah or Uncle Saul must have answered, and he sat down again.

Nili had taken a cookie, but she felt too nervous to bite into it.

"I've got to ask you something," Gadi said.

"What?" Nili realized she was holding her stuffed turtle, Koko, like a little kid. She stuck him under the pillow behind her.

"You know what they're thinking?"

"Who?"

"The police." He looked around the room for a second, then ashed the cigarette into his hand.

"Don't do that! You'll burn yourself." Nili found a small ceramic bowl in which she kept "stuff." She emptied the contents, mostly shells and beads, into a drawer of her desk and handed him the bowl to use as an ashtray.

"Thanks." For a moment he just stared at his cigarette; he didn't even smoke it.

"What about the police?" she asked.

"They think Lev did it."

"Did what?" Nili felt slow and stupid.

"Killed Mom."

"Gadi! That doesn't make any sense."

"Usually, when a wife gets killed, the first person they suspect is the husband. And Lev's a doctor. He'd know about this drug and he'd have access to it."

"No one would even know about the drug if he hadn't tested for it," Nili objected. "You heard. He said you have to do a special test because it wouldn't just show up in a regular autopsy. Why would he do a test like that if he gave it to her?"

"Nili, Nili." Gadi sighed. "Don't you know people do that

sometimes? They commit a crime and then they feel guilty, so they let everyone know because they want to be caught.''

"But not Dad." She felt dizzy. Maybe it was the cigarette so near to her. She picked up her glass of milk and gulped it.

"Here, have mine." Gadi pushed his milk toward her. "You and I know he wouldn't. I'm just saying it's something the police will think. The other thing they're going to think? If Lev knew about this drug Pavulon, maybe other people in our family knew. They'll look at Lev and you and me, and they'll ask which of us is the most likely suspect. Which of us could commit a crime?" In his eyes she saw the memory of when he'd gone to prison.

"You weren't even there! I waited for you by the women's entrance to the synagogue, and you weren't there!"

"The problem is, little one, I don't have an alibi. Someone who can prove I was somewhere else."

"I saw . . . I bet it was a crazy person! Maybe an Arab. They just wanted to kill somebody on Mount Meron, it didn't matter who. They carried a syringe of Pavulon to Mount Meron and they found Mom in a place where they wouldn't be seen."

"Nili, what did you see?"

"When?"

"Lev asked if you saw Mom on Meron and you said no. But you did see her, didn't you?"

"Only for a second!" Nili cried. "She walked past when I was waiting for you, that's all."

"Did you talk to her?"

"No. She was talking to someone else."

"Who?"

It couldn't matter if she told. Still, she felt as if her mouth was stuffed full of cookies and she could hardly speak through them.

"Who was it, Nili?" Gadi repeated.

"The American lady who watched the movie with us yesterday. Audrey Siegel."

Part Four /
Murder

At the core of the Cain and Abel story is the insistence that every murder is the murder of one brother by another.

Rabbi Joseph Telushkin, *Jewish Literacy*

Twenty-nine /

Thursday—the 36th day of the counting of the Omer

"How do you feel, Mom?" Margo, driving the little rental car back into Safed, glanced at her mother in the passenger seat.

"Great." Alice sounded as good as her words. Her voice was strong and she seemed not much more fatigued than Margo or Audrey after the busy day they'd had.

The busy, wonderful day.

A drive of about two hours that morning had taken them to a rustic, charming restaurant—picnic tables on a shaded wooden porch—beside the Dan River. The restaurant, part of a fish farm, served them mouthwatering fresh trout, as well as salad, baked potatoes, and pita. They lingered over the meal, talking nonstop and polishing off a bottle of Israeli wine. Mildly tipsy, they giggled and joked as they wrestled with three forks over a piece of the restaurant's special apple strudel.

After lunch, they put on extra insect repellent and napped in the shade on the riverbank. Alice stayed there reading while Margo and Audrey went for a short hike. On the way back, Alice insisted she felt well enough to stop at a kibbutz that manufactured sandals, an Israeli factory outlet store.

Margo was breaking in her new green sandals, executing a dance step on the cobbled street to Bernice's house. A pirouette thrust her into a large, red-haired man.

"Oh! Sorry," she said. Where had he come from?

"No problem," the man responded in Israeli-accented English. "Are you Mrs. Audrey Siegel?" he asked. "Or Mrs. Margo Simon?"

"Who are you?" Margo didn't like the way he'd suddenly appeared outside Bernice's gate, as if he—and the young woman with him—had stepped from the bougainvillea on the wall.

"Sorry, I forgot to introduce myself. Police Lieutenant Eli Pincus. And this is Officer Efrati. We want to talk to Mrs. Siegel and Mrs. Simon."

"Can I see some ID?"

"Margo!" her mother whispered, appalled at her lack of courtesy.

The man and woman weren't in uniform, however, and no way was she, an American urbanite, going to take the word of someone who merely said he was a cop.

"Some . . ." Pincus's English was good, but apparently not perfect.

"Identification, Eli," said Efrati.

Pincus slapped his forehead. "Of course, like on the American cop shows."

They held up photo ID cards. Pincus's photo must have been taken ten years ago, when he was about Margo's age. Efrati looked as cute and perky in person as she did in her photograph.

"You're from Haifa," Audrey said, reading the Hebrew on their cards. Haifa, Margo knew, was the largest city in the area; it was about equally far north as Safed but on the Mediterranean, over an hour away.

"The police department in Safed is small," Pincus said. "Sometimes we work with them."

"We'd like to ask you a few questions," Efrati said.

"What about?" Margo said, but Audrey was smiling and opening the gate for them.

"I'm Audrey Siegel," she said. "This is my sister, Margo, and my mother, Alice Simon."

What was Audrey going to do next—offer them tea and cake? Margo felt as if she'd wandered into a play where everyone except her knew the lines.

"Mrs. Simon." Pincus beamed at Alice. "How are you feeling?"

"Better, thanks."

"Please, come in," Audrey said. They hadn't moved toward the gate she held open.

"Thanks," said Efrati. "But it's better if you and Mrs. Margo Simon come into the station."

"What the hell is going on?" Margo whispered to Audrey, when they got in the backseat of the officers' car.

"I made a complaint!"

"About . . ."

"The way the Safed police dealt with Mom's poisoning." Audrey sounded giddy with triumph. "Sunday afternoon, when you were visiting Mom, I managed to reach someone at the American embassy." She must have burned up the phone lines after her talk with Batsheva. "I didn't want to mention it, because I didn't know if anything would come of it."

When they arrived at the police station, Pincus said they'd like to interview Audrey first; would Margo wait in the hall?

"Don't you want to talk to both of us together?" Margo asked.

"Oh no, this is how we do it in Israel," Efrati said breezily.

Margo supposed it was because Audrey was the one who'd called the embassy.

Half an hour later she was ready to file a complaint herself. Did the cops from Haifa really intend to investigate Alice's poisoning, when the Safed police had decided it was nothing but a silly tourist making herself some henbane tea? Or had they pulled her and Audrey in to harass them for complaining in the first place? Maybe they'd stuck Audrey in an interview room and left her there, the same way they'd stuck Margo in the hall. There weren't even any magazines.

But it made no sense to harass two American tourists, especially one who had already shown herself capable of getting the ear of the American embassy. And why would officers come all the way from Haifa to do it?

Margo went over to the high desk staffed by a young uniformed policeman.

"Can I talk to Officer Pincus?" She enunciated clearly and slowly.

"They'll come get you when they want to talk to you." His voice dripped Texas.

"Where are you from?"

"Galveston."

The Texan Israeli pointedly returned his gaze to some papers on the desk.

"Do you have anything to read here? In English?" she asked.

He started to shake his head, but then said, "Yeah, all right. Just don't lose my bookmark." He reached into the desk and handed her a book.

If she'd suspected the police were trying to get back at her and Audrey, she felt sure of it when she tried to read the tome the desk cop had given her: *Major Trends in Jewish Mysticism* by Gershom Scholem. She'd made it through only five pages of dense prose when Efrati came and led her into the interview room. By then, she and Audrey had been at the police station for an hour.

At least, *she* had been there for an hour. Audrey wasn't in the small interview room, nor had Margo passed her going down the hall.

"Where's my sister?" Margo asked.

"She went back to where you are staying," Pincus said. "Please, sit down."

Margo kept standing. "I didn't see her."

"She went out the back way. One of the officers is giving her a ride."

"What's going on here?"

"Just a few questions," Pincus said.

"Would you like some coffee?" Efrati added brightly.

Did you know that perky people make me want to scream? Margo thought. *Especially when they jerk me around.*

"I want to know what's happening," she said.

"Sure you won't have some coffee? It's good."

"Fine." She sat across the table from the cops. She might as well reserve her indignation until she could use it, when she spoke to Audrey's contact at the embassy.

"Sugar? Milk?"

"A little milk."

Efrati fetched cups of coffee for Margo and herself. Pincus nursed a bottle of seltzer water.

The first questions were benign—a technique she knew

well. Relax the interviewee so you can sneak up on them with questions they might not want to answer. Except, what did the Israeli cops plan to ask that she'd have any qualms about answering?

When did you arrive in Israel? In Safed?

Why did you come?

Pincus did most of the questioning. Efrati smiled encouragingly and took notes, although the interview was being tape-recorded.

"Your mother came to Safed about . . . what, five weeks ago?"

"Yes." She sipped her coffee. It *was* good. It was also so strong that each sip electrified her nerve ends.

"Did she come to study with Mrs. Halevi?"

Hadn't they already heard this from Audrey?

"She didn't actually intend to study. She spent a day in Safed on a tour. When the tour ended, she wanted to spend some more time here. She met Mrs. Halevi shortly after she came here."

"And Mrs. Halevi convinced her to enroll in classes?"

"Yes. But I wouldn't put it that way. She was interested in what Mrs. Halevi was teaching, and wanted to learn more."

"She decided to stay in Israel, yes?" Pincus said. "She canceled her plane ticket to come home?"

"She decided to stay longer."

"How did you feel about that?"

"I was pleased for her, that she was enjoying herself."

"You know," he said, "often people come to Israel and get religious, and it's natural for their families to worry about them."

"I wasn't worried." Careful not to hesitate. She saw where his questions must be going. He wanted to establish that in deciding to study with Batsheva and prolong her trip, Alice Simon was already a woman behaving strangely—a woman who, a month later, might conceivably pick henbane and brew a pot of tea. And therefore the local police had shown no negligence in dismissing the poisoning as an instance of yet another American who'd gone native in a slightly lunatic way.

Nevertheless, bringing in two officers from Haifa seemed like a lot of trouble for a complaint. Margo wondered just how forcefully her sister had complained, and to whom.

"Did your whole family feel the way you did?" Pincus asked. "Your sister who came to Safed with you? And you have a brother, also?"

"A brother back in the States. Audrey was a little concerned that Mom had been taken in by some kind of guru. But all of us were pleased she was so happy, probably the happiest she'd been since my father died a few years ago."

"About your mother being poisoned."

At last!

"Did you feel Mrs. Halevi was responsible?" Pincus said.

"Not at all. But I don't agree with the conclusion the police came to, that my mother—"

He held up his hand. "Your sister thought Mrs. Halevi should have done something about some earlier incidents that took place, some problems with her other students."

"I didn't see it that way." And what did it matter?

"Your sister told this to Mrs. Halevi on Saturday night, yes? She was extremely angry, yes?"

Margo nodded.

"Please answer for the tape," Efrati said.

"Of course. She was upset about a lot of things—the fact that my mother had gotten so ill, the way the police weren't taking it seriously, everything."

"So upset that she struck Mrs. Halevi?"

"She grabbed Batsheva's arm. That was all."

She was confused by the direction the interview was taking. It wasn't until Pincus's next question, however, that she felt afraid.

"Tell me what happened on Erev Lag B'Omer," he said.

Thirty /

"On Erev Lag B'Omer?" Margo repeated.

She felt an eerie sense of dislocation, like the second after a fender bender when you haven't yet assimilated what's happened. You know you were driving down the street, maybe you remember hearing a crunch, but you can't understand why you're sitting in your car feeling dazed.

On Erev Lag B'Omer, Alice was in the hospital. If the police wanted to know about Erev Lag B'Omer, then they hadn't brought her in because of Alice's poisoning. Everything she had assumed was wrong.

"What's this about?" she said.

"Please." Pincus smiled. He had a sad smile, as if he'd seen too much in life. "If you could answer the question."

She could think of only one reason that police officers, especially officers called in from Haifa, would want to know about Erev Lag B'Omer.

"Is this about Batsheva? Are you investigating her death?" *But hadn't the boy who found her said she looked like she was sleeping?*

"A few questions came up. That's why we need to talk to you and your sister, since you went with her to Mount Meron."

Margo barely heard him as she reframed everything he had asked—and she'd answered—only moments before. Some of the questions about Batsheva had surprised her, but she'd figured he was getting background. Knowing he was looking into Batsheva's death . . . Oh, hell! Hadn't she more or less said that Audrey had seen Batsheva as an unscrupulous guru? And the local rumor mill must have magnified Audrey's argument with Batsheva into a violent attack.

"I thought she had a heart attack."

Margo didn't expect a response, she just wanted to buy another minute to think. If she told them about Erev Lag B'Omer, was there anything that could hurt her sister? Trying to reconstruct what had happened that night, her thoughts kept slipping like a bicycle chain fallen off gear. She got a vivid image of the Hasid pushing the collection box into her face— that and nothing else.

At last she remembered. And realized Audrey was in no danger.

"When do you want me to start?" she said. "From when we got separated?"

"How about from the time you arrived at Meron? You and your sister went with Mrs. Halevi and her husband, Dr. Blum, yes?"

"Right. We met at nine and took a shuttle bus from Safed to Mount Meron. We walked around together for about half an hour. Then I lost everybody, and I guess Batsheva did, too. I found Lev and Audrey at eleven-thirty. They were together at the place where we'd agreed to meet, a falafel stand. I'd gotten mixed up and I kept going to a stand that sold corn. But Audrey and Lev remembered."

"They were together," she repeated, to make sure the police got it: Audrey couldn't have killed Batsheva, because she was with Lev.

"What did you do during the time you were separated from your friends?"

"Wandered around. We agreed to look for each other every half hour, so at ten-thirty and eleven and again at eleven-thirty I went to the corn stand to try and find them. I stayed there for five or ten minutes each time."

"Did you see anyone you knew?"

"No."

Margo's sense of relief dissolved. She'd been so concerned that the police suspected Audrey. What if *she* were the suspect? Of the three people who had accompanied Batsheva to Mount Meron, it was she, not Audrey or the victim's husband, who had spent an hour and a half with no one to say where she'd been—unless the vendor at the corn stand remembered her, or the aggressive Hasid with the collection box. She'd escaped from him and run up the mountain, probably close to where Batsheva's body was found.

She thought longingly of the vial of Xanax in her purse, a hedge against occasional panic. But she doubted Pincus and Efrati would understand about post-traumatic stress. If she gulped a tranquilizer now, would they take it as a sign of guilt? Like the accused in medieval times, forced to prove their innocence by taking a mouthful of pebbles? Those who salivated lived and the dry-mouthed died.

Pincus's next question wasn't, however, about how she had spent the ninety minutes for which she had no good alibi.

"Your sister and Dr. Blum never got separated, yes?"

"I don't know about 'never.' But they knew where we were supposed to meet, so it would have been for less than half an hour."

"What did your sister say about her conversation with Mrs. Halevi that night?"

What conversation?

"Things were so crazy, after we started searching for Batsheva," Margo improvised. *What hadn't Audrey told her?* "And the next morning, finding out she was dead. We didn't really . . ."

"Have you heard of Pavulon?" Pincus asked. If he was trying to keep her off balance, he was succeeding.

"No."

"You don't have any idea what it is? You don't ever remember hearing that word before?"

Margo shook her head, then remembered the tape recorder. "No."

"What about pancuromium bromide?"

"No."

Efrati said, "Your sister, when we asked her about Pavulon, said she wouldn't speak to us any further without an attorney."

"Why are you telling me this? If she wouldn't say any more without an attorney, then I won't, either."

But Audrey was certainly going to say a lot to *her.* What

the hell had happened between her and Batsheva on Mount Meron?

"We talked, that's all."

"You said you were with Lev the whole time!" Margo sat on their bedroom floor; she'd have preferred to sit on Audrey. She wanted to pummel her the way she had when they were kids.

"Look, what we need to focus on is our meeting with the lawyer tomorrow morning." Audrey had been active on the phone after her return from the police station. She'd contacted an attorney recommended by Bernice, as well as the American embassy. "I need to know what you told the police."

"You first. What went on with Batsheva that night? I thought you met with her in the afternoon."

"Shh. Not so loud." Audrey glanced toward the wall they shared with their mother's room. Alice had gone to bed early after their all-day outing.

"Tell me or I'll scream."

"When I got to her house that afternoon, she said something had come up, and could we talk that evening instead?"

"Why were you so secretive about it? Why did you lie?" Margo couldn't believe she'd felt so close to Audrey last night she had even confided about the problems between her and Barry. Obviously, the confidences didn't go both ways.

"I knew you wouldn't like what I was going to discuss with her."

"Which was . . . ?"

"I wanted Mom to come home as soon as she was well enough to travel, and I wanted Batsheva's cooperation in telling her that was the best thing for her."

"What did Batsheva say?"

"She thought Mom should stay in Safed and continue her studies. The fact that Mom was almost killed didn't mean a thing to her!"

"Did you tell the police this?" *With the same degree of indignation?*

"Of course not."

"How did they know you were talking to Batsheva in the first place? Did you tell them?"

"They already knew. Look, I wrote down what I remembered of the interview for the attorney tomorrow."

Margo's heart sank as she read the handwritten transcript. The police had taken a different approach with Audrey, the kind of approach they'd use with someone whom they expected to lie. Efrati and Pincus had batted questions back and forth like tennis balls. And they'd asked more in the beginning about Alice's poisoning, as if to lull Audrey into believing that was the real purpose of the interview.

Their first question about Erev Lag B'Omer wasn't an open-ended "What happened?" but, "When you and Mrs. Halevi talked on Erev Lag B'Omer, did you settle your differences?"

Audrey: I think we understood each other's points of view.

Pincus: What did you discuss?

A: What does that have to do with what happened to my mother?

Efrati: You never know what's going to be relevant.

A: We talked about my mother's health and her plans to return home.

E: Where did you have this conversation? By the stalls where they were selling things? Or higher up the mountain?

A: This can't possibly have any bearing—

P: Just a few more questions, okay? So we can fill in the forms. What kind of work do you do in the States?

A: Marketing.

E: For what kind of company?

A: I don't . . . Pharmaceuticals. A pharmaceutical company. What does this have to do with—

P: Are you familiar with a drug called Pavulon?

A: You're not trying to find out who poisoned my mother.

E: Have you heard of Pavulon? Pancuromium bromide? Since you're in the pharmaceutical business, I thought you might have.

The transcript ended there. Margo looked up.

"That was when I asked for an attorney," Audrey said. "What's Pavulon? Some kind of drug?"

"Yes." Audrey described how it immobilized most of a person's muscles, including the muscles controlling breathing, to enable a doctor to establish an airway.

"Could that be what killed Batsheva?"

"Yeah," Audrey said softly. She hugged her knees to her chest. "It would be a quick death, but . . . Oh, God. From what I understand of how Pavulon works, for the first minute or two she would have still been conscious. She knew she wasn't getting any air—Margo, she had to know she was dying—but she couldn't call for help. She couldn't thrash around and hope someone noticed her. She couldn't even blink her eyes."

"Oh." Margo had just taken a bite of a tuna sandwich. She gave up on trying to swallow, and spat it into a napkin. "Oh, no. Do you think the person who gave her the Pavulon just left, or did they stay and watch her die? Was the last thing she saw the person who killed her?"

"I guess it depends on how much they hated her."

"I liked the other story better."

"What story?"

"Thinking she went up the mountain and heard the voice of God. Audi, you said she couldn't call for help. If she'd gotten someone's attention, then what?"

"She could have lived. Simple as that. When a doctor gives a person Pavulon, they don't die. You keep them on a respirator until the drug wears off. Or, if you don't have a respirator, you do mouth-to-mouth. You have to work at it, I think the drug suppresses respiration for half an hour. But as long as you don't give up, the person would make it."

"How do you know so much about Pavulon?" Margo asked. Her sister was only a marketing director, not a pharmacologist. Did she have an encyclopedic knowledge of every drug on the market?

"My company manufactures it."

"Oh."

"As in 'oh, shit? oh, hell?' "

"All of the above. And as in 'oh, do the police know that?' "

"If they don't, they will."

"But it's not as if all your top executives carry it when they travel, just in case they want to kill someone."

"It's available in hospitals. I could have picked it up when I visited Mom. Oh, God," she said, her voice breaking.

"Come here." Margo put her arms around her sister and stroked her hair. "They don't really have any reason to suspect you. You talked to Batsheva that night and you know about Pavulon. But what motive do you have for committing a premeditated murder? Maybe if you got furious at her when you were talking, you might have shoved her or slapped her face."

"I wouldn't! I don't think I would," she amended in a small voice, remembering—as Margo did—the argument she'd had with Batsheva.

"If they're looking for credible suspects, what about people who've known Batsheva for decades, not just a few days? What about Lev? If he's no longer your alibi, then you're not his. And talk about having access to Pavulon."

"Margo, I'm scared."

"The police were *trying* to scare you, in case you did know something. But they don't have a case."

Margo had almost talked herself into it.

"Listen to me." Audrey sat up and grasped her hands. "They searched the house."

"Here?" Their quarters at Bernice's were so temporary, Margo hadn't noticed any disruption; she still didn't. Audrey's family photos no longer occupied the top of the bureau, but Audrey had been holding them when Margo returned from the police station.

"They searched the room at Dalia's, too. And Margo?" Audrey's voice sounded thin and scared. "They confiscated my passport."

Thirty-one /

The problem was, he'd already spent the money. Not all of it. He had only needed to settle a few pressing debts. But he'd spent enough that, should his customers insist he return the sum they'd advanced him . . .

They wouldn't insist, however. On the phone tonight, didn't his caller at first sound angry, in that polite Arab way that implied the hand not occupied with the telephone was holding a knife? Naturally, the caller's employer was deeply sorry to hear about the death of Gadi's mother, and no one expected him to move ahead only a day or two after his mother's death. But surely enough time had elapsed—unless they were mistaken and Gadi was a religious Jew?

He was tempted to say yes, and to show up for his next meeting with them with a *kippah* on his head and *tzitzit* fringes showing beneath his Italian designer jacket. But he knew how to work with these people. Jokes about religion offended them. Smooth talk, on the other hand, was a language they understood; they'd invented it, hadn't they?

"You haven't heard," he said.

"Heard what?"

"My mother's death. Everyone thought it was a heart attack. We learned today that she was murdered."

The Arab's wordless murmur managed to convey both sympathy and disapproval for the sort of mother who would get herself murdered. For a moment Gadi experienced a flood of rage—and of something else he'd noticed several times since he'd heard about Batsheva. Not grief. There was too much bitterness between him and his mother for him to feel sad now.

Loss. The sense of loss was so profound he fought tears—and then he stopped fighting them, aware that, with the Arab, tears could give him leverage.

"Of course," Gadi said, broken-voiced, "I'm doing my best to meet my business obligations. But my family. This is such a shock for us."

"Of course, of course."

"Not only that." He pressed his momentary advantage. "Naturally, the police have to question us. I don't want to do anything for the next several days that might look the least bit suspicious. A week from now?"

The Arab went to consult with his boss. It was only a matter of form.

"A week," he agreed, when he returned to the phone.

Hanging up, Gadi realized his body was drenched with sweat. A week. Should he have intimated that the real problem wasn't his mother's death but his associates' absurd hesitation? No, he decided he'd played it perfectly; he *did* understand the Arab mind. Instinctively, he had known they would think him either stupid for choosing his associates poorly or disloyal for complaining about them.

And hadn't his associates assured him they were professionals? He had one week to convince them to behave that way.

Thirty-two /

Friday—the 37th day of the counting of the Omer

A friend of Margo's had once run afoul of the California Department of Motor Vehicles. He'd had a seizure as a one-time reaction to medication, an overzealous (and lawsuit-phobic) doctor reported him to the DMV, and he lost his driver's license. He got a second opinion that he was in absolutely no danger of blacking out at the wheel of a car. Even with the second opinion, however, regaining his license was a semiadversarial process with a skeptical DMV examiner. Suddenly, he'd said, he understood what it meant to be "on the wrong side of the law"—feeling he couldn't prove his innocence no matter how hard he tried.

Margo thought of him when she went shopping in Safed on Friday afternoon.

The morning had been spent with the attorney, a chunky, fifty-something man with two gold teeth. He'd strategized with them as to how much Audrey and Margo should tell the police and how vehemently to demand the return of Audrey's passport. Then he and Audrey went to the police station to resume the interview she'd broken off last night; the police had no further questions for Margo.

"Why don't I do some grocery shopping?" Margo offered, remembering the stores would soon close for Shabbat.

"We'll go together," Bernice said. Bernice had been a life-saver, letting them use her living room for the meeting with the attorney. She'd brought in a tray of coffee and pastries, then spent most of the morning at her friend Chava's to give them privacy. She'd returned at noon with sandwiches.

"I don't mind," Margo said. "Just tell me what you need."

Bernice insisted. On the Jerusalem Street mall, Margo understood why. News had traveled quickly. Other shoppers looked at her and looked away. She wondered if some of the merchants would have refused to sell to her if she hadn't had Bernice by her side.

"Do they really think Audrey's guilty?" she asked Bernice, when they returned to her house and Alice was available to translate.

"Audrey or you."

"That's outrageous!" said Alice. "What kind of evidence do they have? Nothing but rumors."

Alice was holding up like a trouper, all of her walking in Safed—and the exercise bike she rode daily at home—aiding her recovery. She had sat in on the meeting with the attorney, saying it would be more stressful to imagine what was happening than to be part of it. Occasionally she said something that made Margo and/or Audrey want to scream. Most of the time, however, Margo felt the way she had as a child, that everything would be okay as long as her mom was there.

She realized this was a fantasy. She realized Audrey had gone to the police station over an hour ago and hadn't yet returned. None of them spoke of it, but Audrey's absence hung over them . . . like ash hanging over San Diego from a canyon fire.

"Look at the alternatives," Bernice said. "If they don't believe some outsider is guilty, then they have to wonder, is it someone they know? A neighbor? A friend of thirty years? And you're American."

"What does that have to do with it?" Margo asked.

"Murder isn't an Israeli crime."

"Except for the Russian Mafia," Alice and Margo responded at the same time.

"We say that a lot, don't we?"

"Bernice, can you help us?" As Alice translated, Margo dug into her Guatemalan bag for notes she'd made the night before.

Bernice nodded.

"First of all, if Batsheva was found on Monday morning,

why did it take the police three days to start to investigate her death?''

"I don't think Pavulon turns up in a routine autopsy. Lev must have run a special test for it."

"Lev? Why was Lev involved in the autopsy?"

Bernice lifted her big, expressive shoulders. "*That* Chava didn't tell me. My guess is Batsheva never had any trouble with her heart. Maybe she even had a physical exam recently, and they told her she had the heart of a twenty-year-old. A religious person might accept her death as the will of God. But a scientist like Lev? Chava said he was in and out of the morgue all week, doing this test and that test."

"Tell me about Pavulon."

Bernice filled in the information she had gotten from Audrey: that Pavulon was given by injection, that someone could have even slipped behind Batsheva and given it through her clothes.

"Could you inject yourself?" Margo asked.

"Batsheva wouldn't kill herself!" Alice protested. She translated the question for Bernice, who said that in terms of mechanics, Pavulon could be self-injected; but, like Alice, she couldn't imagine Batsheva committing suicide.

"What else did Chava tell you?" Margo asked. "What are people saying?"

"The story is that yesterday afternoon, Lev found some kind of evidence that Batsheva was killed—Chava didn't know it was Pavulon and I didn't tell her. Lev went to the police. The Safed police don't handle major crimes, so they asked for help from Haifa. The police talked to Lev, of course, and also to Gadi."

"Why Gadi?" Alice asked.

"That's the weakest part of the story. Someone thought they saw Gadi go into the police station, with Nili holding his hand."

"What about Audrey and me?" Margo asked. "What do they say about us?"

"That you went to the police station—that the police brought you in—and you were there for a long time."

"What else?" Alice asked. "Bernice, you're not telling us everything."

"Does your mother do this to *you*?" Bernice asked Margo. "Try to read your thoughts?" She took Alice's hand. "Why don't we all rest for a while?"

"I can't," Alice said, glancing toward the door, as if she could make Audrey appear there. It had been an hour and a half.

"A game of hearts? Gin?"

Margo tried to play hearts with them, but she couldn't concentrate. She had a feeling she knew what Bernice had held back: that everyone in Safed had heard about Audrey's fight with Batsheva the night before she died. She left Bernice and her mother starting a gin game and went out for a walk.

A hurried movement when she opened the gate drew her eyes toward the retreating back of an Orthodox man or maybe, from his narrow shoulders, a teenage boy. Was it the same kid she'd noticed yesterday morning?

"Hey!" she called, and ran after him. "Hey!"

Was he one of the kids who'd harassed Batsheva's students—waiting for a chance to unleash some mischief on Margo? Or maybe Margo wasn't the target; maybe the kid wanted a second chance to harm her mother.

"Hey!"

He picked up speed and turned right at the next corner. And vanished. When she got to the corner, she couldn't see him. She ran in the direction he'd gone, but hit another intersection. He surely knew the city far better than she did, the shortcuts and the alcoves where he could hide. He could be on any of half a dozen streets by now.

She turned back toward Bernice's, and saw Audrey walking down the street, her long legs taking big strides and her face heartbreakingly pale. Margo ran to her.

"Not here." Audrey shrugged off her hug, and continued to quick-march.

"I just want to take a very, very strong pill and go to bed," she announced at Bernice's. "I've got a migraine. It wasn't that bad with the police. Really, it wasn't," she said, scanning their worried faces. "I'll tell you about it as soon as I stop feeling like there's an ice pick in my eye."

"I'll make you a cup of tea. A little caffeine will help." Alice touched her cheek, and Audrey wept.

"What I want to know," she howled, "is why, when I walked back from the attorney's office just now, people wouldn't speak to me. I saw a little girl I've talked to before, and I bent down to say hello. Her mother pulled her away like I was going to strangle her."

"We need to do something," Bernice said. She went into another room and came back five minutes later. "It's settled. We're making Shabbat dinner for Lev and his family."

"Inviting ourselves for dinner?" Margo asked apprehensively.

"We can't stay and eat—Ma'ayan invited us for dinner tonight—but we'll cook the dinner and bring it over. Lev would like to see us. All of us," Bernice said firmly. Margo remembered that she'd served in the Israeli underground; clearly, she didn't shrink from a challenge. "Audrey, go take your pill and rest. Alice, you lie down, too. Margo can make the tea. Then, Margo, I want you to go get Danny and ask him to help us. I'll send him to the market. And you can work in the kitchen with me. Do you want to learn how to make *tsimmes*?"

Thirty-three /

Friday—The 37th day of the counting of the Omer

They made a ragtag procession down the streets of the old city. Danny carried a fragrant roast chicken, Margo bore the bowl of *tsimmes,* Audrey had a salad, and Alice held a bouquet of flowers. Bernice trusted no one but herself to handle the dessert, her special plum cake that, according to Danny, was renowned throughout half the Galilee.

Bernice led them on a circuitous route through the busiest part of the Jewish Quarter, where people were taking care of last-minute preparations for Shabbat. She made a point of greeting everyone they passed, never failing to mention that they were providing dinner for Lev and his family, and that Lev looked forward to seeing them.

"Are you okay?" Margo murmured to Audrey. "Really?"

Audrey had insisted her migraine was better and of course she would go with them. But her face looked only a few shades darker than tofu.

"The ice pick has stopped," she said. "Now it's more like jungle drums in my left frontal lobe."

After she'd rested, Audrey had described her interview with Pincus and Efrati. With the attorney at her side, she had gone through the same story she'd told Margo the night before; she omitted only the subject of her conversation with Batsheva on Erev Lag B'Omer and the fact they had argued. She admitted knowing about Pavulon, although she didn't volunteer the information that her company made it. She stressed that even though she was aware of the drug's properties, she was no more able to use it than an MBA who marketed oil-drilling equipment would be able to go out and start pumping crude. She and the attorney tried to suggest some other avenues the police might explore. Pincus and Efrati listened politely. Then they took her to Mount Meron and asked her to show them where she and Batsheva had walked, where she'd left Batsheva, and her route back down the hill. It was a nearly impossible task. "None of it looked the same. Except for Bar Yochai's tomb and the synagogue, there was nothing left from Erev Lag B'Omer except piles and piles of trash." Most disturbing of all, despite the attorney's cajoling that had turned to civilized threats, the police hadn't given back her passport.

Privately, she'd told Margo that they had said nothing to the police about her son, who'd finally stopped wetting his bed after she was able to tell him the date of her flight home. If her return were delayed, how would that affect him? But the attorney had advised her to hold "the Zach card" in reserve.

Tears pricked Margo's eyes as she watched her sister walk like a prima ballerina, her throbbing head held high, through the gate to Lev's courtyard.

Lev greeted them at the door and asked them in. Assembled in the living room were Gadi, Batsheva's brother Saul, and Leah, Saul's wife. Audrey glanced hopefully around the room. Nili, however, was the one member of the family who hadn't turned out to say hello. She was in bed with a stomachache, her Aunt Leah said. A *bad* stomachache, Leah added, turning the polite excuse into an obvious lie.

Leah took the food into the kitchen. Saul offered to serve "soda or—"

"Vodka! Let's have some of the vodka!" said Lev.

Vodka sounded terrific to Margo.

Saul served drinks. Leah brought out dips and crackers. Gradually, several small groups formed, Audrey and Danny talking to Leah, Bernice and Gadi playing a game of backgammon, Alice and Margo chatting with Lev and Saul.

When Lev went to get another vodka—his third?—Margo followed him into the dining room.

"More?" he asked.

"Sure." She let him top off her second glass. She could tell she was precisely on the edge of being fuzzy-drunk. Until she went over the edge, the alcohol made everything seem sharper and clearer. "Lev?"

He hadn't shaved all week, whether as a personal sign of grief or a concession to the Orthodox customs of mourning. The stubble and signs of sleeplessness gave his broad face the slackness of a vagrant's. But the penetrating look he shot her seemed undulled by either grief or alcohol.

"Do you mind if I ask you a few questions about Batsheva?" she said.

"*Lama lo?* Why not?" He gestured her toward one of the dining-room chairs.

"Did she ever talk to you about the mediations she did?" Margo asked as he pulled around a chair to face her.

"Sometimes. The same way I talked to her about patients. Technically, it's a breach of confidentiality, and we took—I take—confidentiality seriously. But sometimes you need to talk things out."

"How often did she do mediations?"

"Sometimes two or three a month. Sometimes nothing for a month or two."

"What about in the past few months? Did she mediate for anyone who was upset with the outcome?"

"The police aren't stupid. They asked about this, too." His tone was matter-of-fact rather than unkind.

"The police don't have as much motivation as I do."

"I violated confidentiality once by giving the police the names of her clients for the past year. I'm not going to do it twice. And I have to tell you, I don't think you will find the person who did this among her mediation clients. These aren't violent people."

"At least tell me, was there anyone who would have known about Pavulon?"

He shook his head. "When I looked through her files to get the names for the police, I didn't notice any doctors or nurses. Of course, you never know what people did in the army, if they served as medics."

In the other room, a man—Saul?—started singing in a low voice. It was a plaintive song, a good accompaniment for drinking vodka. Not that Lev needed any encouragement. He'd downed half his glass.

"What about—" she said. "I heard that she didn't just mediate when people came and asked for her help. That sometimes, if she found out a person was doing something wrong, she went to them. Was there anything like that?"

Lev smiled. "It might depend on what you define as wrong."

"How about breaking the law? Hurting other people."

"Ah. Now, Batsheva would have told you—and I agree—that hurting other people is an absolute wrong. But breaking the law? I grew up in a totalitarian country. It's hard for me to condemn someone only for breaking a law, unless I know who made the law and why."

"Lev, *was* there a case like that?" she pleaded. She'd been sipping her drink slowly, in the hope that if she dripped minute amounts of fresh alcohol into her body, she could prolong the sense of clarity she had enjoyed moments ago. It wasn't working. She felt thickheaded and slow.

"I'm sorry. I don't mean to tease you. But breaking the law . . . Batsheva and I always argued about it. I'll tell you what I'll do. I'll look through some of her other files. If I see something, I'll give it to you. You know that song?" He cocked his head toward the living room. "It's an Israeli folk song about the beautiful evening."

"Why did you tell the hospital to keep my mother in intensive care?"

He had responded easily to all of her previous questions, as if he had answered them all before. Now he looked confused.

"At the end of last week," Margo reminded him, "she was supposed to be moved to a regular bed. But you requested that she stay in the ICU."

He studied his hands; Margo wondered if, like her, he'd passed his limit on alcohol. But when he looked up, his brown eyes were bright with understanding.

"You think there's a connection between your mother's poisoning and what happened to Batsheva."

"I think that just a few days before Batsheva was killed, she started to believe that someone poisoned my mother. I'm right, aren't I?"

He nodded. "The night you arrived in Safed, she couldn't sleep."

"I think once she believed that, she started trying to figure out who was responsible. And if she figured it out, isn't there a good chance she'd try to talk to them herself?"

It was one of the arguments her sister had presented to the police, and Lev seemed about equally willing to believe it.

"A group of kids? Even if it were psychologically possible for a boy to do something so evil, how would he know about Pavulon?"

"What if she didn't talk to boys? What if she talked to their teacher?"

"Yitzhak. Batsheva and Yitzhak don't speak."

"The night I came to Safed, Batsheva said she was going to talk to Yitzhak."

"But . . ." he said thoughtfully. "This didn't come up until Thursday night, when you came. On Friday, Yitzhak would have been preparing for Shabbat, and all day Saturday he'd be in *shul* and with his family. Sunday was Erev Lag B'Omer."

"What about after the procession, before he went to Mount Meron? Oh! On Sunday afternoon, did Batsheva go anywhere? Or did someone come to see her?" At the procession, Batsheva had asked Audrey to meet with her that afternoon. But when Audrey arrived, Batsheva told her something had come up. What had come up so quickly that Batsheva hadn't known about it a few hours before?

"Margo!" her mother called. "We need to go."

"Just a few more minutes, Mom! Can you remember?" she asked Lev.

"I wouldn't have seen anyone coming or Batsheva going out. I was here all afternoon, but I had a meeting in my study. Planning health education programs for the Russian immigrants."

"So she could have seen Yitzhak then?"

Lev thought for a moment, then said, "No. No, it can't be."

"Was he on Meron that night?"

"I suppose so. I think he had some of his students with him."

"How did you know she talked to Audrey that night? Did you see them?"

He shook his head, but looked ill at ease.

"If someone saw them, didn't they see Audrey walk away while Batsheva was still fine?"

"You saw how it was there. You catch a glimpse of someone and then they're swallowed up in the crowd."

"Lev, where were you, when we all lost each other?" She had expected it to be the most delicate question—she'd purposely waited to bring it up—but he didn't seem insulted. She read only one emotion on Lev's face. Anguish.

"Where was I?" he said softly. "I was dancing. While my wife was being killed, God help me, I was dancing."

"With the Hasidim?"

"That's right. Three hundred and sixty-four days a year, I have no use for the black-hats. But on Erev Lag B'Omer—oy, can they dance."

"Margo!" Her mother came over and took her arm.

"Okay." Did Sam Spade ever have to cut short an investigation because his mother didn't want to outstay their welcome?

Wearily, Lev looked at Alice. "You know, I didn't want to be right. Do you understand? I couldn't sit back and accept that the cause of death was heart attack, in a woman with no heart problems. I had to investigate other possibilities. But every time one of the possibilities turned out to be wrong, I was glad. I checked it off my list. I didn't want this to happen."

"I understand," Alice said.

"You said you'd go through her files and see if there was anything," Margo reminded him, ignoring her mother's dirty look. "When?"

"I . . . Tomorrow."

Margo's need to help her sister was far more compelling than the guilt she felt over badgering a grieving man.

A grieving man . . . and also a lying man? He had said it himself: you glimpsed someone for a second and then they were gone. For all his apparent sorrow, had Lev really spent every minute when they were separated kicking up his heels with the Hasidim?

Thirty-four /

Friday—the 37th day of the counting of the Omer

It wasn't just the look on her father's face during dinner. It was a feeling Nili got from him—ESP that something was very wrong. The ESP told her not to ask anything, just to watch. After dinner, Lev and Uncle Saul took their cups of coffee into Lev's study. Nili told Aunt Leah she was going to her room. Instead she waited in the hall outside the study. Her father and Saul stayed there for half an hour, their words unintelligible even when she put her ear against the thick door. When they came out, she hid in the darkness down the hall. She heard Saul say they were going to get Cousin Yitzhak.

She had a hiding place in the study, a corner between the edges of two bookcases where she used to curl up when she was little. It was harder to get into now. She had to move a magazine rack and reach with her toes to move it back after she was in place. She could barely breathe. But she didn't want to breathe. She didn't want to do anything to give herself away.

"What is this all about?" said Yitzhak. "What's the big emergency?"

"We need to ask you some questions," Lev said.

"About religious practices? I can tell you now, Lev, you shouldn't light that pipe on Shabbat."

Nili smiled as she sniffed the aromatic tobacco, a smell that had said "Daddy" to her all her life.

"I want to know," Lev said, "if Batsheva talked to you last week."

"No," Yitzhak answered; but then said, "About what?"

"The things that were done to her students. You must have heard that people said those things were done by students of yours."

"I heard rumors. I never saw any evidence that my students were involved."

"Maybe Batsheva found evidence," Lev said. "Is that what she discussed with you?"

"I don't understand the point of this. It's Shabbat, and I'm going back to my family."

"The point?" Uncle Saul exploded. "The point, Yitzhak, is that Lev and I are trying to decide whether to tell the police that they should consider you a suspect in Batsheva's murder."

"Saul, we've never gotten along, but this is outrageous. That American woman killed her. Everyone knows she had a violent argument with Batsheva the night before, and they were seen together on Meron."

Nili wished she could jump out and hurl herself at him, kicking and scratching. Uncle Saul sounded as angry as she felt.

"A terrible argument?" he said. "You think one argument is enough to establish a reason to kill someone? You refused to have anything to do with your own cousin because you claimed her teaching was dangerous."

"It wasn't what *I* claimed. She went against Jewish law."

"Your students were suspected of harassing hers, even giving poison to one of them," Saul said. "Did Batsheva tell you she had some kind of proof? Did you worry about the impact it would have on your yeshiva if you were known as the teacher who turned a blind eye when his students gave someone poison?"

"She had no proof."

"What about on Erev Lag B'Omer?" Saul went on. "You camped all night close to where Batsheva was found dead—I heard you say it in this house."

"She had no proof!" Yitzhak roared.

"But you and she did talk?" Lev sounded so calm, after the angry cousins, it was almost scarier than if he'd yelled.

"A private conversation."

"When? On Sunday?"

"No, Friday."

"She asked you to question your students and find out if they had anything to do with the harassment?" Lev made it an interrogative.

"Exactly, and I said of course I would."

"Yitzhak!" Saul said. "How long have we known each other? Fifty-five years? You didn't say 'of course' anything. You told her, what? That you couldn't be bothered over schoolboy pranks? Oh, or maybe that the acts against her students were a sign from God that she should stop teaching? And we can imagine what she said then!"

"In fifty-five years, I've never known you to be a mind reader."

Nili thought Uncle Saul and Cousin Yitzhak were going to start again, but Lev said, "What about Sunday night? Did you see her on Mount Meron?"

"When I had six students constantly demanding my attention? You want me to talk to the police, Lev? I'll be happy to tell them the truth. I never saw Batsheva on Erev Lag B'Omer. I didn't see you, Lev. I didn't see Nili. I saw only one person from your family on Mount Meron."

"Who was that?" Lev asked.

"Who else? Gadi."

No!

For a moment Nili thought she'd yelled out loud. But Lev, Saul, and Yitzhak kept talking. Yitzhak said he had noticed Gadi talking to one of the vendors; he thought it was at a stand selling cassette tapes.

Lev asked him to stay. Saul went to get Gadi, who was watching the satirical television program that came on every Friday night, where they had puppets who looked like government officials.

Nili wished she could be anyplace but here. Stuck in her corner, tears dripping down her face, she heard Gadi deny he was anywhere near Mount Meron on Erev Lag B'Omer. Yitzhak asserted firmly that he ought to recognize his first cousin's son, shouldn't he? Someone who'd grown up with his son Chaim, that he'd known from a boy?

"You must have seen someone who looked like me," Gadi said, laughing.

"You had a cap covering half your face, but no! I'd know you anywhere."

"Yitzhak! A cap? Have you ever seen me wear a hat?"

Yitzhak might have mentioned Gadi's name only to divert attention from himself—as Nili's father and uncle speculated after the two other men left the study. But in her heart, Nili knew better. She knew Gadi had been at Meron, just as he'd told her he would be. She didn't mind that he'd lied to her father and the other relatives.

But why lie to her?

And why, if he had been there, hadn't he met her as he'd promised?

Thirty-five /

"Do you believe in God?"

Margo was expecting an automatic no. Instead, her husband nearly half a globe away paused, then engaged in a process of elimination.

"Definitely not the guy with the white hair and the beard," Barry said. "And not a personal God, who knows what I do . . . or cares."

"What about a prime mover?"

"I wouldn't categorically cross that one out."

"Can you believe in physics and believe in God?"

"Einstein did. He said, 'I maintain that the cosmic religious feeling is the strongest and noblest motive for scientific research.' "

"Wow. Do you know that by heart?"

"Sure. All of us scientists carry a little book of Einstein quotes." He laughed, and Margo missed him fiercely. This was the kind of conversation they sometimes had in bed after they'd turned out the lights. But he hadn't yet gone to bed on Friday night, and for her it was Saturday morning. "Actually, it's on the calendar by the phone. What about you?"

"The only quote I know is, 'God doesn't play dice with the universe.' "

"I wasn't asking about Einstein quotes."

"My mother says Jewish spirituality has to do with living in God's presence. She thinks God is more present here than in other places. Sometimes I feel here . . . I don't know if it has anything to do with God. I had friends in high school whose dream was to go to Israel. I never felt that way. I was studying Spanish. I wanted to go to Mexico. I wish you were here. You could tell me if you feel anything. That sounds like a postcard, doesn't it? But I mean it.''

"Has absence made the heart grow fonder?" His tone was light, but brittle.

"Oh, Barry!" she said, stung. *Careful with each other.* It was the first time since she'd left a week and a half ago that either of them had brought up what was going on between them. "I've never stopped feeling fond. I was hurt."

"I never meant to hurt you."

"I know."

Bernice walked through the room on her way to the kitchen. *"Boker tov,"* she said. "Good morning."

"Boker tov," Margo said. "I . . ." But the moment had passed. "That was Bernice," she whispered to Barry. "She's wearing the most wonderful leopard-print bathrobe. I think Bernice is God. Remember the Woody Allen film *Crimes and Misdemeanors,* where a doctor hires a hit man to kill his mistress? At first the doctor feels unbearable guilt. He flashes back to his childhood as an Orthodox Jew; he was taught that God sees everything you do, and judges you. But time passes. The doctor prospers. No one suspects him of the crime. He decides there is no God, and he stops feeling guilty.''

"Sounds like what I had hammered into me by the nuns and priests, the idea of God keeping score. I didn't know that was part of Judaism.''

"Not the Judaism I was brought up with. That's why the film stuck with me. It was my religion, but it was nothing I recognized. I was never taught that the reason not to kill is that God will punish you. It's just ethical behavior. If I believe in God or I don't believe, I'm not going to treat people any differently.''

"Going from believing to not believing made a big difference for me," Barry said. "When I was a kid, I thought everything you did was so that God would let you into heaven. When I stopped believing that, I had to come up with completely new rules.''

"What if you went from nonbelieving to believing?"

"I guess the rules would stay the same. What's going on

behind the scenes would become more interesting.''

"Barry, I've gotta go. There's someone at the door.''

"What time is it there?''

"A little before seven. I love you.''

"I love you, Margo.''

She hung up and hurried to open the door before Nili got cold feet and ran away. The kid looked wild-eyed and disheveled. Had she been out all night?

"*Boker tov.* Come on in.'' Margo stopped herself from putting her arm around Nili. She didn't want to scare her.

"Audrey?'' Nili's shaking voice managed to get out the syllables.

"I'll get her. Stay here.''

She raced upstairs and shook Audrey awake.

"This'd better be good,'' Audrey moaned.

"Nili's here. Hurry! I get the feeling she could change her mind and go.''

"Please, please tell me there's coffee made.'' Audrey was pulling on a T-shirt and shorts.

"I think Bernice was making some.''

"There *is* a God,'' Audrey said. "Why are you laughing?''

"Look at you!'' Margo exclaimed, admiring Nili's red-painted toenails an hour later. She tried out the latest Hebrew word she'd learned. "*Yofi!* Great.''

Nili giggled. She was much calmer than when she'd shown up at the door. Margo, on the other hand, was frantic to know what, besides a pedicure, had happened after Audrey spoke briefly to Nili in the foyer. Whatever Nili said—urgently, in Hebrew—Audrey didn't even stop to get the coffee she craved; she immediately took Nili to talk privately in her room. (Margo came up ten minutes later with coffee and a plate of pastries. Audrey and Nili were perched cross-legged on the deep window ledge, heads together. They stopped talking while Margo brought in the tray—as if she could understand them! She heard their voices start up again the moment she left.)

"Why did she come here? What did she say?'' she demanded the instant Nili left.

"She just felt really bad about the police suspecting me.''

Audrey glanced toward the kitchen, where Alice and Bernice were playing gin rummy. "I haven't even had a chance to brush my teeth this morning. I'm going upstairs."

Back in their room, she sank to the floor. The smile she'd worn for Nili disappeared.

"Oh, Margo," she said. "Oh, hell, damn, shit. Guess who was at Mount Meron on Erev Lag B'Omer? And who lied and said he wasn't?"

"The half brother she thinks walks on water?"

"You got it. The family black sheep, who's been on the outs with Batsheva for the last ten years."

"But the Pavulon," Margo said. "Okay, Gadi had a falling-out with her ten years ago, and maybe if they ran into each other on Meron they would've had an argument. But to do something so premeditated?"

"We know what happened ten years ago, but what if there was something else between them recently? All these businesses Gadi starts and never seems to make a go of—where does he get the money for them? And why did he lie about being on Meron? It will break Nili's heart if he killed Batsheva. It's already breaking her heart that he lied to her."

"How did she find out?"

Audrey explained about Nili being stood up by her half brother on Erev Lag B'Omer; he'd told her he had never made it to Meron. Then last night, she'd heard that Yitzhak had seen him.

"Gadi still says he wasn't there. He says Yitzhak must have been wrong," Audrey said. "But Nili doesn't believe him. I don't either. And now I don't know what to do."

"Audi, it's obvious. You have to tell the police."

"I can't. I promised Nili. Don't jump on me! I didn't say I'd never tell, but I told her I'd wait at least until after we go to the American embassy. If I can get my passport back without having to implicate Gadi—"

"Your passport! What if he killed his mother? You can't let him get away with that. And what about Nili? Is she safe? Does he know she doesn't believe his story?"

"He's leaving this morning. He needs to go back to his business in Tel Aviv."

"Or get out of the country."

"The point is, Nili isn't in danger. Listen. I haven't told you everything I heard from her. Gadi's not the only suspect. First of all, Batsheva did talk to Yitzhak; it happened last Friday. Yitzhak didn't say, but they probably argued."

"First of all? What's second?"

"I may have found out what came up at the last minute that made Batsheva cancel her meeting with me on Sunday. Nili doesn't know if her mother went anywhere, because she was in and out herself. But something did happen after the procession." Her voice dripping scorn, Audrey revealed, "Batsheva Halevi, that paragon of ethical behavior, had a habit of reading her daughter's diary."

"Oh."

"What do you mean, oh? Do you read Jenny's diary?"

"I came really close once. I was putting clean laundry in her room, and her diary was sitting on the bed. You just wish you knew what was going on in her head sometimes! I thought, did she leave it out because she wanted me to read it?"

"But you didn't."

"No. I stood there and looked at it for a full minute. Then I walked out of the room and ate a pint of ice cream. Vanilla Swiss almond."

"Well, Batsheva didn't go for the Häagen-Dazs. Nili knew, because she was setting traps. On Sunday, while Batsheva was at the procession, Nili went out with friends. She got home after Batsheva—not long before I was supposed to come there—and she saw that Batsheva had done it again."

"What could be in Nili's diary that was so explosive?"

"To get back at Batsheva for reading it, Nili made up a fictional romance. In the part her mother would have seen that afternoon, she made it sound like she and the boy had had sex."

"Oh, shit," Margo said, with all the passion of the step-mother of a sixteen-year-old girl.

"You said it."

"Who was she having this fictional sex with?"

"Reuven Preusser. Ma'ayan told us about him. The kid from the Orthodox family who was studying with Batsheva on the sly. Nili figured that would really get Batsheva, to make her think the boy was Reuven.''

"I bet we promised Nili not to tell the police about him, either.''

"Margo, she begged me. She's so embarrassed about the things she made up. If she went to the police, she'd have to show them the diary.''

"We can't just ignore this.''

"She said it was okay if we talk to him. She's going to bring him here this afternoon.''

True to her word, Nili showed up shortly after two with a tense Orthodox teenager. He was the same boy Margo had seen in the street and outside Bernice's gate, the kid she had chased the day before.

Thirty-six /

Saturday—the 38th day of the counting of the Omer

Reuven confessed in the first five minutes.

Tearfully, he admitted that although he'd attended Bat-sheva's classes out of genuine interest, he was embarrassed when he was found out by some neighbor boys. To maintain face with them—and keep them from telling his parents—he had acted as a spy. He told them things he learned about Bat-sheva's students, information the friends used to harass the students.

"What about the henbane? What did he say?" demanded Margo. She had had to watch, uncomprehending, as Reuven and Audrey conversed in Hebrew, Reuven shamefaced and Audrey alternately angry and cajoling.

"He didn't say anything about Mom and the herbal tea. He felt bad about the things they'd done—he had no idea they'd use the information the way they did. He'd already decided not to tell them anything else. And he really likes Mom."

"Sure he does. He hid in the other room, didn't he, during Batsheva's classes? When did he even meet Mom?"

"I hear her in class!" Reuven broke in, in slow but clear English. "I know she nice lady. I . . ." He continued in Hebrew, and Audrey translated.

"He was really upset when Mom got sick. He was terrified his friends found out some other way and gave her the henbane. They said they didn't, but he still felt guilty. That's why he's been coming around here, to make sure Mom was okay. He's been trying to get up enough nerve to ask her forgiveness."

''Please,'' Reuven said.

Margo was barely mollified. She glared at the boy, whose slightly chubby face was tear-streaked, the collar of his long-sleeved white shirt drenched with sweat.

''What are your friends' names? The ones who played tricks on Batsheva's students?'' she asked, enunciating carefully.

Reuven mumbled several Hebrew names.

''Students of Yitzhak Saporta?''

He nodded.

''Did he say anything about talking to Batsheva on Sunday?'' she whispered to Audrey.

''Not yet.''

Audrey spoke to him in Hebrew. Reuven looked puzzled. Several times he said *lo*—no—his face flushed with embarrassment.

Audrey beckoned Margo into the next room.

''He was with friends all day Sunday,'' Audrey said. ''They went to the procession. Then they walked to Meron and set up tents. They were so worn-out from walking all the way to Meron, they fell asleep at nine.''

''What about this thing Nili made up?'' Margo kept an eye on Reuven in case he tried to bolt. However, he seemed to have put himself in their hands.

''I asked if Batsheva talked to him about him and a girl. He said no. He got flustered, but I think that just has to do with being a teenager. Frankly, I think he's decided to tell everything he feels guilty about, and we've heard it all.''

''Well, what do we do now?''

Audrey sighed. ''Take him to the police so he can tell them the names of those kids? Oh, God. I can't bear the thought of walking into the police station. What will the police do to them, anyway?''

''Y'know, I think Reuven has the right idea. They need to ask forgiveness from the people they've wronged. Besides, don't you want to see these little creeps yourself?''

''You think if we talk to their parents . . .''

''I don't know if the parents will listen to us. But they'll listen to Yitzhak Saporta.''

• • •

It was the charming Yitzhak, the man who had fascinated Margo with his comments about the thirty-six righteous *tzaddikim,* who invited them into his study. Faced with Reuven's testimony—and perhaps because of Bernice, who'd come with them and was clearly one of the most influential people in Safed—Yitzhak didn't attempt to defend his students or to dismiss their actions as boyish mischief.

He led them to the homes of the boys Reuven had named, two brothers and a third boy. Both families were spending the Sabbath afternoon at home. Margo didn't need to understand a word of Hebrew to follow what went on. Yitzhak spoke first to the parents of the two brothers. They summoned their sons—a fourteen-year-old and an older boy, a big kid who swaggered in and for whom Margo felt no pity when he started to cry.

At the next house, with the first boys and their father in tow, the admission of guilt came more quickly.

The boys and their fathers agreed to go with Yitzhak to apologize to Bruce, Nancy, and Danny, and to find out how much they owed for the broken flowerpots and Danny's ruined clothes.

They even promised to send a written apology to the student on whose doorstep they had left the dead bird.

Yitzhak had questioned them kindly but with a take-no-bullshit air that reminded Margo of Batsheva. She was convinced they couldn't have lied to him.

And the boys swore, one of them weeping in his teacher's arms, that they hadn't given Alice henbane.

It confirmed Margo's gut feeling that the henbane wasn't the merely nasty act of adolescent boys. Until she heard them deny it, however, she didn't realize how much she had hoped it was true. If her mother's poisoning had nothing to do with smashed flowerpots and ink-splattered clothes, then was it linked to a far greater evil—Batsheva's murder?

She raced, sick with fear, back to the house where they had left Alice napping alone.

Batsheva's killer might have come from any part of the lifetime she'd spent in Israel. But if the same person had poisoned Alice Simon, wasn't it most likely someone from the small circle Alice had met during her month in Safed?

Sitting at her mother's feet while Alice and Bernice conversed in Hebrew, Margo thought of the last time she'd seen her mother's Safed friends—yesterday evening, when they'd had Shabbat dinner at Yosef and Ma'ayan's. It was an emotional gathering, everyone doubly shocked by the news that Batsheva had been murdered and because the prime suspect appeared to be Audrey.

Surely, Margo thought, remembering their expressions of disbelief and pain—and their warm support for Audrey—Batsheva's killer had been one of her enemies, not these friends.

Still, she replayed the evening in her mind, looking at each person who had been there; measuring each one's potential for murder.

She started with her hostess.

The second most benign explanation for Alice's poisoning, Batsheva had said, was that Ma'ayan had given her the henbane in error. Was that the reason Ma'ayan was so jumpy and defensive when Margo talked to her a week ago? And why she'd shown such interest in whether Alice had regained any memory of the day she was poisoned? Maybe Ma'ayan's nervousness wasn't on her own behalf, however. When Margo had insisted that her mother hadn't picked the henbane, suspicion fell quickly on the boys who'd harassed Batsheva's students. Had Ma'ayan feared her older son was involved?

Ma'ayan hadn't been jumpy last night, Margo reflected, remembering the color in the herbalist's cheeks as she engaged in an intense conversation with Bruce. Hardly the drab mouse Margo had met a week earlier, Ma'ayan had pulled the curtain of hair back from her face with a bright cloisonné clip. ("Margo, you should try that with *your* hair," Alice had remarked.) Above a simple dark skirt, she wore a cropped indigo sweater that showed off her slender waist and hips. Ma'ayan, the woman Alice had described as always in the background, glowed.

Was that because something—someone—that had threatened her a week ago no longer posed a threat? But would Ma'ayan have known about Pavulon?

Yosef would. Margo remembered him saying he'd served as a medic in the Army. And he'd taken his children to Mount Meron. How long would he have had to leave them to give Batsheva a fatal injection? A few minutes? Would he have done that, to protect his son or his wife?

Last night, he and Ma'ayan seemed to have traded personalities. She was vibrant; Yosef looked positively dour. Margo had wondered if he could be having an affair. What if it was the other way around? she wondered now. What if Ma'ayan was seeing someone else? Who? Bruce, toward whom she'd leaned closely as they talked?

Bruce must have charms that Margo hadn't detected. Not only charms but depth, she conceded, recalling a letter from Alice that had praised Bruce and Nancy's efforts in the Arab village.

The flower children wouldn't have missed the Lag B'Omer pilgrimage to Mount Meron, Nancy had told her. "Such a high—excuse the pun." Nancy said they'd left the celebration relatively early because they meditated every morning at five. "Bruce would have stayed all night and meditated on the mountain. But I made him stop dancing—I thought some of the men would go ballistic when I invaded their turf. Anyway, I reminded him that the day I hit forty, I made my Scarlett O'Hara pledge: I'm never going to sleep on the ground again."

"Did you see Batsheva that night?" Margo asked. "Or was the last time at the procession?" Bruce and Nancy had stood with them waiting for the Torah to be carried out.

"Know what else I've read, besides *Gone with the Wind?* Nancy said. "I'm a fan of mystery novels. Bruce says they're a decadent literary form, and how can I enjoy reading about people killing other people? I say the best mysteries have dynamite characters. Besides, I think there's a basic part of us, as humans, that needs to read about violence. The Kabbalists would call it the animal soul, although I'm sure they wouldn't approve of the way I'm applying it. What do you think?" She didn't wait for Margo to fumble for a reply to the bizarre change of subject, before continuing, "If you're trying to find out whether I killed Batsheva, the answer is no."

"But really," Nancy added, "why would I?"

"Because you and Bruce are doing something illegal, and Batsheva found out?" She matched Nancy's flippant tone.

Nancy made a show of pondering the idea. "Nah. Someone catches onto us, we don't kill them anymore, we just offer to cut them in. It's another thing I swore off in my forties. No more hit squads. It does terrible things to your karma, you know?"

Margo knew that Danny had been on Meron all night. She couldn't think of a single reason he would have wanted to harm Batsheva, and she doubted he would have known about Pavulon. Bernice, as a nurse, was familiar with the drug and she'd lived in the same city as Batsheva for so many years that some terrible animosity might have festered between them. But if Margo suspected Bernice, she might as well suspect her own mother.

Ronit—Margo had heard nothing of Ronit until the last aerogram she'd received at home before Alice became ill.

A new student joined our group a few days ago, a beautiful young woman named Ronit Laor. Ronit had a vision when she was doing her army service, that she should study how to serve God. How she has studied! She tried an Orthodox community for a short time, but decided it wasn't right for her. She also spent a year in the desert with a community of people who live in tents made of animal hide; the group studies and meditates.

Alice had said less about Ronit than about any of the rest of her fellow students. Was that simply because Ronit was a newcomer, or did Alice—like Margo—find her an enigma? Of all the people Margo had met in Israel, she had the least sense of who Ronit was. Did that mean Ronit was hiding something? Or was she simply, as Dalia had described native-born Israeli *sabras*, prickly on the outside and hard to get close to, but sweet on the inside, like the fruit of the *sabra* cactus?

Dalia had said that about herself, though she struck Margo as neither prickly nor sweet but highly strung—and last night, unstrung. She was smoking steadily, a habit that, according to Alice, she had only acquired since Batsheva's death. And she kept pulling at her short hair, sending a small snow of dandruff onto her shoulders.

"Are you okay?" Margo asked.

"Why shouldn't I be okay, hearing a woman I know for twenty years is murdered?"

"I'm sorry." In fact, Dalia was probably showing the most genuine reaction of them all.

Besides, what motive did Dalia have?

What motive did any of them have?

Margo replayed the evening again, this time at fast-forward. She stopped at her conversation with Nancy Isley. Why did Nancy become defensive when asked about Erev Lag B'Omer? Where did she and Bruce get the money to buy Persian rugs and antique kimonos? What unconscious impulse had made Margo joke about their being involved in something illegal? And what, she thought—rising to her feet and saying she was going for a walk—did the flower children keep in their off-limits room?

No one answered when she knocked at the flower children's door. It didn't surprise her; they'd mentioned that they needed to spend today and possibly overnight taking care of business in Tel Aviv. Still, she called their names at the door and again when she went to a side window, out of sight of anyone passing by.

Thanks to her Swiss Army knife, it took only a couple of minutes to pry off the window screen. She hoisted herself onto the sill. And she was inside.

Thirty-seven /

Saturday—the 38th day of the counting of the Omer

Climbing through the window brought her into Bruce and Nancy's bedroom. Shafts of late-afternoon light picked up the details in the superb rose-colored carpet, where she crouched; listened; heard nothing. They were away, as she'd thought.

Down the hall was the "storage" room Nancy hadn't wanted to show her. The door was locked.

Margo tried to slip the blade of her Swiss Army knife between the edge of the door and the frame. The door fit too securely, more securely than she would have expected in an old house.

Nose to the door, she sniffed for animals. She smelled wood and a little mildew. (If they exported snakes, how did snakes smell? She thought of the reptile house at the San Diego Zoo, a dry, almost musty odor.)

A credit card made it between the door and frame, but nothing popped open.

She went back through the bedroom window. The next window on this side of the house belonged to the locked room. It was a single, high window some six feet above the ground. Beneath it, in the narrow space between the wall of the house and a hedge, lay a stepladder. Weird—she hadn't noticed the ladder ten minutes ago.

Weird and providential. She propped the ladder against the wall and climbed. Tried to see in, but there was a curtain. She went to work with the Swiss Army knife. She removed the screen, opened the window, and pulled the curtain aside.

The room was dark, and she couldn't be sure of what she saw. Alley-oop. The small window required a few contortions to get through. Half falling, she landed on her butt, amid a scatter of hard oblong somethings. Videotapes. She switched on the light. Videocassette recorders, a bank of twenty of them, lined one wall. The place looked like a production studio.

A production studio and a shipping room. Two other walls were stacked with brown cardboard cartons.

She picked up one of the tapes from the floor. It had a white cardboard cover, hand-lettered in Arabic and English. *Independence Day*. All the tapes on which she'd fallen were *Independence Day,* some dozen copies of the blockbuster film about an alien invasion. She opened a carton. These tapes were marked in English and Hebrew rather than Arabic. Like *Independence Day,* they were all big action films.

"How come no *English Patient* or *Secrets and Lies*?" she mused out loud.

Didn't video bootleggers have a market for more sensitive movies? For clearly, that's what Bruce and Nancy were doing. The old hippies were bringing U.S. culture to the Middle East, via modern, high-tech bootleg videos.

That was what had paid for their exquisite carpets and framed antique textiles.

That was what Alice might have stumbled on. And Batsheva? Had Batsheva known?

Quickly she replaced the tapes in the carton and closed it to make it look undisturbed.

What if Batsheva had asked Bruce and Nancy to come see her—on the afternoon of Erev Lag B'Omer, for instance—and had insisted that justice be done? What would have satisfied Batsheva's sense of justice? Would it have been enough if the flower children destroyed all the tapes they'd made, rather than profiting from them? Would she have urged them to turn themselves in? Or would she, a woman who refused to cut any slack for her own son, have simply informed them that she had to report them to the police?

It was hard to imagine the flower children doing anything violent—but even harder to imagine Bruce or, especially, Nancy going gently to an Israeli prison.

Quickly, quickly—listening for any hint of their return—
she turned off the light and stacked the tapes of *Independence
Day*, trying to approximate their original position. She hoped
Bruce and Nancy didn't keep an impeccable inventory; she
took a tape with her.

How to get out without leaving any signs? To go back
through the window, she'd have to move over a carton to
climb on. Hallelujah! The door lock was one you could set
from the inside, then just close the door. She climbed backward through the bedroom window. All she had to do was
shut the two windows and replace the screens from the outside.

She'd finished the window to the locked room and was putting the ladder back on the ground when someone grabbed her
from behind and clamped a hand over her mouth.

Thirty-eight /

Saturday—the 38th day of the counting of the Omer

"Down," the person holding her whispered in her ear. "They're coming."

As if she had a choice. She was already down, her assailant's weight pinning her to the ground. Man or woman? She thought a woman. And an Israeli—the few words had been slightly accented. Whoever it was had plenty of strength. They'd pinned her easily and kept her down in spite of her struggles to escape.

"They're coming," her captor repeated urgently, and jammed Margo's head into the earth for emphasis.

She didn't know if the person holding her was friend or foe, but she stopped struggling when she heard the gate open, and Bruce and Nancy's voices as they approached the house. The door opened. The voices got softer and then faded as the door slammed shut.

"We wait," the woman said. "Okay?" She slightly moved her hand from Margo's mouth.

"Okay," Margo whispered back.

The woman relaxed her hold on everything except Margo's wrist, which she kept in a grip of iron. Margo rose to her free hand and knees. She turned her head, wincing—she'd banged her shoulder against the house when she'd been grabbed.

Ronit crouched beside her.

Bruce and Nancy were talking in the bedroom now, above their heads. Which meant the flower children had left the front of the house and could no longer see the courtyard through the windows.

Ronit handed her the Guatemalan carryall she'd left by the side of the house; she would have forgotten it. With a nod, Ronit signaled her to go. She crept close to the ground until she cleared the window, then stood and hurried as noiselessly as possible through the courtyard and out the gate. Ronit was three seconds behind her. She was carrying the stepladder.

"Did you put the ladder there?" Margo asked; she realized it was probably not her top-priority question at the moment.

"It helped, no?"

As they spoke they strolled down the cobbled alleyway. Margo matched Ronit's casual pace by an effort of will, fighting the impulse to run.

"Do you always carry a stepladder?" she said to the Israeli.

"I found it here, in the street." Ronit dropped the ladder and kept walking.

"What's going on? Why did you attack me?"

"Sorry if I hurt you. I knew they were coming and there was no time to explain. You saw, in the room there?"

"How did you know they were coming?"

"I watched at the gate while you were inside."

"Why?" And how had Ronit scurried back to the house without making a sound? Was it part of the religious discipline she'd picked up while meditating in an animal-hide tent?

Ronit ignored the question. "You saw the room?" she asked again.

"Yes."

"What will you do?"

"Tell the police." Or maybe she should tell Audrey's attorney.

"Good. I am police." Ronit must watch more American cop shows than Pincus did. She pulled out an official-looking ID—not that Margo could read any of the Hebrew words.

"What kind of police?"

"Are you hungry? It's sunset, no more Shabbat. The restaurants open again."

"Yeah. Okay."

They bought falafels and sodas at the Jerusalem Street mall. Ronit suggested going to Citadel Park, where they could talk more privately. Margo refused to leave the mall. Her instinct said to trust Ronit. But she'd rather be trusting where people could see them.

"What kind of cop are you?" Margo asked again, when they'd found a reasonably secluded table.

"A minute," Ronit mumbled through a mouthful of falafel. She ate with concentration for several minutes, then sighed happily and explained that she was a government agent operating undercover, closing in on Bruce and Nancy's bootleg-videotape business.

"Why are you telling me?" Margo asked. "How do you know I'm not in on it?" How could she be certain Ronit wasn't in on it herself?

"Number one." Ronit ticked it off on her finger. "You only come to Safed after your mother gets sick. Number two." She moved to the next finger. "Today is first time you go alone to the house of the flower children, and you have to go through window to get in."

"Are you watching their house?"

"Of course."

"If you know what they're doing, why haven't you arrested them? The evidence is there."

"No arrests yet. We wait for them to transfer tapes to distributor. Then we arrest everyone." Ronit frowned. "Should have happened already. We think they got nervous because of Batsheva being killed."

It made sense. Nevertheless. "Can I ask Officer Pincus to verify what you're telling me?"

"Sorry. It's a secret operation. But I can prove who I am. I tell you how much you pay in rent on your house in San Diego and how much is your salary." She did. "I thought Americans made more money," she added sadly.

"Not in public radio. How do you know all that?"

"American authorities checked for us. You have no unexplained income or expenses. That is the third way we know you're not involved."

"You're trying to bust Bruce and Nancy for video bootlegging. But what if Batsheva knew about this and tried to stop it? You've got to tell the officers investigating her murder."

"The flower children didn't murder Batsheva." Ronit licked tehina from her fingers.

"How do you know?"

"We watched them on Meron."

"Every minute? In that crowd?"

"Israeli intelligence is the best in the world."

"What about when they separated?"

"They didn't separate."

"Bruce went to dance on the men's side," Margo said. "Nancy mentioned it last night. She had to go get him because she wanted to leave."

Ronit muttered a word in Hebrew that needed no translation. Curses had the same emotional tone in any language.

"We work with police investigating murder," she said. "As soon as we make arrests for videotapes."

"How long are you going to wait? If they had anything to do with Batsheva's death—"

"Not long. We expect them to do something with the videos soon. They're running out of money. When we arrest for videos, we will ask about Batsheva. But believe me, I think Bruce and Nancy commit only economic crimes. Some people would say not even terrible crimes, since all they do is make ideas available to people for less money.

"You know," she said, "great controversies from the very beginning of Kabbalah involve who gets to hear about ideas. Have you heard about the brother of Hayim Vital?" Although Margo nodded, Ronit told the same story she'd heard from Danny about the Ari's follower whose brother had taken a bribe to let his writings be copied.

"You don't have to keep pretending to be a student of Jewish spirituality," Margo said.

"Is no pretend. I am student. I am cop. That's why I was assigned to join Batsheva's group."

"Did you really spend a year meditating in a tent in the desert?"

"Six months. The first three months I investigated the leader of the group. She went for walk in desert one day and disappeared. Everyone searches for her and thinks she's dead. A week later she gives press conference in Egypt. She said she walked there. Across the desert."

"Was she telling the truth?"

"I think so. After I did my work, I stayed another three

months to keep learning. I had some vacation coming.''

''What about the vision in the army? Did that really happen?''

Ronit nodded.

''What did you see?''

''I think I saw God.''

''What did God look like?''

''That's why I study ever since, to try to understand what I saw. Natan says—you know Natan, my friend who reads palms?''

''Is he a cop, too?'' So much for Natan's ''uncanny'' knowledge. He'd gotten it the same way Ronit had found out Margo's salary.

But she said, ''No, he's a friend. He wants to marry me.'' She sounded dubious.

''Do you want to marry him?'' Margo asked.

''I marry Natan, I stop being cop, I have babies. That's okay. But I want to keep studying. He says he'll let me, but I don't know. What do you think?''

''Maybe it's a problem of translation, but anytime a man says he'll 'let' you do something, sounds like he thinks it's his right to let you or not let you.''

''I think that, too.'' Ronit sighed. ''Anyway, Natan says he thinks *you* see God, but a face of God—not really bad. But you see a face of fire, a face that scares you.''

If the burning canyon had been God, Margo preferred to be an atheist.

''Natan says you need to see God's opposite face, a face of water, so you stop being afraid.''

''What does he mean by that?''

''What Natan means, I don't always know. I am literalist. I think you should take a *mikve*.''

''I don't think so.''

''Many women take *mikves* now, not just Orthodox. You immerse in water, holy blessings are made for you. It's very beautiful.''

Margo wasn't entirely won over by Ronit's disarming ''honesty,'' her easy confession of her real purpose in Safed and the girl talk about her love life. Late that night, when her mother, Audrey, and Bernice had all gone to bed, she slipped the tape she'd taken—she hadn't mentioned to Ronit that she'd put it in her Guatemalan bag—into the VCR and fast-forwarded all the way through. As advertised on the box, it was the movie *Independence Day;* it was subtitled in Arabic.

There was probably a big Arab market for a film that showed the White House exploding.

Thirty-nine /

Sunday–Thursday—the 39th–43rd days of the counting of the Omer

She believed Ronit's account of who she was and why she was in Safed, Margo reflected as she drove toward the coast the next afternoon.

She was less convinced by the Israeli agent's assurance that Bruce and Nancy couldn't have killed Batsheva. Ronit's colleagues had botched their surveillance of the couple on Mount Meron. Ronit herself—a young woman just starting to climb the career ladder—cared more about bringing her bootleg-video case to a successful conclusion than about finding Batsheva's murderer.

"Water?" Alice held out the bottle.

"Sure." She took her right hand from the steering wheel and drank, then handed the water bottle to Audrey in the backseat.

For the next day or two, at least, they would be safely out of the flower children's range. Audrey's attorney had called this morning. He had made no progress on recovering her passport, and advised her to cancel the flight she'd scheduled for Tuesday.

Half an hour later Margo, Audrey, and their mother were on the way to Tel Aviv. To the American embassy.

Really not his turf, they were told by the one embassy official they were able to hunt up late Sunday afternoon—although Sunday was an Israeli workday, the embassy maintained U.S. hours. Why not enjoy being in Tel Aviv and do some sight-seeing and shopping, then come back tomorrow when the *proper* official would be able to give her more information?

"Unctuous prick," Audrey fumed as they left the building. She passed the same judgment on the man they saw on Monday, who told her to return the next day.

In between the meetings at the embassy, they visited museums and strolled down the city streets. An arts festival was taking place, and they caught a dance performance by a French troupe that was so breathtaking Margo was able to forget for a few hours that they were fighting for her sister's freedom to go home.

By Tuesday morning, however, she gave up any pretense of acting like a tourist. Before leaving Safed, she had picked up the files she'd requested from Lev Blum. While her mother and Audrey went shopping she plopped the file folders—half a dozen of them—on her bed in the hotel, and dug in.

It wasn't, Lev had said when he handed her the bursting folders, that Batsheva found so much criminal activity among her neighbors; a given article didn't represent a specific instance of wrongdoing. She was simply interested in ethical issues in general and collected information about them.

About half the material was in English. Margo skimmed articles about medical technology, international trade, and problems that arose when the customs of an immigrant subculture conflicted with the dominant culture. Predictably, there were quite a few articles that dealt with Jewish-Arab relations.

Nothing, however, rang a bell. Maybe the hot information was hidden in one of the notes Batsheva had penned in the margins, sometimes in English and sometimes in Hebrew? She set aside the Hebrew-annotated articles, along with those written in Hebrew, for Audrey to check.

After a lunch that none of them tasted, they made a third visit to the embassy. Audrey was told that the wheels were turning to retrieve her passport. This time she was given a date: within a week.

As they left the man's office Margo waited for her sister to say, "Unctuous prick." But Audrey was silent.

"Unctuous prick," Margo said on her behalf; it didn't feel the same.

"You know, you don't have to stay. You could both go home."

"All for one, and one for all." Alice embraced her; and Audrey sagged against her body. A born scrapper, she seemed utterly defeated.

Alice still didn't know—Audrey hadn't wanted to worry her more—about the problems Audrey's son was having. He had developed a skin rash after he heard that she couldn't fly home on the day she'd promised; it would have been today, Margo realized. Zach again wet his bed nightly; and every night Margo tried to comfort Audrey when she cried in bed.

Their mother-son bond made Margo think of another mother and son. The discovery of the bootleg-video operation had focused her attention away from Gadi Halevi. But it was Gadi, more than anyone, who had felt injured by Batsheva. And if his reasons for being on Mount Meron on Erev Lag B'Omer were innocent, then why had he lied?

Although she had a vivid sense of Gadi, Margo had never had more than a brief, superficial conversation with him. Her impression of him came primarily from other people's stories, most of which involved, in one way or another, his relationship with Batsheva. What was he like in his own element, out of his mother's shadow?

She checked the pocket of her wallet where she threw coupons, cards, and various detritus. There it was, under her ticket stub from the dance concert—the business card for Gadi's store in Tel Aviv.

If you grew up in Safed, did it infuse you with, if not a sense of God's presence, at least a sense of beauty that stayed with you forever? Did Gadi, passing his days in a drab shop in a less-than-bustling Tel Aviv neighborhood, feel visually starved?

Knowing that he sold cellular phones, Margo had expected some equivalent of an American electronics store, hardly lovely but with its own gleaming chrome-and-glass aesthetic. Instead, she and Audrey (having left Alice lounging happily by the hotel pool) entered a claustrophobically small storefront with too many empty spaces on the shelves, the sign of a business that couldn't afford to order new merchandise until it moved what it already had in stock.

Although he was alone behind the counter, Gadi insisted on closing the store for the rest of the afternoon to show them around. "Have you been to Jaffa yet?" he asked. "Oh, you have? It doesn't matter. I know places there you would never find."

Jaffa's cobbled streets and picturesque galleries and shops reminded Margo strongly of Safed. When she said so, however, Gadi protested.

"Safed is so stuck in the past, if you tried to take its pulse, you wouldn't find one. Everyone looks backward. I don't just mean the Hasidim. The artists, too, they're content in their little provincial town. Cigarette?"

"No, thanks."

He lit one for himself. "Jaffa, you know why it's so attractive and so many people come here? Because it's a smart commercial venture. Businessmen looked at this place when it was nothing but dirty ruins, and they had the vision to see stores and restaurants right on the sea. They were seeing the future, not the past. In Jaffa, the heartbeat doesn't come from a bunch of rabbis who died centuries ago. It comes straight from Tel Aviv. Here, this is a great café. Do you want a drink? A coffee? My treat."

Over drinks, he regaled them with plans for the restaurant he intended to open in Jaffa. How many square meters, the elegant decor, the kinds of drinks he'd serve.

"Do you have a location picked out?" Margo asked.

"Not yet. I need two adjacent storefronts. I have to wait until the right spots become available. I've already decided on the chef. I'll have to lure him away from a place near Ha-Bimah, you know, the national theater. . . ."

Margo could hardly bear even to ask polite questions. The posh restaurant was so obviously a fantasy, and Gadi's need to appear important rawly obvious as well.

A sweet temper, a weak nature, and the belief that life owed him something had, according to Bernice, characterized Gadi even as a child. Still, Margo wondered what he might have become without the time in prison and the sense of betrayal he'd felt when Batsheva wouldn't help him. Was that why his relatives were protecting him now?

Audrey, dispirited, barely spoke. Margo waited until she went to the ladies' room to say, "You know we're still trying to get my sister's passport back. Can you help us at all?"

"I might know a few people," Gadi said. "You want me to make some calls?"

"I meant, did you see anything on Mount Meron?"

"On Erev Lag B'Omer? Sorry, I wasn't there." Not a hint of nervousness.

"Oh, I thought I heard . . ."

He didn't even take the bait and demand to know who'd told her. "When I was growing up, I couldn't wait to get away from Safed. Believe me, hanging out at a rabbi's tomb has never been my idea of a good time."

She had wanted to see how coolly he'd lie. She wondered if he'd do as well with Pincus and Efrati, after they returned to Safed and told the police that he'd been spotted on Meron.

Feeling a little as if they were on the lam (although it was a small country; and they kept the police informed of where to reach them), they spent the next two days making the long-delayed visit to Alice's cousins in Jerusalem—"Not more than an hour from Tel Aviv!" Alice said. "And they might forgive me for not coming sooner if I bring my daughters!"

Alice's cousins were gracious hosts. They were also the most dynamic septuagenarians Margo had ever met, chattering constantly in Hebrew and Hungarian; their sturdy legs pumping as they led the way to museums and through the Old City. Alice had no trouble keeping up with them. Only surface bruises seemed to remain from her brush with death.

"How do they do it?" Margo moaned. She and Audrey, both conceding that they were wimps, had begged off a stroll through the Ben-Yehuda Mall after dinner Wednesday night.

"Coffee," Audrey said.

"I drink coffee. Well, usually decaf after the middle of the day."

"See, that's our problem. Did you say you had some things in Hebrew for me to look at?"

Margo handed her the Hebrew articles she'd set aside from

Batsheva's files, and resumed her study of the English-language articles.

The story about the international crime of video pirating was in English. So was the note Batsheva had written on it.

Talk to Danny, it said.

Forty /

Nili wiggled her toes, aware of her red-painted toenails but unable to see them. It was too early, still too dark to distinguish colors. Besides, all of her concentration was focused on another sense, her sense of hearing, as she knelt beneath a window at four A.M.

She had guessed right in what she'd made up about the tragic lovers, at least partly. One of them was already married. Maybe she had recognized something about the married one without being aware of it. Although if someone had told her the name, she wouldn't have believed it!

She didn't know who they were until she saw them for the second time, on Friday night. So upset about Gadi that she couldn't sleep, she had gone out at two A.M. and walked and walked. She'd recognized the shape of them as they clung together. Then she realized she had forgotten to take off her hated glasses and she could see them; this time, they hadn't seen her.

Since then, she couldn't stop thinking about them. She had gone out looking for them again, but it must have gotten too dangerous for them to be together. It was probably still dangerous, but they felt that without each other, they would die.

Both of them were crying. Nili thought her own heart would break, knowing that no matter how much they loved each other, they could never be together. Knowing that if they found her now, they would hate her for the rest of their lives. She would never be able to make them understand how tenderly she felt toward them, how their doomed love and her mother's death and her decision to dedicate her life to writing all went together like instruments in a symphony that was beautiful and sad.

The spring when I was sixteen years old, she would say someday, when she was very famous and she was being interviewed, *my life changed forever. That was when I stopped being a child.*

Part Five /
Torah

Organized religion is our attempt to keep visions of other worlds present in this one. And this is why the religious endeavor tangles us in self-contradiction. For to speak of the other world in the language of this world is impossible.

Judaism focuses on the point where two worlds meet: Sinai. And the inscrutable record of that encounter: Torah.

Rabbi Lawrence Kushner, *Honey from the Rock*

Forty-one /

"I was knocked to the ground!" the rabbi would say when he told people about the tragedy at the Abuhav Synagogue six days before Shavuot.

After the morning service, he shooed everyone from the synagogue and locked the door. He said the Sh'ma. Then he opened the ark upon the synagogue's great treasure, the Torah written by Rabbi Yitzhak Abuhav in Spain five hundred years earlier. It was the rabbi's privilege to prepare the Torah for the three holy days each year on which it was read.

He reached for the wooden box in which the Torah reposed and lifted the box from the ark. The holy text was such a joy to hold; it weighed no more than a feather! Gently he lowered the box to the table and opened it.

The first doubt entered his mind. He had had this honor for only two years, had gazed so closely at the precious Torah no more than half a dozen times. But something alerted him, and as he turned the spindle to advance the holy text he was filled with dread.

Later he would say that from within the box, he felt a rush of air. That he was knocked down by God's angry breath.

For a moment, as he regained consciousness, he didn't understand why he was lying on the floor of the synagogue. Then he remembered and a fresh wave of faintness assailed him. He forced himself to remain conscious.

At the ancient temple in Jerusalem, the high priest was the only person permitted to enter the Holy of Holies. When he did so, a rope was tied around his ankle; should he die of a heart attack while inside, his body could be retrieved without placing anyone in danger.

There was no rope around the rabbi's ankle. He sat on the floor until he felt able to stand. Slowly—feeling as if in only minutes he had become an old man—he pulled himself to his feet. He examined more of the scroll, suppressing his tears lest they wet it. Then he closed the box, returned it to the ark, and locked the ark.

Only then did he leave the synagogue and run to share the terrible news.

"The Torah was blank?" Audrey said. They'd returned from Jerusalem just in time to have Shabbat dinner at Bernice's and to hear the story that had brought people running from their homes and businesses to the courtyard of the Abuhav Synagogue. Even the most secular residents of Safed, Danny told them, were drawn there, united in shock and grief.

"Completely blank," Danny responded. "As if to mock the mystics who say there's as much meaning in the white spaces between the letters as in the letters themselves," Danny responded. "Now there's virtually nothing but white space."

Some people claimed the "erasure" of the Abuhav Torah was an act of God, Danny said, a punishment for the sinful times in which we live. As the story of the letterless Torah had spread that afternoon, all of the synagogues had filled with people praying. Many of the very devout had undertaken a fast until Shavuot six days from now, or until God made the letters reappear.

"What most people think," said Bernice, "is that God had nothing to do with this. The Torah must have been stolen and sold to a private collector. A fake Torah was substituted to give the thief more time to get away." Especially, she added, since text appeared in sharp, clear letters on the several inches of the scroll that would have been seen if someone had simply opened the Torah box and closed it again.

"Why was the Torah in a box?" Margo broke in. She had only partly followed the conversation. *Talk to Danny.* Why had Batsheva written that on an article about bootleg videotapes? "Don't Torahs have cloth covers? And they're all rolled up. Wouldn't you have to unroll it before you could see any text?''

"You're thinking of Ashkenazic Torahs," Danny said. "Sephardic Torahs are kept in wooden or metal boxes. They're the shape of the Torah and they're often beautifully decorated. The spindles or rollers are part of the box, and the Torah stays inside the box when you read it. When the box is open, you see a column of text.''

"The six-hundred-thirteenth *mitzvah*," Alice said. All through dinner, she'd been distracted and dreamy.

"What?" Margo asked.

"The Torah has six hundred and thirteen *mitzvot*—commandments," her mother explained. "The final *mitzvah*—number six hundred thirteen—is that in your lifetime, you should write a Torah.''

"Do people who are religious actually do that?"

"Usually you just contribute so a scribe can write or restore a Torah. It's an incredible task. For a trained scribe, it takes about a year. I've even heard that every time you write the name of God, you're supposed to bathe in a *mikve*.'' Alice shook her head. "This gives me such a feeling. Not exactly déjà vu. Just that I've been thinking about Torahs for days. Do you ever feel that God is calling you to do something? Lately—I don't understand it—I've felt called to fulfill the six-hundred-thirteenth *mitzvah*. To write a Torah before I die.''

"I don't think the person who stole the Abuhav Torah was trying to fulfill any *mitzvot*," Danny said.

"No, and I can't tell you why it feels connected. Maybe I should see Hillel Gebman and make sure my brains didn't get scrambled." She tried to make it a joke, but she looked troubled. "It's been a long day. I think I'll lie down and read.''

"Do you feel called? Is that why you're studying to be a rabbi?" Margo asked Danny. She had volunteered to wash the dishes, and he'd quickly offered to dry.

Batsheva could have meant another Danny. Israel must be swarming with Dannys—but how many who had drawn back guiltily when Margo came upon them engaged in an intense conversation with Bruce?

"I feel called all the time," he said. "For instance, at the moment I feel called to ask you what's up."

"Other than a Torah being stolen and my sister being a murder suspect?" she said, her hands plunged in dishwater.

"Other than that. Is it anything I can help with, or should I just ignore the fact that you keep looking like you're going to cry?"

Talk to Danny. Had that been Batsheva's fatal mistake? Margo should probably give the information to Ronit to help with her investigation, or mention it to Audrey's attorney.

She dried her hands, took the article from the pocket of her sundress, and unfolded it so he could see the headline and the note.

"Are you the Danny she wanted to talk to?" she said.

"Sure am." He'd hesitated only a moment. And he didn't ask what "she" Margo was talking about.

"How come?"

"I'd like to learn to mediate. Batsheva and I used to discuss hypothetical cases—whether something might be acceptable morally even if it was against the law. Or vice versa, if something could be totally legal but still morally wrong. You don't have to look hard to find examples of that. We talked about whether to intervene and the best way to do it. Why don't I wash the rest of these, and you dry?"

"Sure." The relief she felt was palpable. She could easily imagine Danny Rubicoff finding out about the bootleg operation and seeking advice, just as all of her instincts had screamed that he couldn't be involved in the crime. "So you and Batsheva talked about what to do if you found out someone was making bootleg videos? What did you decide?"

"Assuming this was a basically decent person, we thought it would be best to ask them to destroy the videos and get rid of the equipment for making them."

"With the implication that if they didn't do it, you'd have to tell the police?"

He devoted great attention to a serving bowl he was washing.

"You *would* tell the police, wouldn't you?"

"In Deuteronomy," he said, "there's the statement 'Justice, justice you shall pursue.' Martin Buber writes about a very wise rabbi who was asked why the word 'justice' was repeated. The rabbi said it's because you don't achieve a righteous end by unrighteous means; both means and end have to be just. Have you ever reported someone you know to the police?''

"I've never known anyone making bootleg videos. Unless you and Batsheva decided it wasn't morally wrong?''

Bernice's dishes were going to be spotless, she thought as he energetically scoured a pot.

"It's not that I agree with people who say bootlegging is a victimless crime because it only hurts multinational corporations. I'm aware of intellectual-property rights, and the fact that every time someone buys a bootleg tape, they cheat actors and writers out of royalties. If bootlegging were the only thing these people—this person—did, I'd definitely go to the police. But what if the person does something else that's really important, and if you turn them in for bootlegging, you prevent them from doing the good work?''

"Like starting a crafts cooperative in an Arab village?''

"Let's sit down,'' Danny said. "You want a glass of wine?''

"Soda.''

He poured a soda for her and wine for himself.

"Did you tell Bruce and Nancy you'd report them if they didn't destroy the tapes by a certain time?'' she asked.

He smiled ruefully. "I have a few things to learn about mediating. They haven't destroyed the tapes. But they haven't sold them, either.''

"How do you know?''

"I check two or three times a week.'' He sounded miserable. "I've talked about it with them several times. They're thinking about doing the right thing.''

"Or waiting until you leave Safed and can't check on them anymore.''

"I know I have to do something before I leave. I wish Batsheva were here.''

"When did you talk to her the first time?''

"Five or six weeks ago. I used the wrong door in the flower children's house when I was looking for the bathroom. It was supposed to be locked.''

"Did you tell Batsheva who was doing the bootlegging?" Ronit had arrived on the scene about a month ago. Was that because Batsheva had summoned the authorities?

"I didn't name names. She might have guessed. But if you're thinking they killed her to keep her from reporting them, it doesn't make any sense. If Bruce and Nancy were capable of murder—and I don't think they are—why not kill me? But really, I don't think it's in them."

"What are you going to do now?" Margo asked.

"I guess I'll give them until I come back after Shavuot. That's just one more week."

"Where are you going?"

"To Jerusalem, to make trouble. You haven't heard about this? The tradition on Erev Shavuot is to stay up all night and study. At dawn, thousands of people go to pray at the Western Wall. Every year a group of men and women pray there together—Reform and Conservative Jews, also some modern Orthodox. The *haredim* spit on them and yell. Women praying with men, it's kind of a Jewish version of a sit-in at a lunch counter. You want to go?"

"No, and don't you dare encourage my mother."

Forty-two /

Dalia arrived twenty minutes late, clutching an art portfolio under her arm.

"Sorry, sorry!" she said. "When you called yesterday and asked if you could look at drawings to buy, I didn't know I would have to—"

"We didn't mind waiting," Alice assured her. "We sat and admired your flowers."

"I'm sorry." Dalia rummaged in her pocket for her keys. In her haste to unlock the door, she lost her grip on the portfolio; she hadn't tied it carefully and half a dozen drawings scattered on the ground. She let out a wail.

Alice put her arm around the artist. "Don't move. Margo and Audrey will pick up the drawings. We've come at a bad time. We'll leave you alone."

"It's all right. Come in. Please. It's just that this is just so upsetting for all of us who live in Safed," she said, when they were sitting in her living room.

"The Abuhav Torah?" Alice said.

Dalia lit a cigarette. "The Torah. The officials from eight different branches of the government who all decided they had to come here and say something. The delegation of rabbis that arrived for Shabbat. Most of them, the officials and the rabbis, all they care about is to get their faces on television with the Abuhav Synagogue in the background. And the reporters! Every time you walk down Jerusalem Street, someone asks you how you feel about the Abuhav Torah. You know what a lot of people say? You know about the Torah, what's supposed to happen to anyone who even looks at it at the wrong time? People say they hope whoever took it will die a horrible death. Friends of mine, people I've known for years, they want vengeance." She ashed the cigarette into a saucer already full of butts.

"And I keep getting calls from dealers," she continued. "Not just in Israel but in New York, Los Angeles. Everyone wants my drawings of the Abuhav. A gallery I tried to get into for years, now they have to have a one-woman show. Business is booming," she said bleakly. "Oh, I forgot! You want soda? Coffee?"

"I'll get it," Margo offered. "Soda okay for everyone?"

If Dalia was considered the most efficient woman in Safed, she'd hate to see the least, Margo thought as she navigated among unwashed dishes and food in varying states of rot. She found a couple of bottles of soda in the refrigerator and washed four glasses; having gone that far, she scraped the decayed food into the trash can and stacked the dirty dishes by the sink. She would have washed them, but feared Dalia would be offended.

When she returned to the living room, Dalia had brought several thick portfolios to the table. The detailed synagogue drawings were lovely. Alice, Audrey, and Margo took their time deciding. Dalia smoked.

"Do you sell any like this?" Margo indicated one of the drawings on Dalia's wall; less precise than her synagogue pieces, it had more energy.

"I mostly do those for myself. But I have some you can see." She took another portfolio from a shelf. "Ai, the phone!"

"Is she always so nervous?" Margo whispered to her mother, after Dalia raced into the back of the house to answer the telephone.

"Dalia's a racehorse. I'm sure that's what makes her a good artist. And who wouldn't be upset, with the terrible things that have happened here? Do you like this?"

"Mm, yes. I wish she did more of the nonsynagogue drawings. But I guess she has to focus on what will sell."

"There's another portfolio over there," Audrey said. "Why don't we look?"

"We should ask," said Alice, but Audrey had already snagged the portfolio from a shelf.

"Has she ever been married?" Margo asked.

"Dalia? No."

"A boyfriend? A girlfriend?"

"She has a boyfriend."

"Really?" Audrey paged through the portfolio she'd opened. "Does she ever take him out in public?"

"Girls! I shouldn't have mentioned it. It's none of our business. Oh! Oh!"

"Mom, what is it?" her daughters said in unison. Alice had gone pale.

"That drawing."

The pen-and-ink drawing Audrey had flipped to showed a long-skirted woman, her back to the viewer as she walked down an alley in the Old City.

"This is silly," Alice said. "It's just that I had a strong sense of déjà vu. But everything lately seems to give me déjà vu. The Torah being stolen, this drawing."

"Do you think you saw the drawing on the day you got sick?" Audrey asked.

Alice shrugged. "Maybe I saw the drawing. Maybe I saw the woman. Dalia really captured her, didn't she? It's so simple, but I feel like I know her life story. I want that one." She added it to several synagogue drawings she'd selected.

Dalia refused to sell the drawing of the woman, however. It was one she'd done for herself, like everything in that portfolio; she would have told them if they'd asked, she said, jamming the drawings back in. Did they take anything else from that portfolio? she said, and scanned the drawings they'd picked despite their apologies and denials.

"Dalia, could my mom have seen that drawing on the day she got sick?" Margo ignored her mother's glare.

"Not if she came when I was here and I showed her my work." The only way Alice would have seen the drawing was by snooping, she implied.

"That boyfriend of Dalia's," Margo said as they walked back to Bernice's, each of them carrying a cardboard tube containing several drawings. "Is it a boyfriend she's not supposed to have? Like a married man?" *Like Yosef,* she added to herself.

"Poor Dalia. I hope not. She turned forty this year, and she's dying to get married and have a child."

"Don't you know who he is?"

"I never saw him and she never said. It's just . . . This makes me feel like a voyeur. Staying in her guest room for a month, sometimes I couldn't help but hear."

"What if she realized you knew about the boyfriend—maybe you saw him *and* the drawing that afternoon—and she wanted to get you to leave Safed?"

"And she poisoned me? It didn't make me leave, did it? It just brought both of my inquisitive daughters here. Besides, why go to so much trouble when all she had to do was ask me to keep her secret?"

"She might not have realized."

"Speaking of biological clocks, I've been very good up until now about not asking you how yours is doing."

"Mo-om!"

Alice had distracted her as skillfully as when Margo was six and wanted the most sugary cereal at the grocery store.

Nevertheless, she had a gut feeling the henbane could have come from Dalia, who might not have understood that Alice was too discreet to tell tales about her landlady's love life. And what about Batsheva? Could she have known about Dalia's inappropriate lover? Or, if Dalia was responsible for the henbane, had Batsheva learned about that?

Margo planned to mention it to the attorney the next day. But the attorney greeted them with big news: Audrey's passport was being returned. She should have it back before Shavuot.

"See! I was right to go to the embassy!" Audrey said. (The attorney had advised her to wait.)

"Actually," he replied, "I think what happened is the police have too many other things on their hands."

"Because of the Torah being stolen?"

"Because of the arrests they made last night. Some people you know."

The attorney, who had a flair for drama, waited for Audrey to ask, "Who?"

"A Canadian couple. They were making bootleg video-tapes. Their Israeli distributor was arrested, too." He paused, then dropped the distributor's name. "Gadi Halevi."

In a city already shaken by the disappearance of the Abuhav Torah, business virtually stopped and housewives left meals half-prepared as they discussed the latest crime in their midst—and the local boy who had gone over to the *sitra ahra.* The other side.

It was a blessing in a way, people said, that Batsheva was no longer alive to feel the shame.

That led people to remember the last time Gadi Halevi had brought shame on his family, and to wonder how deeply he had yielded to the evil impulse this time. Didn't he go to prison once for selling antiquities? they asked. A habitual criminal with his finger in who knew how many illegal goings-on, a man who had already shown disrespect for his nation's heritage—would it not require such a person to commit the sacrilege of stealing the Abuhav Torah?

When it became known that Gadi was seen on Mount Meron on the night his mother was killed, people began to speculate about a third crime, even more terrible. They wondered if Batsheva had found out about her son's latest wrongdoing and tried to stop him. Everyone knew Batsheva would have reported him to the police; look how she'd reacted when Gadi was scarcely more than a boy. What if this time Gadi had stopped her?

They began to see Batsheva's horrible, unnatural death as the first sign of the Torah's power.

Forty-three /

"If I could go to jail in his place, I would do it. I would! My mother always talked about *lashon ha-ra,* avoiding gossip. Everyone in this city acts so holy, but the way they're gossiping, Gadi committed every crime that's happened in Safed. Someone had ten shekels stolen at Purim two years ago? Gadi Halevi took it. A boy came by on a bicycle, riding too fast, and knocked over an old man? It must have been Gadi Halevi."

"Nili, Nili." Audrey rubbed her back while Margo looked around Nili's bedroom and found a box of tissues for the weeping girl. "You love your brother very much. You'd never believe anything bad about him."

"Yes, I would! I believe he was going to sell those videotapes. He admits it—maybe not to the police, but he told us. That was why he went to Meron on Erev Lag B'Omer. He talked to the people who sold audiotapes there, because a lot of them sell videos, too. He was asking it they wanted to buy from him. That was why he didn't want anyone to know he was there. But he would never take the Abuhav Torah. He isn't very religious, but he knows how dangerous it would be. It's dangerous even to look at the Torah at the wrong time. And my mother. He wouldn't. He never saw her!"

"Please!" Nili said. "You have to help me."

"We'll only be in Safed for a few more days."

"But until you go, you and your sister, can't you keep asking questions?"

"Yes, of course."

• • •

"You told her what?" Margo said. While Nili went to get cold drinks, Audrey had translated the conversation.

"I said we'd help her."

"Audi, I'm sorry for Nili and her family, but how can we believe a word Gadi says? The guy's one of the smoothest liars I've ever met."

"I think Gadi's a jerk, but do you really see him as a murderer?"

"Don't you? He's a con man."

"Right, he's a minor-league con man. He likes to make deals. That's what he was doing when he tried to sell stuff from the archaeological dig ten years ago. Same thing with the bootleg videos. But I think Nili has a point. Gadi's involvement in one crime is making everyone think he committed the other crimes, too."

"Come on. You don't think he stole the Abuhav Torah?"

"The Torah, probably. But to kill his mother? He's not that kind of criminal."

"This is what my father thinks," Nili said in English as she returned to the room. She handed them sodas and sat crosslegged on the bed. "My father says," she continued, switching back to Hebrew, "that Gadi cares most about comfort, and it's no big deal for him to steal from a giant company that makes videos. It doesn't feel like stealing, it just feels like doing business." Margo wondered if Lev had stated his own opinion, and if that was why he'd been so coy when she had asked about Batsheva's mediation cases.

"But to kill a person," Nili said, "he says you have to feel something passionately. He says that for Gadi, that would be too much work."

"Lev's right," Audrey said after she finished translating.

"Can we talk to Lev? Is he at home today?" Margo started to get up, but Nili had already zipped out the door.

She came back with her father, who pulled up a chair beside the bed.

"Did Batsheva know about the video bootlegging?" Margo asked him.

"Yes and no." Seemingly unconscious of what he was doing, Lev cradled Nili's stuffed turtle. His eyes were heavy with pain. Was Lev's analysis of his stepson's character so astute because he felt the kind of passion Gadi lacked? "She knew someone in Safed was doing it. She didn't know who," he said. "She had no idea Gadi was involved."

"Are you sure she didn't find out it was Bruce and Nancy, and try to talk to them?"

"Danny was going to try to mediate. She wouldn't have interfered."

"Why not?" Audrey asked. "She didn't mind interfering with all kinds of things."

Be nice or shut up! said the look Margo shot her sister. This was no time to parade her antipathy toward Batsheva.

"You didn't understand her. Look." He dropped the stuffed turtle and stood up. "What has my daughter talked you into doing?"

"Interfering," Margo said, smiling. "Just a few more questions?"

Lev managed a half smile.

"Sunday afternoon, before Erev Lag B'Omer, you had a meeting here, right? A group of doctors? Who was at the meeting?"

"You're thinking, they're medical people who would know about Pavulon?" Lev said.

"I don't know. I'm thinking, Batsheva would have had a chance to talk to one of them."

He shrugged. "Hillel Gebman was here. You've met him, of course. Also another doctor, Raya Davidov, she's a Russian immigrant. And Ma'ayan Gilboa."

"Ma'ayan? Are you doing something with herbal medicine?"

"Ma'ayan's training is in public health. I think I told you, we're planning a health education program for Russian immigrants. But there were no suspicious absences. No one left the meeting to make a phone call, was gone for half an hour, and came back looking upset. Anything else I can tell you?"

After Lev had left, Margo asked Nili, "In your diary, did you write about any of those people? Hillel Gebman or Raya Davidov or Ma'ayan?"

Especially Ma'ayan. How long would it have taken, on the afternoon of Erev Lag B'Omer, for Batsheva to draw Ma'ayan aside and suggest she had given Alice the henbane, whether by accident or for reasons Batsheva might have guessed? And then—had the herbalist turned to her knowledge of Western medicine?

Although Nili seemed proficient enough in English to understand the question, she looked confused. Audrey translated.

"I didn't write about any of them," Nili said.

"Would you mind if we looked at your diary?"

"Margo!" Audrey cried.

"How could you ask, after her mother already violated her confidence by reading it?" Audrey scolded her as they walked toward the Artists' Quarter.

"How could you ask me to help and then keep getting in my way?"

"I wasn't getting in your way. In spite of that nasty look you gave me. You think I'm some kind of tactless bulldozer, don't you? That crack you made about us playing good cop, bad cop. You think I'm the bad cop—"

"What crack?"

"When we were leaving the police station."

Margo drew a blank.

"The day after we got here," Audrey said.

"Audrey, that was over two weeks ago. I don't think you're tactless. But I do have some professional training in doing interviews, not that you ever give me credit for having a real job."

Margo couldn't have reconstructed the argument, how the emotional volume amplified and the content deteriorated. There was something about their father's mother's candlesticks that they'd both wanted but Audrey got, and a bitter exchange over Margo's living on the other edge of the continent and only visiting when it was convenient, whereas Audrey came running whenever Alice needed her—and yet, which of her daughters did Alice love best?

It all happened in five minutes. By the end, Margo couldn't stand the sight of her sister. Audrey must have felt the same. She strode beside Margo but kept the width of the cobbled alleyway between them. At the Ma'alot Olei HaGardom, Audrey took off to the left, toward the Jerusalem Street mall. Margo, seething, turned right.

She shouldn't have gone to see Ma'ayan alone. Fueled by the fight with her sister, however, she felt ready to take on a barrelful of bears.

As it turned out, Margo didn't have to confront Ma'ayan Gilboa. The danger was of a different kind.

Ma'ayan had taken their youngest child to a doctor's appointment this morning, Yosef told her. He invited Margo in and gave her a friendly hug. The hug somehow became an embrace.

Forty-four /

Monday—the 47th day of the counting of the Omer

She had wondered how kissing Yosef would feel. It felt exciting, wild . . .

And absolutely forbidden.

She didn't know which of them pulled away first, and for a moment she didn't realize that the tears wetting her face weren't hers.

"I should go," she said.

"Wait. Wait." Yosef was weeping too hard to speak.

Maybe she should stay and clear the air.

Margo, don't be a fool! Get out of here.

"Outside. We'll sit outside." Sobbing, he stumbled into the courtyard, to the wicker table beneath the pergola where Margo had first talked to Ma'ayan, the woman they had almost betrayed.

Who cares about Ma'ayan? What about Barry?

How much betrayal is one kiss? Yes, but would it have stopped at one kiss if he'd wanted to go on?

"Water? Can I have some water?" he got out.

"Um. Okay." She went into the spotless kitchen and ran a glass of water. Was this a ploy to get her back in the house? Not that Yosef seemed like a man who'd need ploys. That thought kindled a memory of his kiss—a visceral memory that made Margo's body tingle. She hurried back outside.

Yosef hadn't moved from the table. She handed him the glass of water and a box of tissues she'd snatched on her way through the house. His tears subsided as he drank.

"Are you okay now?" She moved to leave.

"Please. I haven't been able to tell anyone. Please," he said again as she hesitated.

She took the chair opposite him, the table between them.

"I don't do this—try to make love to other women," he said, then added sheepishly, "well, not for a long time. But Ma'ayan . . ."

That was why she'd come here, Margo dimly recalled. To find out about his wife. She took a deep breath and tried to silence the panicky voice—*what have you done? what were you about to do?*—that kept chattering in her mind.

"You hear everyone talk about how different Ma'ayan is from way she used to be?" Yosef said.

"She's nothing like the way my mother described her."

"Did you guess why?"

"No," Margo lied. She thought of her suspicion that Ma'ayan was having an affair. Was that why Yosef had come on to her? Sauce for the gander? Had that been *her* motivation?

"Prozac," he said.

The answer was so diffferent from what she'd expected that for a moment she thought he'd slipped into Hebrew.

"The antidepressant?"

He nodded and mopped with a tissue at a few fresh tears. "All the time I've known Ma'ayan, there is a sadness to her. I thought it was her nature to be sad and shy, the way it's my nature to like parties and cafés and having people around. But four years ago—please, she doesn't want anyone to know this—she tried to kill herself. You see how she always wears shirts with long sleeves?" He gulped the rest of the water. "After that, she got help from a psychiatrist. Different treatments. Drugs, psychoanalysis. Herbs, too. That's how she got interested in herbal medicine, she doesn't like putting chemicals in her body. Sometimes she was happier, sometimes not so much. Last month, the doctor convinced her to try Prozac."

"It must be working. Everyone says she's much more outgoing and confident than she used to be."

"Yes, it works great," he said miserably. "At the very beginning, when she was adjusting to it, she couldn't sleep. She was tense. She got angry at me and the kids a lot. Remember I told you I was away from home the night before your mother got sick? Ma'ayan and I had a terrible fight and I went out. Since then, the Prozac works better. Ma'ayan is happier. Stronger." He sighed.

"And you don't like that?"

"I want Ma'ayan to be happy. I want it more than anything in the world. When she tried to kill herself, I thought I would die. But it's like she's a different person than the one I married. I have to change now. Do you understand?"

"Oh. Oh." Now Margo was crying. Weeping, sobbing, blubbering, she didn't think she'd cried so hard for years.

"I'm sorry!" Yosef pushed the box of tissues across the table to her. "Please, tell me what's wrong." She couldn't speak, and he went on, "Are you upset that I don't love you? I think you're very nice. You're—I wish I had more words in English!"

"No! No!" She was laughing as well as crying, "I don't love you, either. Really." She knew without having to ponder it that her feelings toward Yosef were utterly uncomplicated— fondness seasoned with a significant dash of lust. Between tears, she continued, "It's just . . . It's all the times I couldn't let myself cry. I had to be tough when I came here because my mother needed me. Now I have to be tough for Audrey. And I was in a fire. And it's . . . it's . . ." *More than anything.* "What you said about Ma'ayan not being the person you married and you're the one who has to adjust to that. Oh!" She was sobbing again.

"Wait, don't leave!" Yosef ran inside. He came back with a big glass of water for her.

"Has your husband changed?" he asked when the latest storm abated.

"Not at all. But my idea of him. Something I found out. He didn't cheat on me, it happened before he ever knew me." She paused to blow her nose. Then she told Yosef the whole story. Barry's one-night stand, who it was with, how she'd found out, and how it had made her feel. It was more than she'd told Audrey. More than she had shared with anyone but her counselor.

Before she left, she collected her thoughts enough to wonder how much the Prozac *had* changed Ma'ayan. She was bouncing off the wall when Margo had met her two weeks ago. Had her judgment been affected?

"Yosef, I have to ask you something. If Ma'ayan wasn't sleeping while she adjusted to the Prozac, could she have made a mistake with the tea for my mother?" Ma'ayan had waved a plastic bag of herbs and said it was Alice's tea; but if she were trying to cover up a mistake, wouldn't she do exactly that?

Yosef shook his head emphatically. "Ma'ayan is a perfectionist. Prozac makes her a better perfectionist."

"I hope you won't be insulted if I ask one more thing. Could Ma'ayan have given my mother the henbane on purpose?"

His response was immediate. "Why?"

It was the same question Margo found it impossible to answer. And hardly the biggest issue currently clamoring for her attention.

"Will you tell your husband about this?" Yosef asked as she put on her sunglasses to hide the signs of weeping before she went into the street.

"About our talk?"

"We didn't just talk."

"Yes, but—"

"I thought what hurt you most about what he did was that he didn't tell you."

Gulp. "Yosef, you're a wise man. Maybe you're one of the *lamed-vav tzaddikim*."

He laughed. "In that case, the world is in trouble."

They almost hugged, but both thought better of it.

Back at Bernice's, Margo went to bed with a headache (a real one, after all the weeping).

To her surprise, she didn't feel guilty and scared about "the kiss," as she found herself thinking of it. Illogically, primitively—comfortingly—she felt instead as if she'd evened the score.

Forty-five /

Nili hadn't expected to find them together, so close to daybreak—so close to when his family would wake up. But she had crept beneath the window just in case. At first they talked too quietly for her to hear. Then their voices rose in desperation.

"We have to leave the country now!" she said. "We can't wait any longer."

"You're right. It's not safe for you to stay," he replied.

"Not safe for *me*? Are you saying you won't go with me?"

"Of course I will. Just not immediately. How can I?"

"How can you? You put a toothbrush and a change of underwear in a bag, we take your car to the airport, and we get on the next plane to Canada."

"My love, my love!"

Nili nearly fainted at the agony in his voice.

"We're going to spend today going around and saying goodbye to everyone," Margo informed Barry. She wasn't going to *tell* him anything, certainly not over a less-than-perfect international phone connection. But she wanted to hear his voice. "Tomorrow we drive to Jerusalem. Mom's cousins invited us for Shavuot. Then on Friday, at five A.M., I get on a plane and come home!"

"What do people do for Shavuot?" Barry asked.

"If you're not religious, the main thing is you eat cheesecake."

"Come on!"

"Okay, not necessarily cheesecake. But the tradition is to eat dairy foods. Of which cheesecake has to be the most important food group."

He laughed. "I love you."

"I love you," she responded.

She'd never stopped saying it or feeling it. But something—what?—had changed. What happened a moment later, however, drove that and all other thoughts from her mind.

"Another letter came from your mom," he said.

"It took weeks."

"It looks like someone stuck it on the sole of his shoe and walked all the way. You want me to open it?"

"Sure."

"Margo, it's dated the day she was poisoned."

"Oh, read it! Read it!"

"Please, darling, don't you see?" he said.

Who would have believed Dr. Gebman would say words like *darling*? Nili hugged herself, so glad that she hadn't betrayed him. Audrey's sister had asked her if she'd written anything in her diary about any of the people who'd met with her father before Erev Lag B'Omer—Dr. Gebman, Mrs. Gilboa, or Dr. Davidov. Nili didn't want to lie. Then she'd realized she didn't have to. She had never written the names of the secret lovers in her diary; until ten days ago she hadn't even known who they were.

"Darling, how can I leave with you," he said, "when we don't have any money?"

"We have money. He paid me part of it. It's enough to start with."

"Enough for you and me to make a start. But I have to leave enough to take care of—"

"She always comes first!"

Nili cringed at the pain in Dalia Weiss's voice—the pain she was turning against the man she adored.

"It's not just her," he said. "It's the children."

"*I* want to have your children. I would have had one already, if you hadn't—"

"In Canada, we can."

"You're never going to go to Canada with me. You never meant to."

"How can you say that, after . . ."

Dear Margo [Barry read over the phone],

Every day here is remarkable, but today I feel especially blessed. This afternoon I stopped in at Dalia's—you know, my landlady. I wanted to go through her drawings and pick out a few to buy. I've seen the work she exhibits locally, the synagogues. But she let me see all of her work, even things tucked in the corners of her studio. I found the most exquisite drawing. It's of a woman hurrying down the street—you only see her from the back but you know she's in a hurry. It's very simple, done with more fluid lines than the things that are Dalia's big sellers. I can't explain why it grabbed me the way it did. She was thrilled I chose that drawing because it's one of her favorites. She insists on giving it to me as a gift! She's going to frame it for me.

"You want to hear all this?" Barry asked.

"Yes!" Croaking the word through a tight throat, Margo realized how tense she felt. Was the drawing Alice had left for Dalia to frame the same one Dalia had refused to sell her yesterday? Was that the reason for Alice's sense of déjà vu?

Whether or not the drawing was the same, why had Dalia never delivered the gift she'd promised? And why had she denied seeing Alice on the day she'd drunk henbane?

They were angry now, harsh and accusing.

"How could you make a deal where you didn't get all the money on delivery?" he said.

"He insisted on having it authenticated before he'd pay the full amount."

"It's been three months. We were supposed to have the money and be able to leave weeks before Shavuot."

"Don't you think I know it's been three months? In fact, three months and five days?" Her voice was ragged.

"Shh," he said. "What about your lodger? Won't he hear?"

"He's in Jerusalem for Shavuot."

"He has no intention of paying you. You've been taken."

"What do *you* suggest I do?" Dalia shot back. "Hire an attorney and sue because I haven't received the money I was promised for stealing a Torah? I know! I'll say I have to be paid right now because my lover refuses to leave the country unless he can make sure his wife and kids will be millionaires."

Dalia stole the Torah? Nili was afraid she'd gasped out loud, but the lovers continued as if they hadn't heard her.

"Do you think this could be the Torah's curse?" he said.

"Don't talk to me about curses! It's because you believe nonsense like that, that you panicked."

That's not even the most wonderful thing that happened today!

You know there are 613 mitzvot—*commandments— in the Torah. The very last, the 613th, is to write a Torah scroll during your lifetime.*

It was the same thing her mother had brought up the other day. As Barry continued reading, however, the letter told an additional story, one that had vanished from Alice Simon's memory three weeks ago.

Imagine my amazement to find out Dalia is writing a Torah! When I was looking at her drawings, I noticed the scroll at the back of a shelf. She told me that from the time she was a child, she's been fascinated by the 613th mitzvah *and wanted to do her own Torah. She's doing it the hard way. (As if there were an easy way!) Rather than writing on separate sheets of parchment and then joining the edges of the sheets together to make a scroll, she created the entire scroll first. That's all she has so far, just the scroll with nothing written on it.*

"Omigod," Margo said.

She asked me to keep it a secret [Barry read], *because it's a very private project. Of course, I'll tell no one in Safed. I probably shouldn't tell you, but I'm in a strange mood tonight, sort of dreamy and wild. Too much sun? Anyway, I'm sure Dalia wouldn't mind my telling you.*

Isn't it wonderful that just when you think you "know" someone, you discover there's some dimension of them—something much deeper—that you never guessed at!

"*You* were the one who panicked," he said. "First, that insane idea about the henbane tea."

"What's insane about it? I thought if she got a little sick, she'd go home."

"A *little* sick."

"How could I know she'd be silly enough to take a walk instead of getting in bed like a sensible person, and that she'd fall down the Ma'alot Olei HaGardom? What was I supposed to do? Wait until the missing Torah was discovered, and then she could tell everyone, 'Oh, I saw Dalia with a blank Torah just like the one you found in place of the priceless Abuhav Torah?' "

"That was just one you did for practice, anyway. Why didn't you get rid of it?"

"I forgot, okay? How did I know she'd snoop in my studio? The point is, the henbane didn't really hurt her. She's fine now. I," she said emphatically, "didn't kill anybody."

"Your hands, my love, are as immaculate as Lady Macbeth's. You only begged me, after Batsheva told me she knew about us, to do something about it. What did you think 'doing something' meant? Should I have offered her a share of the profits? Do you think Batsheva would have gone for that?"

Something Nili had written in her diary must have made her mother guess who the secret lovers were. She knew she should run and tell the police. Now! But she felt dizzy, as if her legs could barely hold her. From her crouch, she sank all the way to the ground.

"I didn't tell you to kill her," Dalia said. "I said exactly what I'm saying this minute. That we have to leave. We can't wait for the rest of the money."

"You said . . ." His voice trembled with anger. "You said no matter when we left the country—whether we were already gone when the Torah was discovered missing or it was five years from now—Batsheva would figure out that was how we got the money to leave. You said she would track us to the ends of the earth to see that justice was done. What did you think you were asking me to do?"

"I don't know, I don't know," she sobbed.

Margo ran upstairs. She found Audrey throwing on clothes.

"I had the most awful dream," Audrey said. "Nili was in danger. It sounds crazy, but I feel like I have to go to her immediately."

While Audrey shoved her feet into her sandals Margo telephoned Lev. He couldn't find Nili anywhere in the house.

"Call the police," Margo told him. "Tell them to go to Dalia Weiss's."

"Dalia's?" Audrey said when she hung up.

But she didn't press for the answer. She followed Margo out the door.

"My darling, there's something else we can do," he said.

"What are you talking about? What have you got there? Is that Pavulon?"

"It's about time you knew what it looked like."

Nili inched herself up until she could just peek through the window. Hillel Gebman was holding something small—she supposed a syringe of Pavulon. Dalia was across the room.

"Don't even think about it, Hillel," Dalia said. "It isn't the least bit romantic for us to die together. I want to go to Canada. I want to leave Israel today."

"We can't," he said, his voice breaking. "We can't."

"Then take me to the airport and I'll go alone. My parents survived a concentration camp. I can't commit suicide. I won't let you, either. Give that to me." She started to walk toward him, but then she stopped.

"What?"

"You only have one of those," she said quietly. "Were you going to use the same syringe for both of us? Or is that just for me? That would work, wouldn't it, dear? I'm found dead with the Pavulon next to me—and my fingerprints on it, I'm sure you'd think of that—and everyone assumes I murdered Batsheva and I couldn't bear the guilt, so I killed myself the same way? No one has to know about you at all, do they?''

''It was your idea from the beginning.''

''To kill her?''

''You and me. I admit, I wasn't happy in my marriage, but it would never have occurred to me—''

''You're right. You don't have enough imagination to try to grab some happiness. And now you don't have to. Kill me, and you can go back and spend the rest of your life with fat, complaining Ofra. I just want to know, which of us will be more dead, Hillel? You or me?''

He walked toward her, taking the plastic cover off the needle.

''No!'' Nili screamed. ''No!''

She ran inside.

She didn't know Hillel Gebman could be so strong. The skinny doctor grabbed her and she couldn't get away, couldn't even yell with one of his hands firmly over her mouth. She couldn't kick him, either, because he'd hooked one of his legs around hers. Was he still holding the Pavulon? Or had he dropped it?

''Where did she come from?'' Hillel asked. He maintained his hold on her, but his voice sounded strangled in his throat, as if he was as scared as Nili.

Dalia ran outside for a moment, then came back. ''Under the window. There are marks.''

Dalia's eyes were like a wild horse's. Did Hillel look that way, too? Had they both become more animal than human?

''We don't have a choice anymore,'' Dalia said. ''Inject her with the Pavulon. We'll put her fingerprints on the syringe and carry her into the street. Then we go to the airport.''

''And the police pick us up as soon as they find her?''

''Not if she's down the street. I'll check to make sure no one's coming and you can take her a few hundred meters away.''

It was a stupid plan, Nili thought. If she was found dead close to Dalia's house, and Dalia and Hillel had just left the country abruptly, of course they'd be suspected. If they wanted to get away with killing her, they should act as if nothing had happened for three or four months and then leave. But she guessed if they did that, Dalia would never get Hillel to come with her.

But how could she still want him to, after he'd nearly killed her?

"Do it," Dalia said. "Give her the Pavulon."

Nili felt the arm around her body shift. He must still be holding the syringe in that hand. She tried to move, but only managed to squirm a little. She waited for the prick of the needle, trying to think of what her father had told her about Pavulon and if there was any way she could minimize the effects. She took the deepest breath she could. At least she would start with her lungs full of air.

"Forget it," Hillel said. "I'm not going to do it."

"What do you propose we do? Let her go, and she'll run right to the police station."

"What if we tie her up and gag her, and then leave?"

"And when we land in Canada, they're waiting to extradite us. Give me the syringe. *Give it to me!*"

Nili felt the pinprick.

She wasn't aware of Hillel Gebman leaving. But he lowered her to the floor instead of carrying her outside. And she heard Dalia scream, "Hillel! Hillel!"—her voice raw like an animal's.

Forty-six /

Margo and Audrey pounded down the street.

The door to Dalia's house stood wide open. Dalia lay on her side, crumpled, on the floor. They ran in and knelt beside her.

"Oh, no!" Audrey cried, turning the limp body over. "Oh, no no no."

The stricken woman wasn't Dalia. It was Nili.

"She's not breathing." Audrey leaned close to Nili's mouth and nostrils, at the same time Margo put her ear to the girl's chest.

"Audi, her heart's beating."

Without another word, Audrey started giving her artificial respiration.

Margo had seen nothing but the girl on the floor. Now she took in the rest of the room.

Dalia sat in a corner, her face blank with shock.

"What happened?" Margo asked her. "Was it Pavulon?" She had looked for a syringe, but hadn't seen one.

Dalia didn't respond.

Margo slapped her face. "Was it Pavulon?" she repeated.

"Yes," Dalia whispered. "Hillel did it."

Hillel Gebman? Dalia's married boyfriend? Her partner in crime? There was no time to think it over.

"How do I call an ambulance?" she said, but got no response.

Not wanting to waste precious seconds, she phoned Bernice. Bernice said she would put in the call to the ambulance and come immediately to Dalia's. She should be there in a few minutes.

Margo relayed the news to Audrey. "Will you be okay until Bernice gets here?" she asked.

"Fine," Audrey said quickly, then sucked in more air and bent her head to breathe it into Nili.

Dalia had gone.

Margo took off after her.

Dalia had a head start. Still, she was barefoot and the cobbled paving slowed her down. At the end of the street, Margo spotted her going downhill.

"Dalia, stop!" she called.

Dalia looked over her shoulder, and dashed across the Ma'alot Olei HaGardom into the Jewish Quarter.

Had Dalia blindly panicked or did she have friends in the Jewish Quarter who would hide her? Maybe she thought she could lose herself in the alleyways of the Old City she knew so much better than Margo. But the police would look for her. How could she keep hidden then?

Margo kept her in sight as she turned up the next street. What if her real destination was at the top of the hill—the highway, where she could hitch a ride? Where Hillel Gebman might be waiting in his car?

Margo turned at the same place. Dalia was gone.

"Dalia!" She ran, hoping she'd glimpse the artist down the next side street. "Turn yourself in."

"What is it?" A Hasidic man came up beside her. "What's wrong?"

"She . . ." *She poisoned my mother?* Had Dalia murdered Batsheva, too? How much would she have to explain, while Dalia made it to the highway and escaped? "She stole the Abuhav Torah!"

The man yelled in Hebrew. Suddenly two dozen Hasidim joined the chase.

Margo tried the next street to the left. Some of the Hasidim went with her. Others took the street to the right.

She caught a glimpse of Dalia, limping. "There she is!" she yelled.

The street filled with Hasidim. A few of the men picked up stones.

"What are you doing?" Margo said to the man running next to her, who had a stone clutched in his hand.

He replied in Hebrew. She understood one word—*Torah.*

"Dalia, please stop!" She had to get to Dalia before the mob did.

What had she set into motion? Were tensions between religious and secular Jews so volatile that they would condemn Dalia without proof? She recalled what Danny had told her about Shavuot. Not only had the ultra-Orthodox yelled abuse at the mixed-sex prayer group, people had even dumped excrement on them from the windows of yeshivas.

She ran faster. She was close enough to see blood on Dalia's feet, where she'd cut them running.

Another part of the mob emerged from an adjacent alleyway. Dalia was trapped.

Margo ran toward her, screaming, "Stop! Don't hurt her!"

Already a stone had been thrown.

The stone didn't hit Dalia. It connected with the broad chest of a white-haired Hasid who somehow materialized in front of her.

For a moment a buzz of voices informed the people at the back of the crowd of what had happened. Margo saw a man releasing the stone he'd held—not dropping it but placing it gently on the ground. Then came a silence so profound she felt as if she were about to hear the voice of God.

The elderly Hasid spoke for a minute or two in Hebrew. He must have invited the men to join him in prayer. They prayed until the police arrived.

"She could have been killed. And I was responsible." Eight hours later Margo was haunted by the scene that morning— the mob she had provoked and their anger that had needed no provocation.

"You didn't know what was going to happen," Alice said.

"As far as I'm concerned, she deserved it," said Audrey. "Weren't you listening just now? Dalia lied to us. *She* gave Nili the Pavulon. She told Hillel Gebman to inject her, but he wouldn't. She took the syringe and did it herself. *I* would have thrown stones at her if I'd had the chance!''

"No, you wouldn't," Nili said.

She sat, propped up with pillows, in her bed at home. Her skin was pale, but Lev said that was probably more from the scare she'd gotten than from any aftereffects of the Pavulon. She was strong enough to demand to see them this afternoon and tell them what happened at Dalia's before they arrived. Nili had also insisted—with a force of will that reminded Margo of Batsheva—on hearing about the chase through the Old City. Every time Margo had hesitated, worrying that the story was too awful, Nili pressed her to go on. She was more her mother's daughter than she realized.

"Why wouldn't I?" Smiling, Audrey stroked Nili's hair.

"In school, I learned a saying from the Mishna. Someone who destroys one life destroys the entire world. And someone who saves a life saves the entire world. You're a person who saves lives. You breathed for me until the paramedics came. Will you write to me?"

"Absolutely," Audrey said. "And how about E-mail? Do you have a computer?"

Margo and Alice left them to say their good-byes. Alice translated what Nili had said as they walked through the Old City—so peaceful now. The feel of the stones under her feet reminded her of the chase that morning, and filled her with shame.

"How could I be so stupid," she said, "not to know the effect it would have if I announced in the Jewish Quarter that Dalia stole the Abuhav Torah?"

"You were willing to risk your life to save hers."

"Only after I almost got her killed. I didn't have to chase her in the first place. I could have waited at her house for the police to come. She wouldn't have gotten far. They arrested Hillel Gebman when he was putting his suitcase in his car. Why was it so important to me to catch her myself?" As she said it Margo knew the answer: *To make up for feeling helpless in the fire.*

"We're going to take a trip tomorrow," Alice said, "before we drive to Jerusalem."

"Where?"

Alice wouldn't tell. She only said that they should pack their bathing suits where they could get to them easily.

Forty-seven /

Wednesday—the 49th day of the counting of the Omer

> *Water is so precious in this desert country that even a scummy pond no bigger than a child's wading pool might inspire reverence. But here is the miracle. When water does appear, it is often in settings of extraordinary beauty. . . .*
> *At Sachne, Ein Harod (the spring of Harod) comes to the surface and forms a natural swimming pool so large that it's divided into four different pools with walkways between them. There is even, between the first and second pool, a small waterfall. . . . The water feels delicious to swim in. . . . And the setting! Because of Ein Harod, the precious water, the pools are surrounded by trees and bushes, and there are grassy lawns for relaxing and picnicking.*

Sachne, to which Alice directed them from Safed, was just as she had described it. The water was caressingly warm from the underground spring of Harod, the surface of the pools utterly peaceful except for the splashing of children.

It wasn't a *mikve,* but when Margo immersed herself at Sachne, she felt as if the water touched not only her body but her spirit. The part of her that still had occasional nightmares from the fire felt stronger. The tense fear she had felt—for her mother, for Audrey—finally released.

And Barry? On the phone yesterday, she had only known something felt different. In the silky water of Sachne, she understood: she had said "I love you" with her whole heart for the first time in months. She leaned her head back and let the warm water embrace her; let it dissolve even more of the hurt, unforgiving place inside her.

The Kabbalist palmist had said she needed to see God's water face. If there was a God and if such a face existed, she was seeing it now.